TRADING TEAMS

ROMEO ALEXANDER

JOHN HARRIS

．

Trading Teams
A Jock Nerd Romance

Romeo Alexander

Published by BUP LLC, 2018.
Copyright © 2018 by Romeo Alexander

CHAPTER 1

The office is large and impeccably decorated. Stone paperweights carved into abstract shapes add a sophisticated vibe. The walls and bookshelves are lined with awards, diplomas, certificates, and framed pictures of the dean shaking hands with various people, posing in front of various buildings. There's not much in here besides bookshelves, filing cabinets, and a large, pristinely organized wooden desk.

Jake sits in one of the dark green plush chairs across the desk from the dean, watching as the old man talks. He has a friendly face, with wrinkles in his forehead and laughter lines around his eyes. His smile has always been warm and welcoming, and Jake remembers the distinct pride he felt the first time he was in this room. He remembers feeling nearly lightheaded, giddy, as the dean congratulated him on his first winning home game and told him they made a good decision when they offered him a full ride scholarship.

Now he sits here, dread feeling like lead in his gut, as the dean tells him that due to changes in the system, he's in danger of losing that scholarship.

"Two points may seem like a daunting task," the dean says, not unkind and not without sympathy as he leans back in his chair, elbows perched on the arms, and fingers steepled in front of him. "And doesn't need to be immediate. If we see you're making steady progress, we can give you the time needed to raise your GPA. You're a smart kid, Jake. If you simply apply yourself, spend time studying, and perhaps look into some tutoring options, you'll find yourself excelling in no time."

Despite the dread coiling through his chest, Jake manages a tight-lipped smile. "Thanks, Dr. Harrison. I'll do my best."

The man's smile widens a fraction. "I know you will, Jake. Our team needs you, and I know you won't let us down."

He stands to leave and shakes the dean's hand, feeling robotic and stiff as they go through the pleasantries of saying goodbye. His smile feels painted on poorly, cracking at the edges. His voice sounds hollow and distant.

He leaves the dean's office, closing the door gently behind him, and he pauses, glancing around the empty hallway. His eyes linger on the white cinderblock walls and the way the artificial lights reflect off the cheap linoleum floors. He feels numb and hollowed out. A lump has formed in the pit of his stomach, and it's making him nauseous. There's a buzz creeping across his skin, an itch that crawls beneath it, making him feel restless and anxious. His fingers curl into fists then relax, over and over.

How the hell is he supposed to raise his GPA by two points? No matter what the dean said, two points is a lot. A lot more than Jake ever thought he'd be capable of. And he has to make immediate progress or risk his scholarship being pulled. That can't happen. He can't afford to be here without it. His family doesn't have the money, and the idea of applying for loans large enough to cover tuition and living, when he should be getting a full ride, makes him dizzy with worry.

All he wanted to do was play baseball on one of the most well renowned teams in the region, get discovered professionally, and leave college with a passing GPA that barely matters in the long run. He's not an academic. He never has been. School has never been his thing. It's just a means to an end. A necessary evil if he wants to play ball.

Pace brisk, body anxious and running on far too much chaotic energy without an outlet, he goes down the stairs two at a time, leaping the last three before every landing.

Whatever. He'll deal with this later. He'll think about it tonight. Or tomorrow. Or...sometime. For now, he's just gotta get through the rest of his classes. Get through practice without his teammates knowing anything's wrong. He'll deal with it all later.

As he steps out of the building, the rush of crisp, autumn air cools his heated skin. He breathes it in deep, letting it fill his lungs and calm the ache. They're well into the first semester, and autumn brings the promise of winter. From winter, spring will come. He hopes he's still on the team when the official season starts.

His phone buzzes in his pocket, snapping him back to the present. He digs it out and glances at the lock screen. It's a text from his girlfriend. Once upon a time, that mere fact might've given him a thrill. A little shiver down his spine. Now he feels nothing. He wonders when it happened, but he's not surprised that it has. It always seems to happen with his relationships, and he's never been able to figure out why.

Unlocking his phone, he reads the message.

CINDI: *Where are you?*

IT TAKES a moment for the context of the message to sink in. For memory to dredge up the remnants of what he's forgotten, with everything that's happened this morning.

Right. He's supposed to meet her before their next class, and he's late. Great.

Shoving his phone back in his pocket, he jogs down the steps in front of the administration building and starts off across campus.

He finds her in their usual meeting spot in the quad. She's sitting on the crest of the small hill that rises to the sidewalk leading to the student union. It's a hill overlooking the rest of the quad, stretching the length of it, giving students a good spot to sit, relax, and be out of the way of both the activities in the quad and the foot traffic on the sidewalk above it.

She has her back to him as he approaches, one hand holding a coffee cup and the other holding her phone. Despite the slight chill in the air, she wears shorts. Her long, smooth legs are stretched out in front of her and crossed at the ankles. The back of her shirt dips, giving him just a teasing view of her shoulders and spine. He remembers a time when a glimpse of her skin would've made heat rise in him and hunger fill his gut. Now he simply feels numb.

He wonders how long it's been like this without him noticing. When did she go from a successful conquest, the nabbing of a beautiful girlfriend, into just someone he was obligated to see. He used to feel pride having her on his arm, reveling in the looks others gave him, and he used to feel lust rumbling in his chest whenever she was around. She used to get such a reaction out of him, but the novelty of it had worn off so quickly. Quicker than his last girlfriend, and the one before that.

How long had they even been dating?

"Hey, babe," he says as he sits down beside her. She hums a greeting, not even bothering to look up from her phone as she leans toward him, presenting her cheek. He hesitates, but she doesn't look at him, and he eventually gives in to the routine and pecks her lightly on the cheek.

"You're late," she says as she leans away from him once more.

He leans back on his hands, not even bothering to put an arm around her like he usually does. He's normally a touch kind of guy in relationships, but not when he's in a funk. She doesn't even seem to notice the change. "I was in the dean's office."

"Cool," is all she says, sounding indifferent and robotic. She never once stops scrolling through her phone.

He frowns. "He said if I don't raise my GPA by two points, I'll lose my scholarship. I'll be kicked off the team."

"That sucks," she finally puts her phone away, slipping it into her backpack. She turns to him, and for a second, he thinks he's finally about to get some sympathy. Anything, really. Instead she turns to him with half-lidded eyes and a coy smile on her lips. "Wanna have a quickie before class?"

His brows furrow, and he leans away as she leans into him. "I just told you I might lose my scholarship."

She shrugs, dragging painted nails lightly down his arm. "You'll figure it out. So...about that quickie," despite his frustration, his body reacts to the touch. Goosebumps rise on his skin and he shudders, a spark of interest running southward, betraying him. He can't deny she's hot, and she does know how to get what she wants. She smiles at him, knowing and triumphant.

He's really not in the mood, but...

His phone rings in his pocket, the incessant vibrations offering the excuse he needs.

He digs it out, glancing at it for a second before holding it out, disentangling himself from Cindi's hold, just moments before she could attach her lips to his neck and slide her hands beneath his shirt. He may not be in the mood, but he's a weak man. Instead, he pushes himself to his feet, holding his phone out for her to see. "Sorry, it's my mom."

She pouts, clearly disgruntled but still playing coy. "You never answer calls from your mom."

He shrugs, grabbing his bag that had fallen to the ground. "Yeah, well, you know. Better late than never."

She huffs, gathering her things and pushing herself to her feet. Her coy look is gone, as is the lust in her eyes, replaced only by a cold but subtle fury. "Whatever," she turns on her heel, stalking the rest of the way up the hill toward the sidewalk.

"I'll see you later?" he calls out after her, but all he gets is a vague wave in response. He sighs. Just another thing to fix later. Maybe he'll buy her flowers. She's always been a soft touch for flowers. Or...was that the last one? He can't remember. His relationships come and go so quickly he's stopped learning much about them. None of them try to learn much about him either.

He answers the call, turning to walk in the direction of his next class. "Hey, mom."

"Jake! You actually answered."

There's disbelief in her voice, along with a teasing tone, but also joy. He finds himself smiling. "It was bound to happen eventually."

He talks to her as he makes his way to the Business building. She carries most of the conversation, and he supplements it with muttered sounds and one-word responses. She tells him how she and his dad have been doing. How the dogs are. What the neighborhood gossip is. And when she asks how he's doing, he just gives her short and vague replies, keeping a tight-lipped smile on his face in the hope it'll make him sound more genuine.

Then she tells him they're proud of him, and that his dad will be driving up to watch the first home game.

He feels like he's been kicked in the chest, all the air rushing out of him and leaving an ache in its wake. He doesn't have the heart to tell them. Not when it's not certain yet, and not when all it'll do is make them worry. He doesn't want them to think he's a failure. So instead he just gives her a strained response. Something vague but positive that he barely hears past the panicked ringing in his ears.

"Jake," her voice goes soft, concerned, in that way it does when she knows something's wrong. "Is everything alright."

"Fine, Mom, I just gotta go to class now. Love you, bye!" He barely gives her time to say her own goodbyes before ending the call, breathing out a sigh of relief and feeling guilt rush into his lungs.

Just another thing to deal with later.

It's not until the call fades, phone returning to his home screen, that he realizes he's late.

"Fuck!" he shoves his phone away and rushes inside, climbing the stairs two at a time.

His economics class is in a large lecture hall in the Business building. He rushes through the door right as the professor is about to begin and receives an annoyed glare. He smiles sheepishly, pushing the door shut as quietly as he can before rushing to take the first available seat. Backpack thrown to the floor at his feet, he leans back in his chair, hands on the empty table top in front of him.

He never brings his textbook, and he never takes notes. He realizes, with the same rolling dread in his stomach that he's going to need to start doing both of those things. Just as he should start paying attention.

He tries, he really does, and he makes a valiant effort for all of ten minutes. It doesn't take long for his mind to wander though. The subject is boring. A lot of words and a lot of numbers. The professor's voice drones on, talking about business practices or something like that. He doesn't really care about business, it just seemed like an easy major to pick. He's here for baseball, anyway.

As his mind begins to wander, so do his eyes. He sits at the end of a row, and if he turns in his chair, he gets a good view of the whole room. So, leaning an elbow on the desk and resting his cheek against it, he lets his gaze look over his classmates. A lot of them look like him. Jocks who thought business would be an easy way to pass through college. There are a lot of girls as well, and most of them fit the definition of his type.

He doesn't realize he's looking for tutoring material until his attention settles on a guy at the back. He looks younger, and he's definitely smaller. Small frame. Small build. Delicate features. Glasses perched on his nose. None of the fresh-from-Greek-life the rest of his classmates seem to exude. He looks almost bored, but despite that, he's scribbling quickly in his notebook, occasionally glancing up at the professor.

To be completely honest, he looks like an absolute nerd. The typical, cliché smart kid who listens and writes down everything in class. Jake thinks he'd make a good tutor.

As he watches, the boy lifts a hand to scratch his face. The sleeves of his hoodie envelop most of his hand, leaving just his fingertips visible. His eyes are focused intently on his notebook, brows pinched and nose wrinkling slightly in thought. As he scratches his cheek, he doesn't seem to notice the pen in his hand leaving a streak of black along his jaw. It's cute. Really cute. Adorable, even.

Despite the tightness in his chest and the anxiousness crawling beneath his skin, Jake finds himself smiling.

CHAPTER 2

*K*yle makes his way through the halls of the Business building with his head down and eyes on the floor. He's smaller than a lot of the others that frequent this building. Well, smaller than a lot of the dudes, anyway. A lot of jocks tend to pick business as their major. That's not to say there aren't the occasional squadron of geeks and actual aspiring entrepreneurs, but the jocks are the big ones. The ones who take up space in the halls and talk loudly. The ones Kyle keeps his head down to avoid.

There are plenty of girls, too, but they tend to flock to the jocks. They're a strange mix of dressed up and dressed down, but that's college life, he supposes. They cling to each other and to the bigger guys, laughter piercing through their conversation. He knows the odds of them even noticing him long enough to comment on him are slim to none, but that doesn't stop the bristling anxiety whenever he passes a group and hears giggling, a voice in the back of his mind whispering that they're laughing at him.

He just hunches his shoulders and pushes on, making a beeline for his classroom. He feels much more at ease in the

Science and Technology buildings, but he chose business as his major, so he's stuck here most of the time.

It's okay. He can handle it. If he doesn't draw attention to himself, he'll graduate in a couple of years and move on with his life.

He gets to his lecture hall earlier than most. Those who are late always get stared at, and he hates the weight of all those eyes. He hops up the steps to one of the rows in the back, to his usual seat. He's had this seat since the beginning of the semester, and he doesn't plan on changing it now.

Once seated, he automatically goes through the motions of pulling out his textbook and notebook, flipping through the pages to the right chapter and pulling out a pen, but his mind is already elsewhere.

During the test run last night, what went wrong? The graphics on the grass were fine. The dirt splatter was delayed—need to fix that. The trees have a fifty percent chance of glitching when a player is knocked into them—wait, no, that's environment. Focus on one thing at a time. This week I'm working on combat problems. Damage. The health bar wasn't always accurate, and critical hits aren't calculating right. There's a delay between characters taking damage and their health bars showing zero, causing players to be in combat longer than they should and seemingly dying randomly...

He sets a second notebook over the top of the one for his class, already flipping through it to the first blank page. Then he's scribbling down his thoughts, furiously and fervently. His hand desperately tries to keep up with his mind as he mentally rattles off the current algorithms for damage calculation and output. By the time he's done and looks at it, the page is a mess. His handwriting is terrible, but at least he can read it. It's chaos, but it's his organized chaos.

His brother used to joke that Kyle's handwriting was code in itself, and it was one that only the two of them could decipher.

The memory is only half formed before his heart squeezes, stomach clenching and rolling. He shakes his head, pursing his lips as he shoves the memory aside. He's gotta figure out how to eliminate the calculation delay when characters take damage.

The door to the classroom slams open, and Kyle's head shoots up automatically. Out of the corner of his eye, he can see the rest of the class do the same. All eyes fall on the guy paused just inside the room, smiling sheepishly at their disgruntled professor and closing the door behind him. Kyle watches him, a small frown on his lips, as the guy makes his way to his seat.

See? This is why Kyle hates getting to class late. Everyone stares.

Still, he's smart enough to realize he's staring at the guy long after others have lost interest.

He knows this guy, well, he doesn't *know* him. He knows of him. Sort of. He knows the guy's name is Jake, and he knows from overheard conversation that he's not only on the school's baseball team, but one of the star players. Kyle's never seen a game in his life, and doesn't really plan to, but he hears Jake is good. Not that he listens for specifics on Jake or anything. He's just curious, even though he has no logical reason to *be* curious about Jake.

By all rights, Jake blends into the crowd. He looks like any other jock in their class. He's decently tall, ▄▄▄, with broad shoulders and arms that make Kyle's insides twist. His hair looks brown at first glance, but Kyle's stared enough to notice how it shines copper and red where the light hits it. It's cut shorter on the sides and longer on top, looking almost wispy and wind-swept. His face is classically handsome with a strong jaw, nose and brows, a squared chin, with lips that look like they're always two seconds away from pulling into an easy smile and eyes that were meant for laughter. His chin and jaw are covered in stubble, and Kyle finds himself idly wondering if that's just from one night or several days.

Then Jake sits, the professor is starting, and Kyle realizes he's still staring. He blinks rapidly, shaking his head and ducking down to stare at his notes as heat rises up the back of his neck.

Jake is just another jock, and just another classic straight guy in his major. Objectively, yeah, he's hot, but he's just like everyone else. There's no reason for Kyle to stare, especially when it's a waste of time. He has more important things to work on.

Like Cry Thunder, the video game he's been developing for years. And figuring out this stupid damage algorithm.

He barely pays attention during class. The professor's voice drones on like white noise in the background. He glances up every five minutes out of a carefully formed habit. He barely realizes he's doing it anymore. He just glances up out of reflex, scans the PowerPoint slide the professor is currently talking about, determines if anything is relevant, and then goes back to his task. Occasionally, he'll jot down a note or two, just so he knows where the class is in terms of the chapter.

Thankfully, he doesn't really need to pay attention. Economics is easy, and it's mostly just math. He takes time every weekend to read ahead in the textbook, covering everything the syllabus says they're supposed to go over in the following week, and then all he has to do is show up for class and turn in assignments. Simple and easy. And while he's in class, he can use that time to work on Cry Thunder.

He pauses in his writing, reaching up to push up his glasses and scratch his cheek as he stares at the page. He's changed a few numbers around in his original algorithm, and that *should* fix the problem of calculating critical hits.

This should predict it once the player uses an attack, but before the visual motion is followed through, so the damage calculation is there the moment the visual is. There's no telling if it'll work until he inputs the code and tests it, though. And there are a lot of things that could go wrong. Critical strike calculations have to be pulled from a variety of databases, such as character race, class, items, stat boosts, external influences, rune stones…the list is endless.

Out of reflex, he glances up at the front of the room once more, but as his gaze sweeps across the room, his attention is caught before it can even reach the PowerPoint.

In a sea of classmates, a sea of the backs of people's heads, there's one person who's turned around, their face in full view, and staring *right* at him. His internal monologue is cut off abruptly. His gaze does a double take as it sweeps past the person and then snaps back.

And that's how he finds himself locking eyes with Jake for the first time.

The first thing Kyle realizes is that his eyes are blue. That knowledge is quickly followed by a very startled and very profound question. *What the fuck?*

His eyes snap away instantly, returning to the notebook in front of him as he ducks his head. He can feel heat rising up the back of his neck again, and his hand taps his pen on the paper, mind far too scattered to actually focus on the numbers in front of him.

After a few tense seconds, he's able to get his heartbeat under control. It was probably just a coincidence. Jake must've been scanning the room at the same time Kyle was, and movement naturally catches people's attention. They just accidentally looked at each other at the same time. No big deal. None at all.

Keeping his head bowed, he risks another glance across

the room, only to find Jake is still staring at him, the ghost of a smile playing across his lips.

Kyle looks down again, mentally thanking his bronze complexion for hiding blushes. He can feel the heat settled on his cheeks, and he shifts his weight in his chair. Now he knows, he can *feel* Jake's gaze on him. Hot, heavy and strange. He's not used to people staring at him. He's used to their eyes passing right over him, or regarding him with mild indifference before looking away. This is weird. Very weird.

If he's being completely honest, he's been staring at Jake since the start of the semester. It's not something he's proud of, nor is it something he likes to admit. Especially since there's no logical reason for Jake to stand out in a crowd. But that doesn't stop Kyle's eyes from wandering and locking onto the guy for far longer than any of their other classmates.

But he never thought in a million years *Jake* would stare at *him*.

What the fuck?

Does he have something on his face? Oh god, he probably has something on his face. Or he's wearing his shirt inside out. Was he making a weird expression while he was concentrating? He's not used to thinking about what kind of faces he's making. No one usually notices him anyway. Oh god, what kind of face is he making *now*?

He puts an elbow on the table, resting his cheek on his sleeve-covered hand and uses it to hide his face. He focuses on his coding, and when he glances up to the PowerPoint, he very stubbornly refuses to look anywhere else.

He doesn't get much else done during class, and while he knows it's all Jake's fault, he can't be mad at anyone other than himself. He hates that just making eye contact with the guy caused him to get all flustered and his brain to get jumbled. It's not like he's delusional enough to think he stands a chance, and it's not like he ever plans on even trying. Even if Jake was in his league, which he's definitely not, Kyle doesn't have time for guys right now. Even ones with cute smiles and arms that could probably bench press him.

The professor isn't even done explaining their homework before Kyle is in the process of packing up, and they've barely been dismissed before he has his backpack strap thrown over his shoulder and he's hurrying down the steps. He just wants to get out of there, away from that gaze. He can still feel it prickling against his skin. He needs to get back to his solitude where he feels comfortable.

But of course, he's not that lucky.

"Hey!"

He's pulled to a stop as someone grabs his sleeve, and he freezes at the contact. His entire body tenses and a shiver runs through him. He turns slowly, lips pursed, and brows pinched. He's prepared this time, but that doesn't stop the rush of air from his lungs as he once again finds himself staring into a pair of pretty blue eyes. Jake is close to him now, and wow, he's tall. Like nearly a full head taller than Kyle. And he's sure that spicy smell is coming from him, and it smells really good, which is weird, he normally doesn't notice people's deodorants. Oh god, he's being creepy.

"What?" he snaps, mentally cringing at the abrasiveness of it.

Jake blinks, but it only takes a moment before he's smiling again. "Name's Jake," he holds out his hand, and Kyle stares at it. He has big hands. Nice hands. Hands with fingers that look long and calloused, and those are hands Kyle definitely shouldn't touch.

He looks from the hand to Jake's face, his own hands tightening into fists in his hoodie pockets. "Kyle," and, feeling anxious, uncomfortable and desperate to get out of this situation, he turns on his heel and walks away. His brother always said he was bad at social situations and had declared he'd help Kyle overcome his anxieties.

But he wasn't around anymore, and Kyle has no desire to talk to people. Especially people who make him feel heat flush beneath his skin and butterflies in his stomach.

"Hey, wait!" he hears Jake's voice follow him out into the hall, but he keeps walking, heart hammering as footsteps hurry after him. He pointedly ignores Jake as he falls into step with him. "I saw you taking a lot of notes in there."

Kyle huffs a short laugh, bordering on a scoff. He doesn't feel like explaining that what he was writing had nothing to do with class.

Jake seems nonplused by his silence. "So, you understand economics, right? Like this class? You look like a guy who understands this stuff."

A nerd. He's calling him a nerd. At least he's trying to be nice about it. Kyle bristles anyway, shoulders rising as they tense. "Yes."

"So, uh, I know this is a little out of nowhere, but do you think you could like...tutor me?"

Kyle stops abruptly, turning to find Jake looking at him. His smile is small and sheepish, and there's a look in his eyes that Kyle dares to call embarrassment. His entire body is hunched, slouched in a way that's almost defensive, making him look smaller. A far cry from the boisterous, confident guy Kyle had pegged him for. It's surreal, and far from what he'd been expecting or bracing himself for. Copy some homework? Cheat on a test? Do a paper for him? Make fun of him? Sure. But tutoring? Actually helping him *learn?*

Kyle blinks, confusion and surprise and a strange sort of indignant heat rolling around inside him.

He doesn't have time for this. He doesn't have time for jocks who think they can use him for an easy A. Doesn't have time to tutor someone who doesn't see him as any more than a walking textbook with glasses.

His eyes harden, brows furrowing as he frowns. "No," he says, before turning on his heel and slipping away into the crowd, easily blending into the background and losing Jake in the chaos.

He doesn't have time for pretty boys that are far out of his league. He has work to do.

CHAPTER 3

$\mathcal{J}$ake can be a pretty chill guy. He rolls with the punches, you know? You swing, you miss, and move on. No use dwelling on your strikes. Focus on your hits. But Jake has his own stubborn streak. Once he gets something in his head, it's hard to shake it. And right now, he's a hundred percent convinced that he *needs* Kyle to tutor him.

Just like he thought, Kyle gets good grades. He admitted as much after some hassling, and he admitted it with a lazy pride that told Jake he barely had to work for those grades. While a little jealous, it cemented Jake's determination. He can't say *why* he's so fixated on Kyle specifically, he just knows he is. Rolling with his gut instincts has rarely failed him before, so he figures he'll go with it.

If he can get Kyle to say yes.

* * *

"What's that?"

It's Friday, marking the fourth day in a row Jake has stubbornly put himself in Kyle's path. They don't even have a class together today, but Jake's learned that if he hangs around in front of the Business building long enough, Kyle is bound to show up. The guy looks young, but he's in the Business building *a lot,* and it makes Jake wonder if he even has any gen-ed classes.

He was waiting outside the building, two coffee cups in hand, when Kyle showed up. He initially thought Kyle would be hard to spot in a crowd. A wallflower type. But as it turns out, he's quite easy to find as long as you know what you're looking for. He's small, usually tense and frowning, eyes locked on the ground and moving fast. Jake barely has enough time to leap up and cut him off before he enters the building.

Now Kyle stands there, blinking up at Jake. It looks like it takes him a moment to mentally catch up, like he was too deep in thought to recognize Jake immediately. There are heavy bags under his eyes and lines around his mouth. He looks tired.

Jake puts on his winning smirk: two parts playful and one part genuine. "It's coffee," he'd already been holding out the coffee cup, but Kyle's just been staring at it like he'd never seen one in his life. Which...maybe he hadn't. Jake's taking a gamble here. He moves the cup closer to Kyle. "It's for you."

Kyle's eyes slide from the cup up to him, narrowing slightly. "Why?"

Jake shrugs, head tilting to the side. "'Cause that's what friends do."

Kyle seems to tense at that, lips pressing into a thin line. It might be a trick of the light, but Jake can almost swear his cheeks look a little pink. "We're not friends."

"Okay, no, maybe not. But we *could* be," this doesn't seem to be the right thing to say because Kyle's frown deepens, hand on his backpack strap, tightening it.

"You don't want to be my friend. You want me to tutor you."

"Can't I want both?"

"No."

Jake feels his smile fading. If he's being honest, Kyle kind of reminds him of a Chihuahua. Adorable and small, causing his instincts to protect and coddle to rise to the surface, but at the same time skittish, snappy, and wary. Yet despite how abrasive Kyle's been with him, he can't bring himself to resent it. It's kinda cute, actually. Mostly because Jake can tell Kyle's not really an asshole. Jake *knows* dudes who are assholes. Kyle's seems more defensive and wary. Jake's just gotta get past those walls.

Jake sighs, letting his smile slip as his shoulders slump. "Okay, look. I'll admit, I didn't approach you to be your friend," Kyle just stares, unblinking, slowly raising one eyebrow. Jake raises his hands, and thus the coffee cups, in a placating gesture. "*But,* that doesn't mean we can't be friendly. And that doesn't mean we can't become friends. I'm really serious about tutoring. I don't need answers, I need like...to learn. So I can do this on my own. I don't need to just pass economics. I need to pass *everything.* This year and next year."

He can hear the frustration leaking into his voice, and he can feel a frown forming. He doesn't know why he's sharing all this. Kyle never asked for his baggage, but he has a feeling honesty is the only thing that's gonna get past those walls.

He looks back at Kyle, eyes pleading. "Look, if I don't get my GPA up by *two* points, or close to it, by the end of the semester, I'm gonna lose my scholarship. I can't *afford* to be here without it. *Please,* dude. I can pay you. I'm not expecting this for free, and I'm not above begging right now. I'm desperate. I'll get on my knees right fucking here if I have to."

Kyle's face is closed off and unreadable. His brows are

furrowed as he scowls. His eyes are hard and narrow as they search Jake's face. They're a striking shade of hazel. A greenish brown that looks beautiful framed by long, dark lashes and bronze skin. *Focus, Jake.*

Kyle looks down, the toe of his shoe idly scuffing against the concrete. Then he looks to the side, up and around to the building. And that's where Jake starts to see his mask crack. He bites at his lip, brow pinching in a way that's no longer wary, but more...no, it's still pretty damn wary, but there's indecision there that Jake counts as a win.

When he looks back at Jake, his eyes are still narrowed, and his gaze is still hard, but there's also defeat there. He nods toward the cup in Jake's hand. "What kind of coffee is that?"

Jake blinks, then stares at the cup, his mind taking a moment to catch up to the unexpected question. "Oh, uh...a mocha?" Kyle raises a brow, and Jake shifts his weight. "I figured you might like something sweet? Something chocolatey?"

"You're making a lot of assumptions about me," he grumbles, but he reaches out and takes the cup anyway. Jake isn't above noticing how soft his hands are when they brush against his, and he's a weak enough man to attempt to prolong that contact. Kyle pulls back quickly, holding out his other hand. "Give me your phone."

Jake scrambles to do just that, unlocking and slapping the device in Kyle's waiting palm. He frowns as he enters his number, practically shoving the phone back into Jake's hand before walking past him toward the doors.

"Text me when you're ready to study," he grumbles, refusing to make eye contact, and frowning like he tastes something bitter. But as Jake looks at the new contact in his phone, he finds himself grinning. He'll take it as a win.

He has his victory, but impulse convinces him to push it.

"Hey!" he spins on his heel, grin still fixed in place as he spots Kyle, stopped halfway through the door into the building. He looks back at Jake, an eyebrow raised. "Wanna come to a party tonight? You know, get out, meet some people, get drunk?"

He sees the conflict flicker across Kyle's face, but there are far too many emotions to pinpoint, and they're gone before he can try. Kyle smiles, but it's small, just a tilt of his lips, and it doesn't reach his eyes. "No, thanks," he says, and it sounds hollow.

Jake watches him disappear into the building, grin fading. There's a strange ache in his chest, soft and barely there. Sympathy? Pity? He's not really sure. Jake likes to think he's starting to scale those walls, but now he's wondering what he'll find beyond them. Kyle looks tired, but it's more than that. He looks...sad. Like he carries a dark cloud with him that he can't quite shake.

Jake gets it in his head that he wants to see Kyle smile. A real smile, bright and genuine. And he knows he's stubborn enough to follow through.

* * *

HE SPENDS the rest of the day thinking about Kyle on and off. About the hollow sorrow in his eyes when he attempts to smile and the conflict on his face when he decided to help Jake. About his hair, dark and messy, windswept in a way that looked completely natural but also in a way Jake can imagine it being spread out across a pillow as he throws his head back...

Whoa, okay. Wrong train of thought.

Jake shakes his head, running his fingers through his hair to clear his thoughts. He'll have plenty of time to dwell on his tutor later. Right now, he has a party to get to and a girlfriend to meet. Get drunk and probably fuck. A normal Friday night. He's got his favorite jeans on, the ones that are comfortable and make his ass look great, and a fitted ▃▃▃ t-shirt. He looks good, he feels good, and he's ready to forget the world of academia for a while.

The walk to Cindi's apartment isn't long, but he takes his time, letting the night air rush over him. It's crisp and cold against his bare arms, and it feels good. The plan for the night is simple, pick up his girlfriend, walk to the party ten minutes away, get drunk and walk back to her place. Just like they have several times before.

The routine is already thrown when he finds her waiting for him in the parking lot. Even more so when he realizes she's leaning against one of her friend's cars. He can see several of them piled in it through the windows, and he tries to ignore their stares.

"Hey, babe," he says as he approaches, hands in his pockets, smiling despite the tension coiled in his gut. She looks up from her phone, but when he leans in for a kiss, she leans away. It surprises him, but he's even more surprised by the hand pressed to his chest, keeping him at arm's length. He looks down at it, then up at her.

She frowns, full red painted lips turned down at the edges, delicate brow furrowed. "Look, Jake, we've got to talk."

He glances at the car, then at her, speaking slowly. "Oookay?"

He follows her as she leads him away from the car, turning to face her when she stops. One hand on her hip, she holds her phone in her other hand. She looks determined but nearly bored. "Listen, I think we should break up."

He can't say he's surprised to hear it. Not with how she's been acting. He's been broken up with before, and he's learned to recognize the signs. He waits for the mounting tension in his gut to squeeze, to come to a head, to make him feel desperate and nauseous. But it never comes. Instead, the twisting knot relaxes, leaving him strangely at ease.

He blinks, slightly surprised. He'd expected *some* sort of ache. If he's honest with himself, he hasn't felt much for Cindi in a while. Sure, she's hot as hell and a damn fine catch, but the chase had been more fun than the relationship that followed. In the end, there were very few things special about her, and he hadn't felt a connection. Nothing to make his insides all jittery or sparks when they touched.

Still, it *should* hurt when someone decides they no longer want him. Even if it's just for a second. Instead, he only feels relief.

He shifts his weight onto one foot, shoving his hands deeper into his pockets, head tilting to the side as he frowns. "Okay," he says slowly, eyes narrowing. "Can you tell me why?" Because despite lacking any sort of devastation, he thinks he deserves that at least.

She just shrugs, waving her phone hand around in vague gestures. "It's just like...you're a great fuck, Jake. You really are. But you're not very...smart?" he snorts a short, humorless laugh, and she frowns, pointing a finger at him and jabbing it into his chest. "Laugh all you want, but it's true. You even said you're in danger of getting kicked off the team, and I don't want to be the one who drags you down."

He can't help but roll his eyes at that. What a load of shit. If that were true, she would support him. Not ditch him. More like she doesn't want to be seen dating the dropout. It's bad for her rep.

She doesn't seem to notice, gaze already drifting away. He can't tell if she's unable to make eye contact or if she's just bored. "Besides, right now I think I just wanna like, have time to find myself, you know? Be me instead of being in a couple. That's what college is about, right?"

More like she wants to find someone she's not bored with, but he keeps that thought to himself.

"Whatever. Live your life, Cindi," it doesn't come out as cynical or bitter as he thought it might. If anything, he matches her indifference.

If she's offended by his lack of devastation, she doesn't show it. Instead she smirks, patting him on the shoulder as she walks off. "I knew you'd understand. Bye, Jake. Good luck with your grades, or whatever."

He scoffs, practically rolling her touch off his shoulder as he mutters. "Yeah, you too."

He doesn't bother watching her walk away. He just starts off down the street, in the direction of the party. He hears her get into her friend's car, hears it tear out of the parking lot and down the street, but he doesn't look up.

He gets about halfway to the party before he stops. He's not *sad* about the break up, per se, but he does feel strangely hollow. It's not the ache of a break up he's used to. It's not a black pit in his chest and nausea in his gut. It's just a strange numb feeling, like nothing. He stares distantly down the street, lips pursed. He *could* go to the party alone. Drink until he feels *something*.

But he's surprised to find he really doesn't want to.

He's even more surprised when a whispered voice in his mind offers an alternative.

"I can't believe I'm doing this," he mutters to himself even as he turns on his heel, stalking back toward campus with renewed purpose. He pulls out his phone, finding Kyle's new contact and fires off a text. "Studying instead of partying. Who am I?"

But despite the sardonic tone of that thought, there's a strange buzzing thrill that vibrates beneath his skin as he gets a text with Kyle's dorm number.

CHAPTER 4

*K*yle stares down at the phone in his hand, eyes narrowed on the text from Jake that says he's on his way over. It seems far too enthusiastic for a study session, especially given that he was supposed to be going to a party tonight. Kyle sighs, setting his phone face-down on his desk as he pushes away from it. So much for getting work done on his damage algorithm. Maybe if he can convince Jake to read for a bit, he can type up some of the test code strips he came up with earlier.

He twists in his seat, gaze flickering around the room. His dorm isn't exactly big, but he thinks it's a decent size, for a dorm. His roommate is out tonight, as he is most weekends, so at least they'll have the space to themselves.

His heart does a weird little skip at that thought, and he puts a hand to his chest, frowning. That's...weird. And not okay.

Shaking his head, he slides out of his chair, setting to work picking up enough of their stuff to make his room a little more presentable. They have their beds bunked to one side, the other side occupied by a small bookshelf stocked with video games and consoles, a flat screen set up on top. Their mini-fridge-microwave combo is shoved over to the side, two worn but comfortable beanbags taking up the center between the TV and the beds. Their desks and wardrobes are puzzled into place around the rest of the room.

His roommate, Jasper, isn't exactly the cleanest guy, but he's not too messy. Not any more than Kyle. His desk has books, papers and wrappers scattered everywhere, but at least it's confined to his desk. Kyle's own desk has more things, more books and notebooks and knickknacks, but it exists in its own organized chaos.

He does a sweep of the room, picking up trash and tossing their clothes into the appropriate hampers. He makes his bed meticulously and wonders why the hell he cares. It's not like he thinks Jake would care. If anything, he's willing to bet Jake's room is also messy.

Standing back, hands on his hips as he glances around the room and its strange mix of personality from him and Jasper, he wonders for the millionth time why he agreed to this. He doesn't *want* to tutor anybody, let alone some meathead jock. He doesn't have time. He has his own school work to do, and when he's not doing that, he's working on Cry Thunder.

He still has *so* much to do before he can even release a playable beta for testing, and he really shouldn't be wasting his time tutoring. Besides, what're the odds that it'll actually help Jake? Sure, he might pass one class, but to bring up his entire GPA by two points this semester alone? Still...Kyle can't help but feel a little bad for him. The way he talked about it, how desperate he sounded, it's clear it means a lot to him that he passes. Maybe it was the pity that temporarily overtook his common sense and caused him to say yes.

Besides, Jake said he would pay him, and Kyle needs to

start building funds if he's going to start investing in servers and storage space for his game.

He gave in for the money, he decides. Getting money for something that'll be easy, that he can do while still offhandedly working on his game, will be worth it.

He hopes.

Lost in thought, he jumps when there's a sharp knock on his door. It's a strange sound, and one he doesn't hear often. Jasper rarely has friends over, and Kyle never does. The only visitors they ever really get are his RA and occasionally neighbors asking for something.

Heart hammering far too wildly for a simple knock on the door, Kyle scowls as he walks across the room. Lifting his chin, he swings the door open and ignores the weird squeeze in his chest when he finds Jake standing there. It's a stupid reaction. He *knew* Jake would be there. Still...it's one thing to know, and another to see him there, in Kyle's hallway and in Kyle's doorway. Wearing nice jeans and a fitted T-neck that stretches across his broad chest and shoulders, hanging to a tapered waist. He has a backpack thrown over one shoulder, and he smiles sheepishly down at Kyle.

"Hey, uh, sorry about the sudden change of plans," he says, rubbing the back of his neck. His eyes wander away from Kyle to the room behind him.

Kyle shrugs, stepping back and gesturing him in. "It's fine," he doesn't mean for his voice to sound so clipped, but it comes out that way nonetheless. He blames the weird heat beneath his skin. "Just sit wherever."

He closes the door quietly and slips back into his seat at his desk, chair turned so he can watch as Jake stands in the middle of his room and turns in a slow circle, taking everything in. It's strange to see him there. He looks nothing like Kyle or Jasper. Tall and broad and more at home in a gym than in their strange little den of a dorm. Still, Kyle realizes it's the first time he's ever had someone over. The first time he's ever invited anyone over. And his chest does that annoying little squeeze again.

He frowns, ducking down to pull his economics textbook out of his backpack, setting it down on his desk loudly enough to get Jake's attention. "Should we get started?" he asks, mindlessly flipping through the book to avoid looking up at Jake.

"Oh, right, yeah," Jake drops his own backpack to the floor and collapses into one of the beanbag chairs. He makes himself comfortable before pulling out his own textbook and a notebook that looks like it's never been used. "Would you believe this is the first time I've ever actually opened this book?"

Kyle exhales a short, sharp laugh, even as he deadpans. "With how often you bring your book to class? No, I never would've guessed."

There's a long silence, and as it drags on, Kyle starts to feel the wriggling of doubt in his gut, anxiety squirming beneath his skin. That was...could that have been considered rude? Shit. It's been a long time since he's been forced to be social with people, and he and Jasper live in a shared state of sarcasm and dry humor.

He glances up and catches Jake's gaze. His eyes are wide, lips parted slightly in shock. And as Kyle watches, those lips slowly curve up into a wide, toothy smile. One that is *definitely* not good for Kyle's heart. "Oh my god. Was that a *joke?*"

Kyle frowns, bristling slightly. "Am I not allowed to joke?"

"No, no! You definitely are. I just wasn't expecting it, I guess? You're always so serious."

Kyle looks down again, digging out his own notebook from class to keep his hands and his eyes busy as he mutters. "You're making assumptions about me again."

"My bad."

Kyle can hear the smile in his voice, but he refuses to look up. He's learning very quickly that Jake's smiles aren't good for his health. The guy is too damn pretty for Kyle's own good. And he's going to be stuck with him, alone in his dorm, for at least an hour. Oh god, why did he agree to this?

"So, uh...what chapter are we on exactly?" there's a sheepishness to his voice, along with an edge of embarrassment trying to hide behind humor.

Kyle finds himself smiling, even as he keeps his eyes cast down. "Five."

"Right, I knew that."

Never having tutored in his life, Kyle has been under the impression it would be easy. Figure out what Jake's been having trouble with, force him to study and do his homework, and that's it. Turns out that's a lot harder when Jake has never read or studied for this class at all, and Kyle quickly comes to the realization that a foundation has to be built before any real studying can happen.

The first twenty minutes are spent with Kyle asking questions, trying to figure out how much of the material Jake knows and where he needs to learn the most. Turns out the answers are not much and pretty much everything, in that order. With a sigh, rubbing his fingers on his temple, Kyle tells Jake to start by reading chapter five. *Actually* reading it. Not just skimming it. At least then they can move forward through the stuff they're learning now in class.

"Just let me know if you have any questions while you're reading," he says as he turns back to his computer, fingers already settling over the keyboard and eyes scanning the strips of code he'd been working on earlier.

It takes Jake two minutes before he asks his first question, and then what feels like thirty seconds after that for the second. They come at such a rapid speed, and Kyle quickly realizes that not having a foundation is a problem. Whenever the book refers to something they learned earlier in the semester, Jake gets confused. But it's more than that. The mere wording of sentences, even those explaining simple concepts, get confusing and muddled in Jake's mind.

Kyle finally sighs, pushing back from his desk and climbing to his feet. He shuffles across the room and collapses into the beanbag next to Jake, his own book open on his lap. He's resigned himself to the fact that he's going to have to go through it with Jake and help him decipher the text.

He regrets moving to the beanbag almost immediately when Jake's cologne fills his nose and his calf brushes against Kyle's foot. Curling up in his beanbag, he focuses on the text, talking through it aloud and answering questions, keeping eye contact to a minimum.

* * *

JAKE SIGHS LOUDLY, the exhale trailing off into a groan as he stretches on the beanbag, arms over his head as his back arches and his head falls back. "██████████, my brain hurts."

Kyle frowns, brows pinching. "We're only half way through the chapter."

"*Halfway?*" Kyle nods, and Jake groans again. He rubs his eyes with the heels of his hands.

"No one said getting your GPA up would be easy," Kyle says, trying to sound gentle.

"I know, I know, just...can we take a break?"

Kyle sighs, closing his book and pulling out his phone. It's been nearly an hour since Jake arrived. "Sure."

"Sweet," Jake rolls to his feet, taking a moment to stretch his hands high above his head and arch his back again. Kyle finds his gaze fixed on the strip of skin revealed as his shirt rides up, and he quickly looks away. Jake's back pops, and he groans, causing heat to rise to Kyle's cheeks. Jake then paces around the room, and Kyle keeps his attention fixed on his phone, determined to ignore him while he attempts to get his traitorous body under control.

"You've got a lot of games."

When he glances up, he finds Jake bent over, hands on his knees, looking over the collection of games on the shelf. Kyle *refuses* to admit that Jake's ass looks really good in those jeans. "Thanks," he says, heat crawling under his skin as his voice cracks slightly. He clears his throat. "Only about half of them are mine. The rest are my roommate's."

"Oh," Jake straightens, pointedly looking around the room with a slight purse to his lips. "I was kinda wondering if you had one. I mean, all the extra furniture comes with the dorm, so you could've just spread your stuff out."

Kyle shakes his head. "No, I have a roommate. He's just, uh...not here a lot on the weekends."

"What kinda guy is he?"

Kyle's face scrunches up in thought, lip curling a little as he struggles to find a word for it. "Um...artistic?"

Jake laughs, and while Kyle's not so sure what's funny about that, he finds himself smiling anyway. He doesn't mind Jasper. He smokes a lot and lazes around their room, but he's a nice enough guy. He talks to Kyle about Cry Thunder and he's offered to be a beta tester. They're not friends, exactly, but he's pretty good as roommates go.

"What about a girlfriend?"

The question catches him off guard, and Kyle blinks, staring up at him. "What?"

Jake is turned back to the shelves of games, occasionally pulling one out to look at the case. "You know, a girlfriend? You got one of those?"

"Uh, no. I don't," his heart feels like it's bruising his ribs, but the accelerated rate is different this time. There's an underlying tension in the air and a squeezing of his lungs. The question isn't pointed or barbed, not prying or searching. Just general curiosity. There's no way Jake could *know*...right? Kyle hasn't been *that* obvious. He scratches his cheek, eyes cast to the side. "I've actually...never had...a girlfriend."

The admission is filled with tension as he bristles, prepared to defend himself if he needs to. But Jake just hums his acknowledgement, not expressing any surprise and no pointed follow ups. In fact, he seems lost in his own thoughts, like he barely registered Kyle's awkward admission at all.

"I just broke up with my girlfriend, so I suppose I don't have one either. Or, I guess, *she* broke up with *me*." He says it offhandedly, but there's something deeper there. Something beneath his couldn't-care-less facade. Something...sad. Something that has Kyle's heart aching for him in a way he's not used to. Jake continues to pick through the games, though Kyle is certain he's not really looking at them. "She said I wasn't smart, or whatever. Which is *rich* coming from her. We were supposed to go to a party together tonight, but I didn't really feel like going after, you know, that happened. I don't even know if she's still going. Not that I really care. It was bound to happen eventually, and it was fun while it lasted, I guess. At least now I can focus on my whole GPA problem without worrying about her."

There's a pause, and Kyle squirms in his seat, not quite sure what to say. He finally settles on, "I'm sorry to hear that," and hopes it comes across as genuine as it feels. There's a hollowness surrounding Jake when he talks about it, and that's something Kyle can relate to.

Jake straightens, blinking in surprise as he turns. He scratches the back of his neck as he smiles. "Oh, uh, sorry. I didn't realize I was rambling. I know you don't wanna hear about my relationship problems."

Kyle waves it off, opening his textbook again. "It's fine."

They end up getting back to work, and Jake has found a new surge of determination and focus. Whether it's to prove himself or distract himself, Kyle isn't sure. He walks Jake through the chapter, explaining concepts and business models while ignoring the twisting leaden knot in his gut.

He's seen Jake around with his girlfriend before, both classically pretty and perfect together. He's known Jake is straight, and it's not like he's deluded himself into thinking anything could or would happen between them. Especially since no one knows Kyle likes men, and he's not about to change that. But just the confirmation that Jake is even *more* out of his league hurts a lot more than he thought it would.

CHAPTER 5

*J*ake has always had a fondness for coffee shops. Coffee itself is a goddamn blessing, but the atmosphere of coffee shops has always been alluring. Meeting up with friends, hanging out and wasting time between classes, meeting dates, all that good stuff.

However, as he sits in one of the tall chairs at a high table in the back corner of the campus's main coffee shop, chin resting on his open palm and eyes wandering around the room, he realizes this is probably the first time he's ever studied in one.

Or at least, he *should* be studying.

"Do you have your practice questions done?" Kyle asks without looking up from his laptop.

"Uh," Jake looks down at his open textbook and his noticeably blank notebook. "Not...exactly?"

Kyle glances up, leveling him with a flat look over the top of his glasses.

Jake leans back in his chair, draping one elbow over the back of it and gesturing at Kyle with his pencil. "Hey! Before you go judging, it's busy in here. There's a lot of distractions."

Kyle blinks at that, owlish and confused. He turns then, glancing around the coffee shop. They're in the corner, away from the main foot traffic, but the rest of the tables are mostly full. The room is filled with the soft, general din of mingling voices. "Oh," he says. "I hadn't noticed."

Jake snorts a short laugh but doesn't call attention to Kyle's single-minded focus. It's cute, kind of. For someone so smart, he's kind of oblivious to a lot of things. "Why can't we just study in your room again?"

Kyle stiffens a little, eyes flicking back to his screen. The sound of typing picks back up again. "My roommate is there now, and I don't want to disturb him."

"Would he get mad?"

Kyle shrugs. "I don't know, but I'd rather not push it."

"What's he like?"

Kyle glances up. "My roommate?" Jake nods, and Kyle's brow furrows like he's thinking of a particularly difficult math problem. "He's fine, I guess. We talk about video games, and sometimes we play together. Other than that, we don't really talk much. He's nice though, that's all I care about."

Jake's eyebrows rise. "Are you guys not friends?"

Kyle tilts his head to the side, eyes wide and curious once more. Jake swears his glasses make him look far too innocent and adorable for his own good. "Why would we be friends?"

"Uh, because a lot of people try to befriend their room-mates? And, I dunno, maybe you guys knew each other before college."

Kyle scoffs lightly, pushing his glasses up his nose. "No, we were random roommates. And he's not really my friend. He's not a bad roommate, though."

"Do you have any friends?"

The question is out of his mouth before he can really register what he's saying, and when Kyle visibly bristles, Jake realizes his mistake. Kyle's eyes narrow, frown becoming more apparent. "What's that supposed to mean?"

Jake sits up straight, hands going up in a placating gesture as he tries to backtrack. "No, wait! That's not what I meant. I mean like...uh...like, what'd you do in your free time?"

Kyle, however, doesn't relax, and when he speaks, it's stiff and closed. His walls are firmly back in place. Dammit. "I play games, and I work," he turns back to his computer, hunching as if that might help him hide behind it.

Jake frowns, leaning forward to rest his elbows on the table. "Yeah, but, like...what about a social life? Like what do you do with friends? Where do you go when you go out? For fun and stuff."

Kyle doesn't look up, nor does his typing slow, but Jake can see the tension around his mouth. His head tilts, catching the light of the laptop screen in his glasses and keeping Jake from seeing his eyes. "You should really work on those practice problems. We have a test on Friday, and we need to figure out where you need the most help."

Jake may not be academically inclined, but he's not stupid. He knows what Kyle is doing. He knows Kyle doesn't want to talk about it, and he gets the impression it's because there's a level of embarrassment there. He should probably back off, but his interest is caught, and he's always been stubborn.

"Come on, you've gotta do something. Any clubs on campus? There's like a million of them. Probably not sports, but like...I'm sure there's even a video game club. Gaming club? Something like that."

Kyle bites his lip but says nothing. He simply ignores Jake and continues to type. He does that a lot in their tutoring sessions. He does some of the work with Jake, but he doesn't need to dwell on it as long. He always ends up back at his computer typing up something Jake can't see.

"Do you go out to eat? Meet up with classmates?"

Silence.

"What about parties? You can't be in college and not go to parties! Plus, everyone gets drunk, and when they're drunk they're super friendly. Everyone becomes your best friend. I'm sure you can meet people if you come to a party with me."

Kyle looks up then, eyes narrowed in suspicion. He doesn't look in the least bit convinced, but Jake has his attention, and that's a victory. He feels his heart squeeze briefly, and yeah, that's weird.

Kyle looks him up and down before slowly speaking. "With you?" his lips twist strangely, like the words taste sour on his tongue.

But the sound of them has Jake's heart slamming into overdrive, and...yeah, that's *really* fucking weird. He smiles, straightening and leaning over his elbows. "Yeah, dude! You can come to parties with me. I can introduce you to people. You can get out of your dorm and enjoy college life a bit," he snaps his fingers, pointing at Kyle as an idea occurs to him. Kyle jumps a little in his surprise, but Jake just grins. "That's it! Not only will I pay you for tutoring, but I'll show my thanks by helping you make more friends. Like, my new quest. You'll be my little buddy. What do you say?"

Kyle's lip curls, nose crinkling and glasses lifting higher. "No."

Jake feels that bubble of excitement that had been building in his chest start to deflate. "Come on, dude, it'll be good for you!"

Kyle shakes his head, nearly dislodging his glasses and having to push them higher up his nose. "I'd rather just be left alone. People are...loud and messy, and I'm better off on my own."

Jake frowns, hunching his shoulders. He feels...off. He knows this feeling, and it doesn't make sense. Disappointment, acute and sharp, twisting in his gut. He doesn't know why it stings so much to have Kyle say no. After all, he's just his tutor. Just some kid Jake was trying to reach out to. Show his appreciation and everything.

Kyle just said he doesn't want to make new friends, so why does Jake feel like he's rejecting *him*?

And why does he even *care*?

"Seems pretty lonely," Jake mutters, tapping his pencil on his notebook. He sounds dejected, and he knows it. He's never been great at hiding his emotions. "You seem pretty lonely. You're just shy and anxious, but don't worry, with my help..."

"I am *not*," Kyle snaps, and Jake's eyes fly to his. He's sitting up straight, glaring at him fiercely. His mouth twisting into a scowl.

"I'm just saying..."

"I'm not *lonely*," Kyle closes his laptop with enough force that Jake winces. "I'm not shy, and I'm not *anxious*. And I don't need your *help*. I'm *fine* just the way I am, and I don't need you to *fix* me."

"Kyle," Jake tries, but the boy is already shoving his laptop and his books into his backpack. "Kyle! Come on, that's not what I meant."

Kyle turns to glare at him, and the look in his eyes is enough to make the words die in Jake's throat. "Finish your practice problems, and we'll meet up before the test to go over them," he says stiffly, with a bite that has Jake flinching.

He throws his backpack over his shoulder and stalks out of the coffee shop, leaving Jake reeling.

Behind the fire in his glare and the bite of his words, there had been genuine hurt. Jake had seen it. There were shadows and pain that made his gaze glassy and his lip tremble, if only slightly.

Jake had hurt him.

Jake had fucked up. He'd fucked up big time.

He'd just been trying to help, but god, he feels terrible. And the worst part is he's not even sure *how* he fucked up. Well, sort of, anyway. He realizes calling Kyle shy, anxious, and lonely probably wasn't a good call. He seemed pretty stuck on that. But Jake isn't *stupid*. He can *feel* there's more to it. There's something a lot deeper and a lot darker that's eating at Kyle. The worst part is he has no idea what, and at this point, he doubts Kyle would be willing to tell him.

Once again, he's stuck with the question of *why* does he *care?*

Jake sighs, staring down at his text book. His foot bounces incessantly, his fingers fiddling with his pencil, and he knows he's not getting anything else done right now. He'll try to do it later. He's got to if he wants to prove to Kyle that he's serious about the tutoring thing. But right now, his mind feels too scattered, and his emotions too unstable and confused.

He shoves his book and notebook back in his bag and swings it over his shoulder. He drops his empty coffee cup in the trashcan on his way out and shoves one hand in his pocket, pulling out his phone with the other.

He doesn't realize what he's doing until he's scrolling through his contacts and stops over a familiar name. A small ghost of a smile tugs at his lips. Of course, his first instinct is to call her. She always has a way of knowing him better than he knows himself, and she's always been able to ground him.

He presses the call button and puts the phone to his ear as he starts off across campus, heading back towards his apartment. She answers on the third ring.

"Hey, loser, long time no talk. You avoiding me?"

He finds his smile widening. "Babe, you know I'd never. Besides, I'm calling you now, aren't I?"

She hums thoughtfully. "Not your babe," she says it offhandedly and light heartedly. It's an exchange they've had a million times. One that means nothing but playful teasing, filled with inside jokes. "Anyway, what's up? I haven't heard from you since you told me Cindi broke up with you. She's not begging for you back, is she? Need me to run interference?"

"Nah, haven't heard from her since that night. And you're acting like I only call you when I need you."

"Don't you?" he can hear the smile in her voice.

"Maybe I just wanted to talk to you."

"Mmm, can't blame you. I'm a gem and a pleasure to be around."

"Damn straight."

"I'm bi, and you know it."

"Damn bi, then."

"Better. So, what's up?"

"Got time to talk?"

"I've got ten minutes before my next class."

"Cool. So, how're things going? How's Becca?"

"Amazing, beautiful and kicking my ass on a daily basis. She misses you, too, by the way. We haven't had time to hang out lately, so we should definitely do that. But I get the feeling you didn't call in the middle of the day when you *know* I have a class coming up just to talk about my relationship. Methinks you're calling about your own love life."

"It's not my love life."

"But you *are* calling about something specific," he can hear the amusement in her voice, and he knows he's been caught.

He sighs. "Fine, yes."

"Good. So, what's up?"

"You know how I told you I convinced this guy in my economics class to tutor me?"

"Mhmm, the cute one."

Jake stiffens. "I never said he was cute."

He can hear the smile in her voice and hates it. He hates how well she knows him, yet at the same time he loves it. "You didn't have to, dude. It was *very* clear in the way you described him to me. In how you talk about him. Are you calling for advice on how to ask him out?"

Jake sputters, heat rising rapidly to his cheeks. "That's not...*no!* He's my tutor, Liddy!"

"So? Isn't that why you asked him to tutor you?"

"I asked him to tutor me because he's super smart!"

"Yeah, but you were very persistent that *he* be the one to tutor you. Hell, dude, you could've asked me when he said no, but you wanted him. I thought it was pretty obvious."

"That's not...I wasn't thinking about *that*," he wasn't...was he? That isn't why he asked Kyle to tutor him. Kyle just looked like the smartest kid in the class, and Jake's decision had nothing to do with how adorable it is when Kyle scrunches his nose up in thought or how he tends to wear hoodies that are too big for him.

"Mhm, sure you weren't, big guy."

"He's not even my type."

At that, Liddy laughs, loud and boisterous. The blush on his cheeks is hot and fierce. He ducks his head as he walks, shoulders hunched and hissing into his phone.

"Stop laughing Liddy! He's not my type!"

"I'm sorry. Oh my god...I'm sorry, Jake, but that's a load of shit."

"What're you..."

"Listen. I don't have a lot of time before I have to get to class, so can I be blunt with you?" Jake makes a disgruntled noise of acceptance, and she steamrollers on. "You've been in a string of short lived, and quite frankly shallow, relation-ships with a bunch of girls who fawn over you because you're a big baseball star. You're hot. You're confident. You're the perfect jock, dude, so you get to have your pick of super-ficial girls, and boy have you been having your pick. And that's fine and all, I'm not shaming you. But when it comes to guys, you have a *very* different taste. Don't even try to deny it. When we dated, you wrangled me into several three-somes, and you were very particular about the kinda guys you like."

"Oh, yeah?" he grumbles, because really, he can't deny it. He's not happy about having to admit it though. "Then what's my type, oh wise one?"

"I know you're being sarcastic, but I'm gonna spell it out for you anyway. You like small guys. Nerdy kinda guys. The soft and vulnerable ones you can pick up, cuddle and protect. The kind that get swallowed by your jackets and clothes when they borrow them. Also, you love guys with dimples and glasses. Does your new tutor check all those boxes?"

He has no idea about the dimples, but he has to begrudg-ingly admit to the rest. "Yes."

"Is he cute?"

Jake sighs, running a hand through his hair and tilting his head back to stare up at the sky. "*Yes*. Are you happy?"

"Yup. I'm glad I could help you have this revelation. Is that all you needed?"

"No."

"You've got thirty seconds before I gotta hang up. I'm about to walk into the classroom."

"I fucked up," Jake admits, exhaling sharply through his nose. "I said some stuff, and now he's mad at me. I think I hurt his feelings."

"Then go apologize, dumbass," she says, but there's a fondness there, soft and gentle. "You can do this Jake. You're a sweet guy, even if you can be a little oblivious. Just *do* something about it."

He finds himself smiling, even if his insides are twisting. He feels bad for hurting Kyle, but mixed with his guilt is a gut churning feeling of...uncertainty? Excitement? It's been awhile since he's felt like this over anyone. "Thanks, Liddy."

"Anytime, dude."

CHAPTER 6

*K*yle has trouble sleeping that night. Curled up on his bottom bunk, he stares at the dark room. He rolls over and stares at the cinderblock wall. He huffs and rolls onto his back, staring at the bunk above him. He can hear Jasper's soft breaths, just a fraction away from being a snore. One of the things Kyle noticed when they moved into the dorm was that Jasper fell asleep fast and hard. He could sleep through anything, and he got there almost instantly. Kyle's extremely jealous of that.

It's always taken him a while to fall asleep. He has too many thoughts and they buzz around too rapidly, either repeating events from the day or thinking about the days coming up or thinking about what he needs to do on his game.

For the past few years, when the shadows creep and his body starts to relax, his mental walls coming down, he dwells on memories of his brother and of the hollow ache that's been in his chest ever since the accident.

He feels empty most days, which he prefers to the sharp

sting when the wound was fresh, but that doesn't stop the ache in his chest that he feels most nights.

Tonight, however, Kyle's thoughts don't linger on his brother, nor do they linger on Cry Thunder or his classes. They linger on Jake, and Kyle isn't sure if that's better or worse. He's going to go with worse.

He can hear Jake's words echoing in his head, disappearing into the shadows of his mind and bouncing back more twisted, more mocking, revealing the undertones that are so easy to hide, but Kyle *knows* are there.

Shy.

Anxious.

Lonely.

He knows what those words mean.

Pathetic.

Pitiful.

Anti-social.

He rolls onto his side, curling in on himself, pulling his knees to his chest and holding his blankets tight. He breathes in deep and tries to let it out slowly, but it just shudders out. He squeezes his eyes shut, trying to will the thoughts away. He tries to focus on Cry Thunder, on his new damage algorithms. They're working so far, but there's still a bug with the ranger class. Ranger damage doesn't always calculate critical strikes the way it should...

My new quest. You'll be my little buddy.

Jake sees him as nothing but a pet project. A doll to have fun with. Someone broken yet fixable. Someone to dress up and parade around to his friends. *Hey, guys, look at this nerd I found. Watch him dance. Watch him try to fit in. Let's have a good laugh...*

It's not the first time he's been used for the entertainment of others. It's not the first time he's been mocked and laughed at. And it wouldn't be the first time someone pretended to be his friend just to make him do things, as a bet or to entertain their friends. Get the nerd to do something embarrassing. Laugh at the geek who's trying to come out of his shell. He's not a stranger to bullying, and experience has taught him that people like Jake are usually the bullies.

And it doesn't help that Kyle usually finds them extremely attractive, and they make him go weak at the knees. He hopes that each one will be different, but they never are.

Is that why he's so hurt over this?

He *did* try to say no, and Jake managed to weasel his way past Kyle's defenses. He knows he's a sucker for a pretty face, but he thought he'd gotten better. Had he convinced himself that Jake was different? That he wouldn't be like all the others who've tried to use Kyle for entertainment or for someone to cheat off?

Oh god, he had, hadn't he?

Jake had spilled his little sob story and batted his eyelashes, and Kyle had fallen for it, hook, line, and sinker. His defenses had crumbled just enough for Jake to sneak inside. Then he starts talking like Kyle is someone to be fixed, sending up all those red flags that he's learned to notice, and...Kyle shouldn't feel so hurt over this. He's not a stranger to this. If anything, he should be mad. He should be indifferent. He should just brush it off as an *I-knew-it* moment and move on. No harm, no foul.

Yet here he is, curled up in bed, unable to sleep, torn up inside, with Jake's words echoing around in his head, haunting him.

He really is pathetic.

What did he think would happen? Jake would walk into his life, pristine and strong, with his pretty smile and scruffy jaw, prove to Kyle that some jocks were different and sweep him off his feet? Yeah, right. He'd like to tell himself that isn't what he thought, but the ache inside him says otherwise. He's an idiot. Jake is straight as a rod, and he's just like everyone else.

Time for Kyle to move on. He doesn't have time for tutoring and cute guys anyway. He has to work on his game. He has to *finish* his game. He has to graduate and release his game. It's what his brother would've wanted. He has to make their dream a reality because he's the only one who can.

He clenches his fists, burying his face in his pillow. Alright, no more tutoring. Next time he sees Jake, he'll tell him it's not working out. He can find another tutor easily. He doesn't need Kyle specifically. They'll both move on before Kyle can get hurt.

It's for the best.

But it still hurts.

* * *

KYLE FEELS like he's in a daze as he showers and gets dressed, partially from drowsiness but mostly because he just feels numb. All his emotions feel muted and inconsequential. It's a familiar feeling lately, and he finds some comfort in it. At least like this he doesn't have to care about Jake.

He packs his bag, pulls on his hoodie, and grabs a nutrition bar on his way out the door. His room is only on the third floor, and he hates having to wait for elevators. So out of habit, he turns away from them, heading for the stairwell and moving quickly down the steps. He has fifteen minutes to get to his next class. Easy enough. It only takes five to walk there, but he likes to be early.

He slips out of his dorm building after a couple of other students, head ducked down as he checks his messages and email on his phone.

"Kyle!"

He freezes, stumbling mid-step and nearly falling. When he finds his balance, he spins around, phone in one hand and nutrition bar halfway to his mouth as his eyes zero in on Jake. He pushes off the wall of the dorm, jogging a couple of steps to catch up to him.

"Hey," he says, smiling sheepish and strangely breathless despite the jog being only a couple of feet. His hair looks messy and still damp from a shower, bag lazily slung over only one shoulder. He holds the strap with one hand, the other shoved in his pocket.

"Uh, hi?" Kyle manages to say. It takes him a second to build his walls back up again and shake out any lingering thoughts that Jake looks...really, really good today. *He looks good every day*, he reminds himself. *Get over it.* He shakes his head, eyes narrowing. "What're you doing here?"

"I, uh..." Jake runs his fingers through his hair, tugging at the strands in what Kyle is learning is a nervous gesture. He looks away, eyes flickering across the sea of students all around them, trudging from their dorms and setting off on the paths to campus. He sighs, posture slumping as he turns back to Kyle. "Look, I just wanted to apologize for yesterday. About the things I said. I didn't mean them *like that.* Like...*bad.* I just wanted to show my appreciation, you know? Help you out for helping me out. This means so much to me. I *really* need this tutoring, and I'd really like for you to be the one to do it, so I'm just...really sorry."

He looks exhausted. There are dark bags under his eyes, and his entire face is open and haggard. None of the posturing or the smirks, he's not trying to hide anything. He looks honest and genuine. Kyle feels his heart squeeze and his stomach flutter, and...

No. *No.* He needs to say no. He needs to tell Jake he won't do it. It's over. He has things he needs to focus on. He can't do this anymore. He needs to end it before he gets hurt.

But when he opens his mouth, the words that come out are not those. "We need to set some ground rules," Jake visibly perks up at that, eyes widening and body lifting. His smile is hesitant, but hopeful, and he looks too goddamn much like an excited puppy. Kyle can feel his heart squeeze, and he *really* needs to get ahold of himself. He holds out the hand with his phone, putting one finger in the air to stop whatever Jake might say. "I'll help you and continue to tutor you, but I manage my own social life. This is strictly academic and professional. I don't need friends, and I don't want them. I have to focus on my studies. I'm not here to party. Got it?"

Jake's shoulders slump again. He doesn't look upset, but he narrows his lips, brows furrowing as he looks Kyle over. There's pity in his eyes, and it makes Kyle bristle. "That's... kinda sad, isn't it? Like, lonely? What's the point if you can't have fun?"

Kyle stiffens, raising himself to his full height and lifting his chin. He glares up at Jake. "Do you agree or not?"

Jake puts up his hands quickly. "I agree, okay. I get it. No dragging you to parties. We're just here to study."

Kyle nods once, and steps past him, continuing along the path to his class. "Good. Meet me here later to go over your practice problems for the test on Friday."

"I'll text you when I'm free!" Jake calls out, and Kyle stiffens, shoulders rising toward his ears. He simply lifts a hand and waves it to show that he heard.

Heat flushes his cheeks and a smile tugs at his lips. He puts his phone away and slaps at his cheek. "Pull yourself together, Kyle," he grumbles, dragging his hand down his face.

Strictly professional. Jake isn't his friend, and Jake isn't interested in him. *He's* not interested in *Jake*. He's just doing this to get a little money on the side. The fact that Jake looked wholly apologetic and genuine doesn't change anything. It doesn't mean he's different than the rest, and it doesn't mean Kyle should let his guard down.

He ignores the fact that by the time he gets to class, the void in his heart is a little less vacant and he feels a little less numb.

CHAPTER 7

*A*fter a fitful night's sleep, haunted by his own words and dwelling in the realm of *what-if-he-doesn't-forgive-me*, Jake is feeling pretty good. Much better, anyway. He's not gonna lie, he's a little bummed. Bummed, but also relieved? He's relieved Kyle didn't decide to just drop him completely, that he'll still tutor him, and Jake doesn't have to worry about finding a new tutor. Because no matter what his reasons, he really does want Kyle to tutor him. He wasn't lying. He likes Kyle.

But he's also kind of bummed because...he *does* like Kyle. He's cute, and yeah, okay, like Liddy said, he's totally Jake's type, but it's more than that. Kyle is interesting. He's not just plain and ordinary. There's something more there. There's something hiding behind the walls he puts up, and Jake has a driving urge to figure out what it is. Every time Kyle pushes him away, Jake is that much more determined to push back. He wants to get inside that head of his and see what makes him tick.

He sees the shadows Kyle carries around with him. It's much more obvious now they've spent some time together.

It's not just walls keeping others out. There are walls keeping something else in and Jake wants to know what. He wants to get in there and battle those shadows and those ghosts. He wants to see Kyle *smile*. A real, genuine, unabashed smile. He wants to know what Kyle's laugh sounds like. He wants to know if the guy has dimples.

So...yeah, he's probably in a little deep and getting carried away. It doesn't help that he's got a voice in the back of his head that sounds an awful lot like Liddy, constantly reminding him that Kyle is fucking *adorable*.

But the fact remains that Kyle said he doesn't want friends. He wants this to be a strictly professional relationship between them. No parties and no hanging out. And as much as that bums him the fuck out, and as much as he'd like to push that boundary, he knows he has to respect Kyle's wishes. His grades depend on it, and his grades should be his top priority right now.

Still, despite being his priority, school work and studying has never really gotten him excited. If anything, he knows he should be dreading it but resolved to deal with it anyway. So, he knows the strange thrill he feels settling in his chest as he leaves the locker rooms after baseball practice that night, has little to do with studying, and more to do with the prospect of seeing Kyle again.

He tries not to dwell on that too much. Overthinking has never done him much good. He's gotten this far in life just following his gut feelings, doing what he wants to do without thinking too much about what it might mean.

"Hey, Jake!"

He turns as a couple of his teammates filter out of the locker room behind him, bags dangling from their shoulders. Their hair is still damp from the showers, shirts sticking where they didn't fully dry off, reeking of freshly applied body spray. It's familiar and strangely comforting, as are their smiles as they catch up to him. These are his teammates and his friends.

"Sup?" Jake says as they fall into step with him, heading across the parking lot that borders the practice field.

"Dude, we heard about the break-up," Terry says, throwing an arm around Jake's shoulders.

Matt snorts from where he's walking at Jake's other side. "Yeah, Cindi won't shut up about it. She's making it *very* clear that she's back on the market."

"Sucks, dude. She was hot," Terry shakes his head, squeezing Jake's shoulders. "So how you holdin' up?"

Jake shrugs, mildly surprised that none of this news stings. Not even slightly. He doesn't really care that she's already moved on from him, nor does he really care that she's apparently looking for someone else after telling him she wanted to work on herself. "I'm fine. It wasn't like she broke my heart or anything. She was getting kinda boring, you know?"

They chuckle, exchanging a few crude comments between them. Jake tunes them out, keeping his easy-going smirk in place, nodding and laughing where he knows he should. He's never been a big fan of locker room talk, of all the gossip and crude comments his teammates like to throw around when they're alone. He's learned to adapt, knows how to get in on it, and sometimes finds it amusing, but right now he doesn't really care.

They rattle on about their girlfriends and chicks they've banged, or their current conquests, Jake isn't really sure. He's stopped listening. For once, he doesn't really care about figuring out who he wants on his arm next. It's surprising, and mildly alarming, that he finds himself thinking about the practice problems he's supposed to show Kyle tonight, wondering if he's done them right.

Then he hears a buzzword.

One that makes him physically recoil, steps faltering as his eyes snap up to Sam. He's walking backwards in front of them, hands shoved into his pockets and with little regard for whoever he might be backing into. Sam is grinning at him, mischief and amusement sparking in his eyes, and Jake doesn't like the look of it. He frowns, eyes narrowing. "What?"

Sam's grin widens, toothy and shark-like. "I *said*, Greg and I saw you at the coffee shop yesterday with that nerdy faggot kid."

Jake bristles, a chilling fear flooding through him, feeling like ice in his veins. *Faggot.*

"Greg said it looked like you guys were on a date," Sam continues, oblivious to Jake's pounding heart. "I said there's no fucking way. You bang like, all the hottest chicks. Break up or not, you wouldn't go after some geeky little gay kid."

"He's not gay," Jake says automatically, something new twisting in his gut. It feels like uncertainty, and tastes like disappointment. He doesn't have time to dwell on that, though, because Terry laughs right next to his ear, joining in.

"What about *you*, Jake? Tired of pussy and looking for a new snack? Didn't know you could switch teams so easily."

Matt chuckles, elbowing Jake in the side. "Maybe Cindi broke him more than he's leading on."

"It looked like you guys were studying. You banging him to get good grades?" Sam chuckles, shaking his head. "I can't blame you for that one. I'd definitely let a dude suck my dick if it meant passing my classes."

"There's a thought," Terry snaps his fingers like he just discovered something, leaning in to loudly whisper in Jake's ear. "Is he good at sucking dick? I heard the nerdy ones are always the horniest. I bet you could get that little faggot wrapped around your..."

"Fuck off," Jake snaps, roughly shoving Terry's arm off his

shoulders. The laughter stops at the venom in his voice, smiles fading into frowns.

"Dude, chill, we're just playin'."

"Yeah, man, don't get so defensive."

"What, are you guys actually dating or something?"

Jake stops walking, letting them pull ahead and stop to look back at him. He glares at them, lips pulled into a tight scowl. "He's tutoring me, so I can pass my classes and keep my fucking scholarship," he snaps, shoving Terry as he storms past them. "Now *fuck off* and mind your own business."

He can hear them grumble behind him and call out after him, but he ignores them. Fuming, he stomps back towards campus, taking another route. He kicks rocks, scowling at anyone who looks at him for too long.

He's not entirely sure what set him off. He's used to that kind of talk from his teammates, and he's gotten good at brushing it off, but hearing them talk that way about *Kyle* just...it pisses him off. Kyle doesn't deserve to be talked about like that, whether he can hear it or not. And being dragged into it himself was just...

He didn't like it. That *word* echoes around in his head, making the ice in his veins sharper with every reverberation, making him shiver with dread.

Did it really look like him and Kyle were on a date in the coffee shop? They both had books and stuff out, and Kyle was clearly absorbed in his computer. Plenty of other people on campus hang out and study with friends. It's normal. It's not weird or date-like at all. And while the thought of it looking like a date makes this weird part of him flutter and melt, it's quickly frozen and shattered by the memory of his team-mate's mocking grins, grating laughs, and sardonic smiles.

By the time he reaches Kyle's dorm, he's cooled off somewhat, but he can still feel anxiousness churning in his gut. He feels like eyes are watching him as he sits on the bench outside the building and pulls out his phone to text Kyle that he's here.

He leans back on the bench, head tilted back to gaze up at the late afternoon sky. It'll be dark soon. His foot bounces incessantly, feeding off the nervous energy that his anger has boiled down to. He can't shake it, no matter how hard he tries.

"Jake?"

His head snaps up at the sound of his name, and he frowns as Kyle walks out of his building. He stands quickly, tilting his head with confusion as Kyle moves toward him instead of waiting to let him into the building. "Uh, what're you doing? Aren't we gonna study in your room?"

Kyle shakes his head. His hair is damp and looks freshly washed. It curls slightly, and something in Jake's chest tightens as Kyle gazes up at him through his glasses. "My roommate's here. I figured we could go study in the quad or coffee shop or something."

"No!" they both freeze. Kyle looks taken aback, confusion pinching his brows as he tilts his head, physically taking a step away from Jake. Jake just stares, wide eyed and horrified at his outburst. "Uh, I just mean..." he wraps his fingers around the back of his neck, chewing on the inside of his cheek. What *did* he mean? He's not even sure, but with his teammates' words still fresh in his mind, the thought of being out with Kyle again, where people can see them, can make assumptions, can make judgements...a shiver runs through him. "I just mean like...studying in the coffee shop was kind of distracting for me? You know, a lot of stuff going on. It's easier if we're somewhere private."

Kyle frowns, eyes wary and calculating as Jake fidgets

under his gaze. "Okay," he says slowly. He sounds reluctant, but more than that, he sounds uncomfortable. Wary, even.

Jake hates it. He hates seeing Kyle retreat back behind those walls, a look of mistrust in his eyes. But really, what has Jake done to make Kyle want to trust him? Still, he's already dug this grave, so he might as well lie in it. He does think it'll be better for them both if they keep their study sessions private.

He smiles, hoping it looks genuine enough to put Kyle at ease. "We can go to my place. My roommates are out drinking tonight and shouldn't be back until later."

He doesn't mention that normally, he would be out drinking with them. He doesn't mention that he didn't even feel disappointed when he told them no because the prospect of hanging out with Kyle made him strangely jittery. He doesn't even want to face that fact himself.

Kyle looks him over for a while and relaxes a fraction, but the wariness remains. Finally, he shrugs. "Sure," He doesn't sound as confident or at ease as Jake was hoping, but he doesn't fight him on it, and that's good.

* * *

A FEW HOURS LATER, Jake has finally managed to cool down and focus. Not only that, he finds he's actually enjoying himself. Sure, the studying part is hard, but Kyle is able to take all the fancy mumbo jumbo the text book says and put it into words he can actually understand. And it's kind of *exciting* that he understands? Like, for the first time, he actually, truly, *gets* it. He understands the material.

That in and of itself, is a thrill that's new and exciting.

They go over the practice test Jake did, and Kyle takes the time to correct his mistakes and explain the right way to do things. Jake listens attentively, determined to forget his teammates and prove to Kyle that he's really here to learn. After that, they end up ordering a pizza, and they eat while Kyle gives Jake more practice problems and has him do those now he has some new understanding.

The atmosphere is relaxed. It'd taken Kyle a while to warm up to his place, but after a while, he did. He relaxed and looked comfortable in Jake's apartment, sitting on his couch with his legs pulled up and crossed, laptop on his lap. Jake can't explain it, but he likes the look of him there. Likes what it does to his chest. He focuses on his work rather than thinking about that.

They're nearly done when Jake's roommates come home. He hears the key in the lock, and his heart immediately sinks. He freezes on the couch, eyes darting to Kyle. He can see him stiffen. Then his roommates are barging through the open door, stumbling over each other and laughing. The door slams shut, and they stumble through the entryway, pausing when they reach the living room. Their laugher dies, and he looks up to find them both staring, openly gawking at him sitting on the couch with Kyle.

Kyle, thankfully, hasn't turned around to see their open stares.

"Jake?" Steve looks puzzled.

Marcus pushes forward, grin wide and toothy. "Jake! You're home! I thought you were gonna go out and *study*. You know, be *boring*," he saunters forward, sitting himself on the arm of the couch, right next to Kyle. He leans back against the cushion, draping his arm casually behind Kyle, who stiffens further. "This the little nerd who you wrangled into helping you out?"

"I thought you guys were gonna be out all night," Jake says stiffly, smile in place but feeling strained.

Steve shrugs, leaning against the wall as he struggles to pull off his shoes. "We got kicked out for being too loud or whatever," he pulls one shoe off with a victorious sound, stumbling slightly when his balance shifts. "Figured we'd come back here and finish getting smashed. You want in?"

"No, I'm fine."

"What about you?" Marcus leans forward, getting in Kyle's face enough to make him lean away. He gazes at Marcus, eyes wide and mouth set. "Name's Marcus, by the way. So, you're the one who got him suddenly all academic."

"You mean boring!" Steve calls from the kitchen where he's rummaging through the fridge.

Marcus laughs, sliding off the couch and sinking into a cushioned chair nearby, one leg hooked over the arm of it. "You two look cozy," he says, grinning playfully as he gestures to the two of them on the couch and the empty pizza box on the table. "Looks kinda like a date."

He waggles his eyebrows, and Jake scoffs. He looks down at the book in his hand, feeling heat creeping up the back of his neck. "Get off it, Marcus," he mumbles.

"Is he the one you dumped Cindi for?" Marcus pushes, and Jake stiffens, heart rising into his throat even as his stomach sinks. His breath comes strained and quick, and he refuses to look at Kyle. "He's kinda cute for a guy. Kinda looks like a girl if you squint."

"Dude, Jake's not gay! He's dated like, all the hottest chicks on campus. He's a fuckin' player!" Steve calls from the kitchen. He leans out over the open bar to narrow his eyes at them from across the room. His attention zeroing in on Kyle. "Are *you* gay, kid?"

"Dude," Marcus snaps, waving a hand lazily at him. "You can't just ask people if they're gay," his reprimand falls flat as he slurs his words, his voice indifferent.

"Why not?"

"I dunno. They don't like it, or some shit."

"Marcus, where'd you put the fuckin' vodka?"

"It's on the top shelf!"

"No, it's not. Get your ass in here and find it."

Marcus grumbles as he stumbles out of his chair, staggering his way into the kitchen. Jake can hear them arguing, but his attention zeros in on Kyle as he slowly closes his laptop. Jake keeps his eyes down, heart hammering in his throat. His blood feels like ice in his veins, but his skin feels hot all over. He watches out of the corner of his eye as Kyle packs his things.

He should say something. He *needs* to say something. But ~~fuck~~ *fuck*, what is he supposed to say?

"Kyle…" he starts, slow and wary, but Kyle cuts him off.

"I'm going to go home," his voice is strained and his words thick. When Jake tries to get a good look, he thinks Kyle's eyes might be glassy, but he keeps his head down and turned away. Jake can see the tension where he clenches his jaw. "You'll do fine on the test. Text me if you have any more problems."

Jake watches as Kyle picks up his bag and leaves. Slinks right out the door without his roommates noticing. A ghost, small and silent. He watches from his spot on the couch, rooted and frozen, heart in his throat and stomach rolling uncomfortably.

He fucked up. He fucked up *again*.

As soon as the door closes, he's off the couch, text book slamming down on the coffee table. He stomps to the kitchen, fury blazing, melting away the ice in his veins. "Guys, what the *fuck?*" he slams his fist on the wall, and both his roommates spin around, eyes wide and mouths gaping, wobbling on their feet and holding cups and a couple of bottles between them.

"Jake, what…"

"Seriously? Did you *seriously* have to pick on him like that?"

"We were just having fun."

"You were being an asshole, Marcus. You both were. Straight up fucking assholes."

They have the decency to look abashed and apologetic, and he knows them well enough to know it's genuine. "We didn't mean it like *that*."

"We were just trying to have some fun with the guy!"

Jake sighs, running fingers through his hair and tugging at it until it stings. "I know, but seriously? Don't be fucking douchebags. He's tutoring me, so I can keep my fucking scholarship and stay on the team, so *lay off him*."

"Sorry, man."

"Yeah, dude, we weren't thinking."

Silence persists, heavy and leaden, for several moments before Marcus lifts a shot glass. "Wanna take some shots with us?"

Jake sighs. He doesn't, but he also doesn't want to dwell on the fact that Kyle has walked out on him *again* because of his own stupid actions. He doesn't want to think about how he feels about that. Instead he holds out his hand. "Sure."

CHAPTER 8

"*S*o, he *does* know how to answer the phone!"

Kyle sinks lower in his desk chair, pulling his feet up onto it and his knees to his chest. He wraps his free arm around them, resting his cheek on his knee as he sighs. "Hi, Mom."

"I haven't heard from you in ages!" her voice is teasing but happy. It makes his insides twist with guilt. It hadn't been *that* long. Had it?

"Well, I'm here now," he picks at the seam of his jeans. "How've you guys been?"

"Oh, same old, same old. Your dad's been working himself into the ground because he can't say no when people need him, and nothing has changed at the bank for me. The dogs are doing well. Mickey learned how to jump onto the counters, so that's a pain."

Kyle hums, a soft smile tugging at the edges of his lips. He misses them. He really does. It's not easy being here on his own. Especially not after everything that happened last summer. He knows his parents aren't fairing much better, but it's hard to talk to them. They call him constantly, and most days he just can't find the energy to answer the phone. He's trying *not* to think too much about it. Forcing himself to move on. But every time he talks to them, he feels like a ghost is hanging over the conversation. An elephant in the room that's clearly there but no one wants to address it.

Still, he hasn't answered one of their calls in a while, and he can only go so long before the guilt starts to claw at him and tear him apart from the inside out. He grits his teeth and bears it, if only for now. She called while he was waiting for Jake to show up for a study session, so at least he has an escape if he needs it.

"Enough about us, though. How are *you?* You've barely told us about anything. How's college life? What's your roommate like? How're your classes?"

"It's fine. He's good. We get along fine. Classes are classes. Mostly boring, but I'm passing," he mumbles. He doesn't really want to get into it, and he doesn't want to *think* about it. College is just something he has to do and something he has to get through. Even if it sucks, and it...no, he's not thinking about it. Everything is *fine.*

His mom hums, but her high energy is flagging. He can hear it leaking out of her. When she speaks again, he can hear how tired she is. He can hear everything she's trying to hide and everything she doesn't want to say. "I'm glad things are going okay. We just...we worry about you."

He feels his chest tighten. His fingers dig into his thigh and curl around his phone. "Mom..."

"We just...we miss you, Kyle. We know you can't come home, but we'd like to hear from you more often. Just to know that you're okay. Even if you have nothing to say, we'd like to hear your voice."

"I know, Mom, I just..." he has to stop and swallow the lump in his throat. He can hear how thick his voice has become, and he clears his throat. "I'm just really busy with school, you know? It's more work than high school, and with everything I'm doing I don't have a lot of time."

It's not entirely untrue. He *is* really busy. He needs to hurry up and graduate as soon as he can. He needs to pass all his classes with flying colors, just like his brother would have. He has to finish his game, just like his brother would have wanted him to, he has to...

There's a sharp knock at the door, and Kyle jumps, head whipping around to look at it. It takes a couple seconds before his mind can catch up.

Right. He was waiting for Jake.

"Hey, Mom, I gotta go."

"Was that a knock I just heard? Do you have a friend coming over?" She sounds so surprised and hopeful, breathless in her shock and glee.

He can't bring himself to disappoint her. "Uh, yeah, so I gotta go. I'll talk to you later."

"Alright! Tell me all about them later, okay? Love you."

His voice feels tight and his words sound thick as he says, "Love you, too, Mom."

He hates how relieved he feels when he hangs up.

By the time he gets to the door, he's more put together, but his chest still feels tight and his breath is straining. And judging from the way his pulse jumps and his stomach flips when he opens the door, he knows it doesn't entirely have to do with talking to his mom.

"Hey," Jake sounds sheepish, hands shoved deep in his pockets and shoulders hiked up to his ears.

"Hey," Kyle says, trying to sound as neutral as possible as he steps aside to let Jake in.

"You okay?" Jake asks, brows pinching as he looks Kyle over.

He looks away, closing the door behind him. "Uh, yeah. Just got off the phone with my mom."

"Ah, gotcha," he sounds distracted. Kyle watches as he paces as far into the room as the small dorm will allow before spinning around quickly and abruptly. His hands fly out of his pockets, going up in a defensive gesture. "Look, I'm really sorry about the other night. I didn't think my room-mates would come home so early, and I definitely didn't think they'd be assholes. I told them off once you left, and they promised not to mess with you anymore."

Even as his limbs feel like they're buzzing with energy, Kyle feels his stomach flip and his insides melt. His shoulders slump as tension he hadn't realize he was carrying leaches out of him. He hadn't realized how much he needed to hear that. He hadn't realized how relieved he would be to hear Jake apologize and look completely genuine about it.

He hadn't expected this much, and the fact that he got it unprompted, means a lot.

The ghost of a smile touches his lips. Not a full smile, but the brief beginnings of one. "Thanks, Jake."

Jake's body sags, bag falling to the floor as he smiles, wide and relieved. "No problem, man. You're with me now. No one is gonna mess with you on my watch. *Especially* my friends."

They take up their usual seats on the beanbags on the floor, their bags and books spread out around them. Kyle shifts, sinking into the seat and pulling his knees up to get comfortable. He pushes his sleeves to his elbows, his glasses up his nose, and pulls the textbook onto his lap to flip to the right chapter.

"So, uh, I was wondering..." Kyle's page turning slows as he glances up, curious. Jake sits in his beanbag, legs stretched out in front of him, bent slightly. He lounges back, arms spread out across the puff of the beanbag. His notebook and textbook sit on his lap, untouched. His gaze is locked in front of him, fixed on the shelves of video games, but his eyes are too still to be reading the titles. "I was just curious, you know? About you…and like, it's no big deal. I just got to thinking…not that you gotta answer me if it's too personal, I just…"

"Jake," Jake's mouth snaps shut as he turns to look at him, and Kyle just levels him with a flat look. Judging from the way he looks abashed, Kyle has a feeling Jake knows he was rambling. He doesn't think he's ever seen Jake this nervous. Not even when he was working up to apologize. "Just spit it out."

Jake lets out a long breath. "Right. I'll just ask then," his hands slap at the beanbag's sides where they hang. He looks away again, eyes wandering the room. "And you don't have to answer if you don't want, I was just really curious, like…you're not really into sports or anything like that, and you don't seem to be really interested in girls, at least I've never seen you check out girls the way my friends do, even when there's a really hot one standing next to you, so like, I was wondering, are you like…" he waves a hand around vaguely. "*You know?* Do you like dudes? Not that it really matters to me. I don't care if that's what you're into. It's not a big deal. Kyle? *Kyle!*"

Kyle hears him as if through a fog. His voice sounds distant and his understanding of words is fuzzy around the edges. His room seems to zoom out, perpetually stretching and blurring at the corners. He stares at Jake, but he barely registers him. Barely sees him. His limbs feel tingly, and his fingertips feel numb. He thinks his mouth is hanging open, and he only knows that because he can feel the coolness from each trembling breath on his lips.

Hazily, distantly, he realizes he's having a panic attack.

His chest is tight. Too tight. He can't breathe. His stomach is hard and clenched and rolling, and *he can't breathe.* There's pain in his fingers, but it's distant. He thinks he's clenching his hands. Everything seems to fade in and out, and his mind is on a mental repeat.

No. No. He can't know. He's not...He can't be. No one can know. No. No. Nonononono.

"Kyle."

Hands are on his cheeks, warm and strong. Calloused and rough. Firm, but so, so gentle. Kyle's gaze snaps to focus on Jake's face. He's closer than he was. He fills up Kyle's vision, eyes holding onto his and refusing to let go.

"Calm down. It's okay. Breathe with me okay? In, out. Yeah, just like that. Follow with me. In. Out. In. Out. You're doing great, buddy. Stay with me"

Kyle focuses on the feeling of Jake's hands as a grounding point, holds onto his gaze for focus, and breathes with him. Listens to his voice, warm and low, rich and smooth like honey. Slowly, oh so slowly, he calms down. Feeling comes back to his body. His breaths even out. His mind slowly settles back into his body.

He closes his eyes, breath stuttering out in a long sigh. "Thanks," his voice is strained and cracked.

He opens his eyes as Jake pulls away, hating that he already misses his touch. Jake's smile is small and apologetic. "No problem. Sorry about that. I didn't think...I just didn't think. We don't have to talk about it. I get it if you don't trust me."

Kyle looks down, mindlessly flipping to the chapter they need to work on. He's never been great at conversation, and he doesn't even know how to approach what just happened. He doesn't know what to say at all, so he goes for a hard segue. "So, about the homework we were assigned."

Thankfully, Jake lets him have it and easily takes the hint.

They spend the next couple hours going over their work. They're getting ahead of the game, going over the chapter they're set to cover in class for the upcoming week. Kyle's plan was to get Jake starting ahead so he understands the lesson before their professor goes over it in class. Hopefully then he can follow along and understand the assignments a little more.

Kyle immerses himself in it, helping Jake read and decipher the over-worded text into something more approachable and understandable. Jake is already getting better at seeing through the complex wording to the heart of the matter, able to spin it into his own words. He does it with lackluster confidence, forming it in the shape of a question and waiting for Kyle's approval and confirmation. The smile he gives whenever Kyle says he's right is blinding. It makes Kyle's stomach flip and butterflies flutter in his chest.

It's stupid. All of it is stupid. Of course, if he's being honest, Jake is attractive. He's always *known* Jake is attractive. He's never shied away from that truth. But there's a difference between acknowledging someone is attractive and being attracted *to* them. He realizes that he's starting to dip into the latter, and he needs it to stop. It's stupid, and it'll go nowhere. Even if Jake is telling the truth and it's no big deal that Kyle...likes...you know. Jake is still straight, and Kyle knows better than to crush on a straight jock.

When they're done for the evening, Jake packs up his things quietly and quickly. There's tension in the air, and it's not until then that Kyle realizes how relaxed the atmosphere is when they're alone. He's gotten so used to Jake's easy presence, how warm and inviting and relaxing it is, he's never realized how much he appreciated that until it's gone. He's never realized how much he enjoys Jake's mindless and idle chatter as he packs up his things. How much just listening to his voice puts Kyle at ease.

It's stupid, and he knows he should just let it go, let Jake drift away, but he can't.

He scrambles to his feet after Jake and grabs his arm as he

reaches for the door. Jake freezes, looking back and blinking at Kyle's hand tugging at his sleeve. Jake's eyes follow the hand to Kyle's face, and Kyle blanches. He hadn't thought this far ahead, but now he has to say *something*.

He bites his lip and looks away, down at his feet and his mismatched socks. "I, uh, just wanted to say sorry, about earlier. I didn't mean to freak out like that."

Jake's hand touches Kyle's, enveloping it in warmth. He shivers at the touch, at how rough his hands feel against Kyle's own. "Hey, man," he says, voice low and soothing. "It's no problem. It happens."

Kyle stands up a little straighter, lifting his chin a little higher. He breathes in deeply, closing his eyes, willing his heart to settle and his nerve to be strong. His words come out in a rush when he exhales. "I don't really know what I am, I...I've never dated anyone, but I don't think I want to date...girls..." he trails off and cracks his eyes open. Jake's expression is hard to read. He looks surprised, but also not? Gentle and encouraging but also...guarded? There's something else there, something Kyle can't put his finger on. He feels lightheaded with the quickness of his pulse. "I'm not out, and no one knows, so please don't tell anyone. I just...I just wanted you to know that I *do* trust you."

He's surprised by how much he means it. He hadn't intended to admit that, but now that it's out in the open he knows it's true. Kyle isn't sure when he decided to trust Jake, but he does. He's not sure if it's smart or not. Trusting Jake gives him the power to hurt him, but it feels exhilarating to say aloud. All of it. He hadn't told anyone this secret other than his brother.

He's trying to decipher the conflicting look in Jake's eyes. His smile is there, but it's strained in weird ways, and his eyes look kind of glassy, and then...

Then Jake is pulling him into a hug. Kyle finds himself

pressed against Jake's broad chest, tightly enough that he can feel the solid strength of him beneath the softness of his shirt. Arms wrap around him, thick and strong. He's so...big. Kyle is enveloped and wrapped up and he feels safe. His nose brushes Jake's collarbone, and he smells really nice. He buries his face in Jake's chest and hesitantly lifts his arms to wrap around his waist, fingers curling into the back of his shirt.

He breathes in deep and lets out a shuddering breath. He's never been held like this. It's hard to breathe, but not because Jake is squeezing him too hard. It's been a long, long time since he's felt the physical comfort of someone else, and it has his skin tingling. But more than that, he's acutely aware of every point of contact and every shift of Jake's body against his own. Far, far too aware.

Jake's cheek rests on top of his head, and he can barely repress the shiver that runs through him. "Thank you for sharing with me," Jake says, mumbling into his hair. "No one's gonna give you a hard time, okay? Not while I'm around."

Kyle sighs, body relaxing into Jake's hold. His fingers clench tightly in his shirt. "Thank you," he says, voice muffled by Jake's chest.

Even after Jake leaves, Kyle finds himself short of breath, heart pounding, and the lingering warmth of Jake's body buzzing across his skin.

CHAPTER 9

"His room doesn't have any movie posters, or any kind of posters, really. Or pictures on the wall. Actually, there's a couple video game posters and a few banners and tapestries hanging around, but I'm pretty sure they're his roommate's." Jake leans forward as he talks, elbows on the table, idly shifting his coffee cup between his hands.

Liddy sits across from him, lounging back in her seat. Her arms stretch out to the table, cradling her own cup between her palms as she watches him talk.

"At first, I kinda thought, like, does this guy have *any* taste? Does he do *anything* besides study and play video games and whatever the hell he's always typing on his computer for? Like, I was fully anticipating him being a boring hermit who needed some culture added to his life."

Liddy hums lightly, lifting her cup to her lips. There's a smile there that Jake *knows*. It's one that's two parts understanding, and one part amused. He knows whatever follows that smile is usually a heavy dose of teasing and playful dragging. He does his best to ignore it.

"But *then* we studied at my place, and you know how I have all those indie movie posters?"

Her smile quirks a little wider around the lip of her coffee cup as she huffs a short laugh. "Yeah, because you're a wierdo who likes wierdo movies."

"They're great movies."

"They're terrible but continue."

Jake leans forward, putting his palms flat on the table, meeting her eyes as he says in a loud whisper. "He *recognized* them."

Liddy's laugh is surprised, choking a little on her coffee. She puts the cup down, one hand to her chest and face twisted as she half laughs, half coughs. "You're *kidding* me."

Jake leans back in his seat, grin wide. "Nope. He totally recognized them, and more than that, he *likes* those movies. I finally found someone with taste."

With her coughing fit subsiding, she grins. "You mean you finally found someone you don't have to force into watching your boring, low quality movie collection."

"They're not *boring*," he argues, but she's already waving him off.

She leans forward, sitting on the edge of her seat with her elbows on the table. Fingers curl delicately around her cup, index finger idly tapping the top of it. Her smile is coy and Jake feels a familiar sense of unease and wariness. "This is cool and everything, but I asked how the *tutoring* was coming."

Jake frowns, brows pinching. "I was *telling* you."

"You were telling me about *Kyle*. I asked you about tutoring, and you talked for five minutes about his room, three minutes about his oversized hoodies, ten minutes about his apparent interests, two minutes about how smart he is, and a four-minute story about the time he smudged his own glasses and how cute it was when he got frustrated over it."

"I..." Jake's frown deepens. "I never called him cute."

Liddy lifts her coffee cup, pointing at him with an index finger. "But you implied it. Pretty heavily, might I add."

Jake scoffs, leaning back in his chair and crossing his arms over his chest. He scowls at her across the table. "I thought we were here to catch up. This is me catching you up with my life."

She nods, but her smile never fades. "That's exactly why we're here, and you certainly are. You trust me, right?"

Jake blinks, scowl fading in his confusion. His hesitance comes from his surprise, not wariness. He answers truthfully and honestly. "More than anyone."

And it's almost startling to realize how true that is. He and Liddy dated back in their senior year of high school and through their first year of college. He's never kept in contact with any of his exes, but Liddy is an exception. They became closer after they broke up, and in a lot of ways, she became not only his best friend, but the sister he never had.

She knows him, inside and out. After seeing him as a boyfriend and as a friend, she knows him far more than a lot of his other friends do. In fact, most of the time, she seems to know him better than he knows himself. She loves him, and she's gentle and encouraging when she needs to be, but she's also blunt as hell and the kick in the ass he often needs. She says the things he needs to hear but is afraid to. She doesn't sugarcoat things for him, but she'd fight to protect him, tooth and nail. And in some circumstances, she has. They've been kicked out of a couple bars in their time.

He loves her, and she's good for him. There are times where he wishes things between them had worked out, but he knows he wouldn't trade what he has with her now for anything. Plus, she and her girlfriend, Becca, are the cutest couple on the goddamn planet, and Jake can see she's a hundred times better for Liddy than he was.

"Okay, so I'm gonna ask you something, and I want you to be honest with me," her smile fades, and her expression takes on something more serious.

"Okay," he says slowly, leaning back in his seat, eyes narrowing slightly.

"Do you have a crush on Kyle?"

"What?" Jake sputters, eyes widening and mouth falling open. "*No!*"

Her lips twitch, the ghost of that smile returning. "Are you sure? Because it sure sounds like you have a crush."

He leans forward, resting his elbows on the table to get closer to her as he hisses in hushed tones. "I'm not...I don't fully like...*swing that way*. Liddy, stop *laughing*. This isn't funny!"

Her lips split into a shit-eating grin, and she has the decency to hide it behind one hand as she smothers her laugh. "I'm sorry, Jake, but *seriously?* You're gonna pull the *I'm-not-gay* card? On *me?*"

He glares, lifting a hand to point a finger at her. "Don't you dare bring up the threesomes, Liddy, I swear to..."

"We *definitely* had threesomes, and you were not only the one who instigated them, but you were also the one who was more interested in adding another guy to the mix."

"I thought it's what you wanted!"

"That's definitely not true, and you know it. I was playing with *my* sexuality and my bisexual identity at that time, just like you were. I wanted another girl."

Jake shifts in his seat, restless and uneasy. He scowls, but he can feel how weak it is. He also knows Liddy can see right through him, right into the heart of things he doesn't want to face. He looks away, glare drifting out across the coffee shop. "I wasn't exploring my sexuality," she scoffs, and it sounds like a choked laugh. He turns his glare back to her, finger coming down to jab the tabletop to emphasize his point.

"Look, all guys know when another dude is attractive. They just don't like to admit it because they're insecure and think it makes them less masculine."

Liddy hums, one arm resting on the table while the other trails a finger around the lip of her coffee cup. She nods. Her smile has gone from shit-eating grin to gentle and under-standing. Kind, but unrelenting. "True, but only a guy who is at least a *little* attracted to other guys can enjoy himself in a threesome," her eyes crinkle at the corners, wry amusement in her features. "There's experimentation, and then there's actually enjoying yourself. And you, sir, were enjoying your-self," he glares, but her smile never fades. She leans back in her chair, stretching her legs out alongside the table and hooking one arm around the back of her chair. "Take it from someone who already went through the whole bisexual crisis, it's not that bad."

He sighs, leaning back in his chair and crossing his arms over his chest again. He stares down at the woodgrain on the table, lost in thought. Brows furrowed, and lips twisted into a frown, he lifts a foot, propping it up on her chair under the table. She doesn't seem at all bothered by it. In fact, she reaches under the table, patting his ankle and calf in a small sign of affection and comfort that he hadn't realized he needed.

He sighs again, letting his frustration leak through. "It's not…I'm not *opposed* to it. I just don't think I could ever like, *date* a dude, you know?"

He's surprised when Liddy laughs, and his eyes snap up to her. Her smile is wry, and her eyes exasperated, but there's a fondness there when she tilts her head. "Jake, can I be blunt with you?"

He raises an eyebrow, amusement tugging at his lips. "Aren't you always?"

"True. Alright, here it is: you were a shitty boyfriend."

His smile immediately falls. "Liddy, what the fuck?"

She lifts a hand, holding up a finger to stop him. Beneath the table, her hand curls around his ankle, as if trying to physically hold him still to listen. "*But*, you're an amazing friend. You're a really good guy, Jake. You don't get swept up in a lot of the bullshit around us. You're open minded, caring, and genuinely kind. If you fuck up, you learn from it and accept responsibility. You actually care about people, and you're loyal as hell. *But*, you're really shitty at being a boyfriend."

"Gee," he says, voice flat and dripping with sarcasm. "Thanks, Liddy. I always knew you cared."

Her smile twitches upward, and the hand on his ankle moves to pat his calf. "Don't take it personally."

He snorts. "Don't take it personally that you just said I'm shitty to date? Alright. Easy."

"Just listen, okay? 'Cause I'm about to tell you something you're gonna hate hearing, but I need you to *listen*," she pins him with a pointed stare, and he purses his lips, saying nothing. She only continues once she's sure she has his attention, and when she speaks, she stubbornly holds eye contact. "You've always been more interested in how *you look* with a girl, than you have been about the girl herself."

"That's not true," he says it automatically, but the trickling of doubt is just as instant.

Her smile isn't triumphant so much as it's sympathetic. "Yeah, it is, Jake. You're better than a lot of guys in your position, but you still care way too much about how you're seen with the girls you date. I bet *I* know more about the girl's you've dated in college than you do."

He looks at her then and really takes a moment to see her. He's always known he had a type, but he assumed it was just that, a type. In high school, she had been exactly like all the other girls he tended to date. Conventionally pretty, outgoing, understands sports but isn't too active herself, and into him. Now she looks completely different. The side of her head is shaved, the rest of her hair sweeping over the top of her head to fall in long waves on the other side. Her ears are decorated with studs, and there are piercings in her eyebrow, nose, and lip. Two more studs shine just below her collarbones, just above her shirt collar.

She doesn't look anything like the girls he likes to date, but she looks a lot more comfortable in her own skin. She's still pretty. It's just in a different way. Still, as much as he loves her, as pretty as she is, he realizes with startling clarity that even if she wanted to date him again...he wouldn't.

Liddy has shattered the glass, and now it falls into pieces slowly, revealing a truth Jake has never considered.

He wouldn't date Liddy again, not because of her or their past, but because she no longer fits his *style*. She no longer looks like the conventionally pretty cheerleader-type that he dates. She has far more personality, far more compassion, and is far smarter than the girls he dates.

How long has he been like this and why hasn't he noticed?

Is it really his *type*, or is it just something that's been programed into him that he *should* like because that's what his parents and friends would approve of? Because that's the type he's *expected* to date?

He shakes his head. It's a lot to take in, and a lot to consider. He feels nauseous, stomach rolling and chest too tight. "I'm not *that* shallow, am I?"

Liddy's hand squeezes his ankle. She leans forward to put her other hand on his arm. Her eyes are gentle and kind, and her smile encouraging, holding him together. "Not on purpose. I think it's just habit. I'm not telling you to go out and do something about it or to declare your love for this kid, but think about what I said, okay? This is the first time I've ever seen you genuinely interested in a person, and I don't want you to deny yourself because he's not your usual type. Just listen to yourself, alright?"

His smile wavers, and his throat feels tight. "Alright," he whispers, taking in a shaky breath. "I'll think about it."

She pats his arm, leaning back and standing up from her seat. "Good. Now enough of this mushy stuff. We have enough time before class for me to kick your ass in a game of pool at the game hall on campus."

His smile widens, gaining confidence and appreciation as the conversation turns to more familiar territory. "You wish."

CHAPTER 10

*J*ake: *I just checked online and guess who got a B- on the test yesterday*

KYLE: *Probably a lot of people.*
   Kyle: *Can't be me though, I got an A*

JAKE: *Haha, yeah yeah, we all know you're super smart.*
   Jake: *Seriously though thank you SO MUCH for your help.*
   Jake: *I couldn't have done it without you*

KYLE: *I just helped you study. When it came down to the test, it was all you.*
   Kyle: *Congratulations :)*

JAKE: *Is this what it feels like to be smart?*

KYLE: *If you're so smart, I guess you won't need me to tutor you anymore*

JAKE: *NO. KYLE DON'T EVEN JOKE.*
Jake: *ONE B- ISN'T GOING TO RAISE MY GPA ALL THE WAY.*
Jake: *HELP ME OBI-WAN KYLENOBI, YOU'RE MY ONLY HOPE*

KYLE: *I can't believe you just quoted Star Wars at me, but people think I'M the nerd*

JAKE: *Don't knock the classics, dude*

KYLE: *I will attempt to refrain*

JAKE: *Seriously though, we should go out and celebrate.*
Jake: *Wanna grab a drink later?*
Jake: *Like tonight?*

KYLE: *I don't really drink*

JAKE: *Ever?*

KYLE: *Not really, no. Not in public, anyway.*
  Kyle: *And I don't really do bars.*
  Kyle: *I don't know if that's a good idea*

JAKE: *Have you ever TRIED?*

KYLE: *Well no*

JAKE: *Come out and try it, just this once.*
  Jake: *Just you and me. No one will try to mess with you when I'm there.*
  Jake: *Lets just go out and hang and relax, we both deserve it.*
  Jake: *My treat.*
  Jake: *Kyle??*
  Jake: *Hello? You can't just ghost me, man, that's not cool*

KYLE: *Fine*

JAKE: *Wait really?*

KYLE: *Yeah, I guess.*
  Kyle: *But just this once*

JAKE: *FUCK YEAH! I'll pick you up around seven. We can grab food in the cafeteria before we go?*

KYLE: *Okay*

JAKE: *See you then*

KYLE: *Yeah, see you*

* * *

BEING with Jake in public feels strange.

He hadn't realized how incredibly vulnerable he'd feel sitting with Jake at a table without the protective wall of his laptop to dive into whenever he felt uncomfortable, or when he felt things he shouldn't. He hadn't realized how exposed he'd feel without books and notebooks spread out over their table to clearly indicate they're studying, not just hanging out. Without those things, and in a bar rather than a coffee shop, people might confuse them being on a date.

And it's definitely not a date. Not at all. It can't and wouldn't be a date because for one, Jake isn't gay, and for two, he wouldn't be into someone like Kyle anyway. Not when he could have nearly anyone else.

It doesn't help that the night feels like it almost *could* be a date. Jake had picked him up, looking nice in jeans that fit snuggly to his legs and ass, along with a shirt that ~~was tight~~ FIT across his shoulders and chest. Kyle had even spent far more time than usual trying to find something to wear, only to realize he doesn't really have *nice* clothes. They'd gone out to eat, and while it hadn't been fancy or anything, it had felt cozy and intimate in ways Kyle hadn't expected.

And now they're at a bar together, in public, sitting at a table in the corner with a drink in front of each of them.

It feels surreal.

Kyle isn't even old enough to drink legally, but Jake had sat him down and gone to buy them both drinks. Now he's sitting alone in a corner with the school's rising star of a baseball player on a Saturday night.

Kyle tucks his feet under his chair, leaning forward just slightly and hunching his shoulders, trying to blend into the background as much as he can. His fingers trail along the condensation clinging to the outside of his plastic cup. He requested a vodka cranberry because it's cheap and he's not a huge fan of beer.

Jake sits across from him and appears far more relaxed than Kyle could ever hope to be. He leans back in his chair, one arm draped across the back. His long legs stretch out by the table, crossed at the ankles, and his other hand lays lazily on the tabletop, fingers idly playing with his beer bottle.

His gaze sweeps around the room, and while he seems at ease, Kyle feels awkward in the silence, with the general din of conversation and clanking glasses around them. He clears his throat, eyes on his drink as he licks his lips before saying. "This was a smart place to come to."

Kyle doesn't look up, but in his peripheral vision, he can see Jake turn to look at him. "Hmm? Why's that?"

Kyle shrugs with one shoulder, wrapping both hands around his cup as he glances around the room. "It's not really a college bar," the bar itself is close enough to campus for them to walk, but by no means convenient. Because of that, its patrons aren't the usual college bar crowd. It's quieter, with less energy and more of a relaxed vibe. The music isn't too loud, and the patrons look older. They look more like grad students than typical undergrads. It's a crowd more willing to stick to their own individual groups than mingle. That, at least, he's grateful for. "People are less likely to recognize us here. You don't have to worry about people seeing you with me."

"That's...Kyle, that's not why I chose this place."

Kyle tilts his head up, just enough to look at Jake through his lashes. He looks genuinely confused, gazing at Kyle with a furrowed brow and a small frown. Jake turns square towards Kyle, pulling his legs up and putting both arms on the table to lean forward. Kyle sits a little straighter, heart beating a little faster. "It's not?"

"No, dude. I just thought this would be more your speed. Like...quieter and stuff," a sheepish smile pulls up the edges of his lips. It makes Kyle's heart flutter and his skin tingle with heat. Jake glances away, scratching the back of his neck with one hand. "Plus, I figured if it's quieter, then we can actually, you know, *talk*."

"We talk," Kyle argues, struggling to keep that wall in place around himself. He can feel it crumbling, brick by brick. He knows his protests are a desperate attempt to block out his feelings, because the fact that Jake can make them start to crumble with a simple smile and an innocent declaration is *terrifying*.

Jake's smile quirks a little wider, eyes finding Kyle's once again. "I mean *really* talk. Not studying or whatever. We don't really know much about each other."

Kyle's eyes tilt down to settle on his drink. The condensation is cold on his fingertips, but his skin feels far too warm. "I don't see why we need to."

Jake reaches out then, hand coming down gently on Kyle's forearm. He jumps, startled, but doesn't pull away. His head snaps up, eyes widening as they meet Jake's. His smile is small and genuine and creates chaos in Kyle's chest. "Like it or not, man, we're friends now. And friends get to know each other."

The walls around him start to crumble, withering at a rate that means he can't even hope to put them back up quickly. He feels himself smile before he even realizes he's doing it, and he sighs, letting his body sag with the long exhale. "Okay."

Jake's smile is blinding and should be illegal. It makes it hard for Kyle to breathe. Jake pulls away, sitting up straighter and letting go of Kyle's arm. There's a knot of disappointment in his stomach, and his arm feels cold at the absence. But Jake remains sitting forward eagerly, elbows on the table. "So, tell me about you. Where are you from? What's your family like?"

Kyle sighs, feeling the rest of his walls crumble to ash in the wake of Jake's earnest smile. He lifts his drink to his lips, drinking half of it in one go and making a twisted face as he pulls it away. Jake chuckles as Kyle coughs. He sets the cup down, takes in a deep breath, and talks.

He starts out stutteringly, halting, uncertainty fringing his words, but he gains confidence as he peeks up at Jake, at his gentle, encouraging smile and the genuine interest in his eyes.

He tells Jake his family is from one of the bigger cities in the state, about a two hour drive from their university. He tells him what his parents do. He tells him they have two dogs, a Labrador and a boxer. He tells him his dad always comes across as really reserved and quiet but has a whiplash sense of humor, if you're lucky enough to hear his mumbling. He tells him his mom is incredibly nice, but her desperate need to coddle him can be overwhelming and overbearing.

He briefly covers high school and moving here for college but doesn't mention any friends. He hopes Jake doesn't pick up on it, hopes that argument won't be reignited, but instead Jake surprises him by touching on a topic that's far more taboo.

"What about brothers or sisters, got any?"

The question is so unexpected and comes with such

genuine innocence and curiosity that Kyle finds himself answering honestly. Where he normally would close off, say no, or redirect the conversation, he finds himself telling the truth. "I...*had* a brother."

It's quiet, hesitant, and Kyle's gaze remains fixed on the table between them. Judging from Jake's soft, "Oh," he understands the weight of Kyle's choice of words perfectly. "I'm so sorry, dude," he watches Jake's hand reach across the table once more, coming to rest on his wrist. Goosebumps rise on his skin when Jake's thumb slowly rubs against his knuckles. "You don't have to talk about it."

Kyle's lips twitch into a small, wry smile, edged with bitterness as he chuckles. "I understand. It's heavy stuff. No one wants to hear about that," he doesn't move and feels rooted to the spot by Jake's hand, but he lets himself wonder what it would be like to reach for him. To place his hand over Jake's. To feel the ridges of his knuckles and the valleys of his fingers.

He wishes he was brave enough.

He's surprised when Jake's hand squeezes, fingers digging just slightly into his skin. "That's not what I meant," Jake's voice is hard enough to make Kyle look up, blinking in confusion at the angry and pinched scowl on Jake's face. For just a second, he wonders what he's done wrong, but then Jake continues, and as he talks, his expression softens. "It's not that I don't *want* to hear it, man. It's that I don't want to force *you* to talk about it if *you* don't want to," Kyle isn't sure what expression he's wearing right now. He's too surprised and concentrating on how rapid his heartbeat is to notice much else, but whatever Jake sees makes his face soften more. His brows furrow in concern, and his voice drops lower with worry. "Have you talked about it with *anyone?*"

Kyle licks his lips, trying to swallow past the lump in his throat. The look in Jake's eyes is far too intense, far too genuine, and threatening to shatter the last of Kyle's defenses. He looks away, lowering his eyes to where Jake's hand still rests on Kyle's wrist. "I haven't really had the time. Besides, it's not like talking is going to fix anything."

"You should tell me about him," Kyle starts to pull away, breath shuddering in his lungs and Jake's touch too warm, burning his skin. But Jake's grip tightens, and Kyle too easily gives into it. He glances up, but Jake just smiles that lopsided smile. "You don't have to talk about what happened but tell me about *him*. What was he like?"

He doesn't want to. He hasn't talked about his brother in a long, long time. He's forced himself *not* to talk about it. The wound of his loss is too much. But Jake is looking at him so earnestly, his hold firm but grounding, and he's just so goddamn *patient*. Kyle feels the last of his resistance melting away, leaving him tired and exhausted but ready to talk.

Besides, talking about his brother is the easy part. The accident is the hard part. He can do this. If it's with Jake, he can do this.

Using his free hand, he lifts his cup to his lips, downing the rest of his drink and shuddering as the vodka bites too strongly. Jake's hand squeezes gently, and Kyle's breath hitches into a small hiccup as Jake's hand slides down from his wrist, easily laying over the top of his, thumb brushing the back of his hand and fingers messily and lazily laying over the slots between Kyle's fingers.

He ignores it as best he can while still committing the feeling to memory. And with a burn in his throat, warmth in his belly, and a prickle of heat rising, he talks.

And talks.

And talks.

He talks about how his brother was always smart, got top grades, and was far better than Kyle could ever hope to be. He was more sociable, kinder, and incredibly charismatic. He had so many friends and so many connections. He was terrible at sports but wasn't afraid to make a fool of himself to have fun. He was older than Kyle and was everything Kyle aspired to be. He was Kyle's only real friend.

He was the only one Kyle ever told about liking guys before Jake. He was the only one he told about his dreams and ideas for a new MMORPG, bouncing ideas between them until the dream became both of theirs. He was the only one who ever encouraged Kyle to chase that dream, and the only one who believed he could. He was the only one who ever really saw Kyle for how he was, never tried to change him, but always encouraged him.

He talks on and on, flood gates opening and the dam bursting. He rambles, and he knows he's rambling, but he can't stop. He starts a story and barely finishes before he's off on a tangent, distracted by stories of things his brother had said or done or things they used to do. In the back of his mind he screams, telling himself to *stop* before Jake gets bored.

But Jake never gets bored. He listens. He actually *listens*. He listens and laughs and asks questions. The whole time his eyes never leave Kyle, never look bored or annoyed.

His hand never leaves Kyle's either, and as he rambles, Kyle starts to idly pick at and play with Jake's fingers. He traces his knuckles and the shape of his hand, and his heart beats a little harder and a little faster when Jake doesn't pull away. When Jake lazily turns his hand over for Kyle to trace the lines of his palm, Kyle's breath momentarily catches, words falling over each other before he pushes on in an attempt to distract from the physical intimacy.

Jake only interrupts Kyle to buy them more drinks, and every time they finish a round, Jake is up to buy more.

They stay out until it's late and Kyle has lost count of how many drinks he's had. Until the room spins and his words stumble much more easily if not more lazily. He doesn't know how long he talks about his brother, but eventually the conversation switches elsewhere. To Jake's life. To his family. To his best friend Liddy, who he says would like Kyle a lot. The conversation moves and morphs and flows so easily from one topic to the next, and Kyle can barely keep up, but it's incredible.

He hasn't talked with anyone this easily or long since his brother was around.

It's past midnight by the time they leave the bar, and the cool night air is a balm on Kyle's heated skin. He stands on the sidewalk, eyes closed, breathing in the crisp air. He sways but thinks little of it. He feels lighter than he has in months.

Then Jake is pulling him into a hug. One moment he's standing there, trying to stay upright, and the next he's in Jake's arms. His body is warm and incredibly firm. Kyle melts into him. Jake's arms are strong around him, tight as they pull Kyle flush against his body. Kyle can feel it all. The firm and fit body beneath the softness of his shirt. He buries his face in Jake's chest, breathes in the scent of his cologne and sweat, and exhales with a sigh.

It's then that he catches himself. He can't do this. No, Jake isn't his. Jake *can't* be his. He can enjoy Jake's company, but this is...he has to be crossing some sort of line.

Kyle is the first to pull away, ignoring the way Jake's arms linger. He looks up, smiling sheepishly as the world around him spins. "I guess I'll see you later?"

Jake smiles, arms dropping back to his sides, hands shoved deep in his pockets. "Yeah, I'll text you?"

Kyle can feel his smile ache in his cheeks, unable to be restrained in his drunken state. "Okay," he takes a few steps back, grin dimming as he glances away. "And thanks. For everything. For being a friend."

He turns quickly, intent on fleeing from Jake, his gentleness, his smell, his arms, and Kyle's own complicated emotions. But as he turns, the world keeps on spinning. His focus blurs, and his balance wavers. He must've drunk more than he thought.

He stumbles, and he hears a car horn blare as a hand comes down on his arm, pulling him back. He stumbles, landing against a firm chest. A warm, solid arm wraps around his waist, and he prays that Jake can't feel his heartbeat.

Jake chuckles, the sound low and breathless in Kyle's ear, rumbling deep in his chest. "Let's get you home, buddy."

Kyle doesn't protest as Jake leads him down the sidewalk, arm kept around his waist for balance. And Jake says nothing as Kyle leans into him, letting himself enjoy this, if only for tonight.

CHAPTER 11

*T*he walk home is both a blessing and a curse.

The cool air is refreshing and grounding. It helps clear his head and fills his lungs with a crispness that's pleasantly sobering. On a normal night, he might be cold, but with alcohol running through his system, the crisp night air feels amazing on his flushed skin.

Now that they're up and moving, exactly how much they drank becomes far more apparent. Now that they aren't sitting down, the buzz flows far more freely though their systems, making their legs wobbly and their steps uncertain.

Jake, thankfully, is used to it. He's at a pleasant state of drunkenness. He's reached his limit, where any more would be too much, but he's stopped so he can ride out the wave before coming down slowly. Things spin a little too much if he turns a little too fast, his skin feels numb, and his words stumble as often as his feet, but he feels good.

Kyle, on the other hand, is struggling a lot more. It's only now that Jake realizes he probably should've paced the poor guy. But they'd been so wrapped up in sharing stories, and he'd been so immersed in learning about Kyle, his smile, the excitement of memory shining in his eyes, the easy way he was talking. It was so different from what Jake's used to, and it was *captivating*. He kind of got wrapped up in the moment. He just kept getting drinks when they were done, to keep the night going. He hadn't considered the fact that Kyle barely drinks and he's significantly smaller than Jake.

That was his bad.

Still, as guilty as he feels, he has Kyle pressed against his side, arm clinging around his waist for support, tucked under Jake's arm and leaning into his side like he's the only thing in the world he can count on, and that, yeah, that's pretty nice.

So, he lets himself enjoy it, if only for right now. If only for tonight.

The walk back to campus takes longer than it did to get to the bar, with them stumbling and giggling the whole way. There are plenty of people still out and about by the time they reach campus, but most of them are far too drunk to pay attention to Jake and Kyle. They stumble along their own paths, laughing with their friends and paying them no mind. Still, Jake holds Kyle close, shielding him from the view of others. He doesn't care that it might seem *more* suspicious if people see them. His only concern at the moment is to not have Kyle recognized at all.

He's not ready to say goodbye or for the night to be over. This has been fun. Far more fun than he was expecting. Once Kyle had opened up, it'd been a whole new world unfolding in front of Jake. And if his heart beat a little too fast whenever Kyle smiled, well, Jake drowned that knowledge in his beer.

By the time they reach Kyle's dorm, he's nearly asleep on his feet. They pause outside the building, and Kyle's fingers are uncoordinated and weak as they try to find his keycard. Face twisted in confusion, he eventually looks up at Jake with wide, pleading eyes. A pitiful whine escapes his lips that's far too cute for his own good and not at all good for Jake's heart.

He can think of a few other instances where he'd like to see those pleading eyes, hear him whine, make those brows furrow with pleasure and lips part in...

Jake shakes his head, firmly holding those thoughts at bay as he reaches into Kyle's pocket to pull out his keycard. When his fingers trail up his hip, shifting his shirt aside for just a moment to feel the soft skin with his fingertips, he blames the alcohol. With Kyle tucked back under his arm, he manages to get the door to the building open and steer him toward the elevators.

Thankfully, no one else is around, and they ride up on their own. Jake leans against the wall of the elevator, hands propped on the metal bar behind him. He let go of Kyle as they entered, not wanting to push his luck, but he's pleasantly surprised when Kyle sways into him anyway. The whole elevator available, and Kyle crowds his space. Without hesitation, the smaller man steps up in front of him, slumping forward to rest his head on Jake's collarbone, body pressed flush against him. His arms wrap loosely around Jake's waist, and he sighs, sounding far too content.

Jake smiles, knowing Kyle can't see it, and lets himself wrap an arm around his back, rubbing an idle hand up and down his spine.

When they stumble down the hall to Kyle's door, Jake props him gently against the wall. Kyle sags there, shoulder slumped against the cinderblocks and head tilted so his temple presses against the cool surface. His eyes close, and if it weren't for the fact that he's still standing, Jake would think he was asleep.

He manages to get out Kyle's lanyard with his keys, but his own coordination isn't great. He fumbles with them, and before he can find the right one, the door opens.

He freezes, standing there and blinking at the guy standing in the doorway. His hair is dark and curly, reaching just past his ears to coil around his neck. Most of it is hidden behind a gray beanie that slouches atop his head. His brown eyes are bloodshot, and stare at Jake with just as much surprise. He's frozen with one arm in his hoodie, halfway through the action of putting it on.

"Uh, hi?" Jake says, Kyle's keys still held between his fingers. "You must be Jasper? Kyle's roommate?"

Jasper looks down to the lanyard, then makes an obvious sweep to look Jake up and down. When his eyes return to Jake's face, there's a small smirk playing across his lips. "Yeah, that'd be me. You must be Jake. The guy Kyle tutors."

Jake blinks, sluggish mind taking a moment to process that. His mouth, however, is way ahead of him. "How'd you know?"

Jasper's smirk widens, lighting up his eyes. "Kyle talks about you *way* more than I think he realizes. Speaking of the little dude, where is…Oh, shit," he takes a step forward, and Jake takes one back instinctively. After poking his head out into the hallway, Jasper's eyes immediately find Kyle, half asleep and propped up against the wall. His smirk widens into a grin, and he laughs. "Oh, *man*, is he *drunk?* you actually managed to get the little nerd *drunk*. I've been trying to get him to loosen up and party a little since week one. Good job, man."

He steps further out into the hall, pulling his hoodie on fully as he moves in front of Kyle. He bends down, hands on his knees to put himself at eye level, tilting his head this way and that to get a good look at him.

"Hey, Kyle, dude," he reaches out, patting Kyle's cheek with enough force to rouse him. His eyes flutter open before narrowing, looking confused and disoriented. "Congrats on your first time getting drunk, dude. And with the school's rising baseball star, no less. Try not to puke on our shit, alright?" Kyle groans, squeezing his eyes shut and rolling until his back is pressed against the wall. Jasper straightens and laughs. "Oh man, I should totally film this. I can't believe you…"

"Leave him alone," Jake snaps, stepping forward and shoving Jasper's shoulder.

The other man stumbles from the unexpected hit, head whipping around to glare at him. "Dude, what the fuck."

"Leave him alone," Jake repeats. Anger simmers beneath his already heated skin, twisting and writhing in his gut. His hands curl into fists at his side. Somewhere in the back of his mind, he *knows* he's overreacting. He knows Jasper is just poking at Kyle in good natured fun. From what he's heard from Kyle, he and Jasper get along just fine. It's no different than Jake's friends and roommates teasing him when he's drunk. He *knows* this, but that doesn't stop the strange and consuming protectiveness that rises inside him.

Jasper puts up his hands defensively, taking a step back. "Hey, man, calm down. It's all in good fun," he frowns as he shoves his hands into his pockets. "I was just leaving anyway. I'll be gone all weekend, so you guys can do whatever. Just take care of him, alright?"

"Of course, I will," Jake says, voice still a little too defensive, with a little too much snap.

Jasper rolls his eyes and shoves past him, moving down the hall toward the elevator, but not before Jake hears him mutter. "Geez, overprotective boyfriend, much?"

Ignoring the flush that rushes up his neck to settle onto his cheeks and the gentle flutter inside his chest, Jake turns back to Kyle and helps him into the room, shutting the door firmly behind them.

Kyle stands in the middle of the room, swaying on his feet. He looks around, but his eyes don't seem to focus on anything in particular. His lips hang open, parted slightly. His face is relaxed and soft, lacking the usual defensive edge and sharp glares. Jake smiles, moving forward to press a hand to Kyle's lower back, his other hand coming down on his arm.

"Come on," he mumbles. "Let's get you to bed."

Kyle takes one step forward before stopping. He digs his feet in, balance rocking but firmly resisting Jake's gentle push. He shakes his head, then groans, instantly regretting the motion as his focus dodges in and out. "No, I..." he pauses, licking his lips as his words slur together. "I gotta...I think I gotta...I'm gonna..." His eyes drift around, from Jake to the rest of his room. His brows furrow, as if deep in thought. Then his lips purse, and there's a resigned sigh when he says. "I'm gonna puke."

It's so determined and exasperated that Jake feels like laughing, but he can see how quickly Kyle's composure is crumbling. With a soft chuckle, he steers Kyle toward the bathroom. He's thankful that it's empty, and thankful he and Jasper have a suite style dorm, where the bathroom is connected between two rooms rather than out in the hall. He knows this isn't going to be a pleasant experience for Kyle's neighbors, but it's less embarrassing than puking in a public bathroom.

He barely manages to get Kyle to the toilet before he falls to his knees and empties his stomach. It's a lot. A lot of waves and a lot of miserable groaning between them. He whines and mumbles that Jake doesn't have to stay for this, but Jake refuses to leave. He squats next to him, back against the wall, idly rubbing Kyle's back and massaging his neck while mumbling soft, barely coherent encouragements.

When they're certain Kyle is done, Jake helps him to the counter, walking Kyle through the process of rinsing out his mouth and brushing his teeth. Kyle is pitiful. His limbs seem heavy and his legs barely hold him. Jake has to pick him up and set him on the counter before he falls over, and he has to keep Kyle going with gentle nudges and firm prods.

Eventually they get Kyle's teeth brushed, mouth washed out again, and Jake ushers him back into his room. Kyle stumbles across it, tripping over the beanbags and falling onto his bed. He curls in on himself, clutching the blankets to his chest as he squeezes his eyes shut. "I'm never drinking *again*," he groans. "Why do people *like* this?"

Jake chuckles, sitting on the edge of Kyle's bed. "It's not so bad when you get used to it."

Kyle cracks an eye, weakly glaring at him while pouting. "It's awful. I feel awful. Ugh."

Jake exhales a short snort, then sighs. Putting his hands on his knees, he prepares himself to stand up. "Well, I guess I should go so you can sleep."

He knows he needs to go, yet he hesitates. And it's in that hesitation that Kyle's hand snakes out, grabbing hold of Jake's and clinging to it. His grip isn't firm. Jake can easily pull away, but he doesn't. He feels rooted to the spot, and his resolve crumbles to dust as he hears Kyle whisper. "Stay. Please?"

His voice is so soft Jake has to strain to hear him. There's so much in those few words. A desperate plea. A fear. A hesitation. A hope. Jake hasn't realized until this moment just how weak he is to Kyle. Just how much Kyle has managed to weasel his way into Jake's heart and bury himself there.

It's with trickling dread that Jake realizes that Liddy might be right.

"Okay," he breathes, the word coming out in defeat. He puts a hand over Kyle's and feels it relax. "Okay, I'll stay."

Kyle's smile is small but far too genuine. "Thank you."

"Come on," Jake turns, reaching out to pull at Kyle's hoodie. "Let's get you ready for bed."

He's helped his friends undress before. He's helped girl-friends undress. Hell, he's helped strangers do it. Nothing about it has ever been sexual. Not when that person has been far too drunk for their own good and struggling to get themselves ready for bed. Half the time Jake has been drunk, too. It's always just been him trying to help someone out, get their shoes and jacket off before they pass out for the night.

But as he helps Kyle out of his clothes, he feels his heart heavy and sharp as it beats against his ribcage. His skin is hot, heat pooling in his gut as it twists. His fingertips tingle where they move of their own accord, trailing along Kyle's skin and lingering even as he tells them not to.

Kyle is really fucking cute. Beautiful, even. Not beautiful like his ex-girlfriends have been. Not classically pretty. But beautiful in his own way. His build is slight and small, but his skin is flawless, smooth and incredibly soft. His eyes remain closed, plump lips moving slowly as he mumbles protests while Jake moves him enough to get his clothes off.

Then he sinks back into his sheets, wearing nothing but his boxers and a shirt. His limbs splayed wide and inviting, head tossed to the side and hair a mess on his pillow. Lips parted, and body curled.

Jake's stomach flips. He wants to ravish him. He wants to leave marks along his neck and collarbone. Wants to feel that small body writhe beneath him. Wants to see Kyle's back arch and head toss back in ecstasy. Wants to see those plump lips red and wet and barely managing to form his name. He wants to see his skin flushed and glistening with sweat as he reaches for Jake.

He wants it. He wants it so bad, and the need crashes over him like a tidal wave. But his hands curl into fists, nails biting his palms. He can't. He can't, and he won't. Not now, and not like this. Not when Kyle is drunk and nearly passed out. He can wait.

He wants more than anything to undress, too, and slide beneath the blankets to wrap Kyle up in his arms. To pull him flush against him and feel their skin together as they sleep.

Instead, he slides to the floor, half-heartedly kicking off his shoes and tugging off his jacket. He builds a barely passable bed on the floor out of spare blankets he finds, sprawled out across two beanbags. It's not too bad. He's slept in worse conditions.

He falls asleep that night torn between the fantasy of Kyle *asking* him to touch him, to crawl into bed with him, *wanting* what Jake wants, and the way his mind pulls back from the insinuation, scared and reeling, convinced that if he were sober, he wouldn't be having these thoughts at all.

He can only hope clarity comes with time, sleep, and sobriety.

CHAPTER 12

$\mathcal{K}$yle wakes up feeling like shit.

Before he's even fully conscious, he groans, curling his body into as small a ball as he can. His fingers tug at his blankets, holding them to his chest and covering his head with them to block out the light. His head hurts. It's pounding and throbbing intermittently between a dull ache and sharp sting behind his eyes. His stomach rolls, not quite nauseous but definitely unsettled.

Why do people actually *enjoy* drinking? This is terrible.

It takes him a moment to rise fully to consciousness, his mind fighting a losing battle to stay down and asleep. When he's fully awake, he keeps his eyes closed against the light, trying to sift through his memories of the night before.

He remembers going out with Jake to a quiet bar. He remembers, with a straining shiver of excitement in his chest, how Jake had insisted he had taken them there, so they could talk and get to know one another. He remembers hours upon hours of just *talking*. He remembers saying far more about himself than he ever intended to, riding the high of Jake's presence, tongue loosened by alcohol, fueled by some sort of misplaced hope that he can't quite shake, no matter how hard he tries.

He remembers talking about his brother, which is not something he ever intended to do. But he didn't talk about his absence or his accident. Jake got him to talk about who his brother was. The good times. And that felt really good, actually.

He only wishes he'd kept track of his drinks instead of just drinking whatever was placed in front of him. He hadn't expected to actually enjoy himself, and he hadn't wanted the night to end, so he just kept going. Now he regrets that decision.

He doesn't really remember when they left or how they got home. There are some fragments, snapshots of memory that lead him to believe they walked back to his dorm together. He doesn't really remember getting *here*, though, or getting ready for bed.

He heaves a heavy sigh, his lungs aching. He probably made a fool of himself, and he probably looked like an idiot. Especially to Jake, who does this often enough to have control over himself. He just hopes he didn't ramble *too* much and annoy him. Whatever he did, it's too late to worry about it now. The damage is done, and he can stew in embarrassment later. For now, his head is throbbing, and his mouth is incredibly dry. He needs a glass of water, aspirin, a long hot shower, and some food. Stat.

He throws the blankets off, both hating and loving the cool air on his heated skin. It's refreshing, clears his head, but he also just wants to curl up and hide from the world for the rest of the day. Groaning, he moves, swinging his legs over the edge of the bed. He rubs his eyes with the heels of his hands until he sees stars. They feel dry and heavy and incredibly tired, despite just waking up. His skin feels sticky and unclean. He definitely needs a shower.

He pushes himself to his feet, arms dropping to his sides as he takes a step.

And nearly steps right on top of Jake.

He lets out a surprised squeal and stumbles backwards, landing heavily on the bed with his heart hammering in his throat. He watches as Jake groans, sprawled out on a makeshift pallet on his floor, body wedged oddly between two beanbags and covered in spare blankets. He stares, eyes wide and mouth agape, as Jake props himself up on his elbow, other hand rubbing at his eyes.

Jake looks around, dazed and disoriented from sleep, but not at all surprised to find that he's in Kyle's room and not his own. When his gaze finally finds Kyle, he smiles, lazy and dopy as his head lolls to the side. "Mornin'."

"I, uh…" Kyle stammers, licking his lips and trying to swallow past the lump in his throat. "Morning?"

Jake sits up, blankets pooling at his waist. He looks around, hand rubbing through his hair and making it stand on end. He yawns, idly scratching at the stubble on his chin. He looks completely at ease waking up in Kyle's room, and meanwhile Kyle thinks he might be having a heart attack. Or hallucinating. "What time is it?"

"I don't know," he doesn't even know where he put his phone last night. It's not under his pillow where he usually puts it, so it might still be in the pocket of his jeans. He's not wearing his jeans. In fact, he's not wearing anything but his boxers and a t-shirt. He immediately grabs the blankets, pulling them over his lap as he sits on the edge of the bed, feeling incredibly exposed all of a sudden. He swallows hard, voice shaking as he tries to find the words to ask what's on his mind. "Did I get undressed, or did you…?"

"Oh, I did that," he says it so casually Kyle feels his breath hitch. Jake glances over at him, blinking in his confusion before understanding crosses his features. He offers a small smile and an offhanded shrug. "I mean, it's no big deal. I've helped drunk people get ready for bed before. And I *do* shower in a locker room full of dudes. It's nothing I haven't seen before."

Jake doesn't *sound* like he's hiding anything from him, but Kyle's heard stories. Not of Jake, but of college in general. Of going to the bar and getting drunk. Ending up somewhere undressed with little memory. He was opening up to Jake last night and high on the adrenaline from it. He wouldn't have put it past himself to get caught up in *things*. Oh god, would Jake even *want* something like that from Kyle? *Would* they have done something like that drunk? Kyle is ashamed to say that he's fairly certain he would have, and *fuck*, what if he tried to start something with Jake and Jake pushed him away and that's why he's on the floor.

"Did something happen last night?" he asks before he can stop himself and before he loses the courage to. It comes tumbling out of him, and he can only hope his voice isn't shaking as much as his hands are. Oh god, what if he fucked up? What if he *really* fucked up?

"Like what?" Jake looks at him, head tilted, and brows furrowed in confusion that's entirely too innocent. Kyle squirms where he sits, struggling to find the words to elaborate. He can feel heat rush to his face and settle on his cheeks, and he can't quite make eye contact. He does notice when understanding flickers across Jake's face. His eyes widen, mouth falling open. "Oh. *Oh.* Like that. No, no, man, don't worry. Nothing like that happened. We just got back, and I got you into bed. You asked me to stay, and I didn't really wanna walk home anyway, you know? So, I just stayed."

He scratches the back of his neck, biting his lip in that nervous way he does, and Kyle looks away. His eyes fix on his hands in his lap, fingers clenching and worrying the blanket.

"Did you *want* something to happen?" Jake asks slowly,

carefully, like he's approaching a wild animal. Kyle refuses to believe there's any hope in that question, only innocent curiosity.

His head snaps up, face on fire as he stammers, "No! No, no, that's not...no," he doesn't know how convincing he sounds.

Jake puts up his hands, defensive and placating all at once. "Hey, it's okay. I was just checking, is all. You know. As a friend, or whatever."

"Right," Kyle says, nodding his head. He lets out a shuddering breath. "As a friend."

Jake's hands lower, and he leans forward, wrapping his arms around his knees. It puts him closer to Kyle, if only by a couple inches, but Kyle can practically feel him moving into his space. It makes his breath short and his heart hammer against his ribs. "Sorry about, you know, getting you super drunk last night. I didn't mean for it to go that far. I just kinda lost track of the drinks."

Kyle forces himself to smile, shaky but genuine, glancing up at Jake through his lashes. "No, it's okay. It was fun. Well...not the last part, but before that it wasn't so bad."

Jake smiles, small and sincere. "I'm glad," he shifts the blankets aside, awkwardly pushing himself to his feet as his body disentangles from his beanbag bed. He groans once he's up, putting his hands on his lower back and bending until he hears it pop. "Oh, man. Remind me never to sleep like that again," it's a casual enough comment, and Kyle hums a vague response. Jake looks around, and it's then the strange tension starts to build. Kyle can feel it like static across his skin. "Well, you seem to be good and all, so I guess I should probably go, or something."

"Uh, yeah," Kyle laughs, but it feels hollow and cracked. "We've got class to get to. Wait, no we don't. It's Saturday." He laughs again and feels his legs shake with it, the skin feels too tight, and they tingle in that way they do before they start to go numb. His breath is short and ragged, and he stares at his hands, clenched, knuckles white around the blanket.

Then the bed dips beside him as Jake sits down. "Hey," he says, voice low and soothing. "Hey, it's okay. Calm down. Everything will be fine," his hand is on Kyle's back, warm and solid, rubbing calming circles.

Kyle knows that. He *knows* it'll be fine. But that doesn't stop the buildup of...*whatever* this is. This strange, unfamiliar energy. The anxiousness that builds and builds with no outlet, sparked by unfamiliar situations. Logically, he knows it'll be fine, but that doesn't stop his mind from dwelling on it and spiraling into a pit that's so hard to crawl out of.

Still, Jake's presence next to him is calming. It's a warm, solid weight that's becoming increasingly more familiar. And when Jake mutters. "Come on, breathe with me, that's it," he does just that. It calms him. He can feel his body relaxing, easing down from the rising panic that had threatened to consume him. He leans into Jake's touch, leaning into his side far more than he probably should. He sighs, letting himself fall and rest his head on Jake's shoulder. He tenses for just a moment, but when Jake doesn't push him away, he relaxes.

Then there's the touch of fingers beneath his chin, gently taking hold and nudging him until he looks up. And Jake is really close. Like, *really* close. He leans down, putting his face close enough Kyle can feel his breath on his cheeks, burning his lips. He gasps, his own lips parting, and the fingers under his chin tilt his head a little more. Jake's head tilts, and their noses brush together. It's such a soft and intimate touch shivers run down his spine and his breath shudders out of his lungs. His eyes flutter shut, and he barely dares to breathe.

It doesn't feel real. It doesn't feel real. This can't be real. It can't be.

Then there's the brush of lips against his own. Wet. Soft. Chapped. Warm. His breath hitches, and he thinks he might have jumped. Jake pulls away instantly, but panic seizes his heart, and unable to let the moment pass, Kyle leans forward, chasing after him. Their lips press together more firmly, awkward at first, until Jake tilts his head more and they slot right into place.

Kyle feels like he's melting. Like he's drifting away. He can smell Jake, hot and musky in his nose. He can feel him pressed against his side, the hand on his back slipping around his waist, the fingers under his chin curling into his skin to hold him firmly in place.

Lips moving across his own in a kiss that's so gentle and hesitant but still firm and needy enough to erase any doubt that it's actually happening.

Then Jake's lips are gone, and he moves back far enough to look at him, but still close enough that Kyle can feel his breath, ragged and panting. Just as lost as his own. Kyle gazes up at him, feeling dazed and more than a little confused. The arm remains around him, though, and the fingers under his chin move to trace light and fleeting patterns up his jaw.

He blinks, licking his lips and feeling them tingle. He doesn't miss the way Jake's eyes lower to follow the movement. "What do you want from me?" Kyle asks, voice broken and ragged, soft as a whisper. He fears the answer, but he needs to know.

Jake's brows pinch just slightly, but he doesn't move away. Instead, he moves closer, pressing his forehead against Kyle's and closing his eyes. "I don't know," he breathes. "Is that...is that okay?"

And because he doesn't want this to stop, whatever *this* is, because his body feels alight wherever they touch and the thrill of it all courses through his veins, urging him onward and giving him strength, he says, "Okay."

He doesn't get a chance to dwell on it or question his choices because suddenly Jake is kissing him again, shifting and pushing and maneuvering them both until Kyle falls back on the bed. Laying on his back, hands clutching desperately to Jake's shirt. Kyle lifts his chin and attempts to give as good as he gets. He's never kissed before, but he finds a lot of it comes instinctually. That, and Jake is a really good kisser, and Kyle finds it easier to follow his lead.

It's sloppy, messy, and distantly he's aware that their breaths are terrible. But he doesn't care. He's kissing Jake. Holy *shit*, he's kissing Jake. And Jake is kissing him back with just as much fervor. He props himself up on his elbows, holding some of his weight up while the rest of his body lays out over the top of Kyle's. He gasps, feeling the larger man's weight blanket him. Feeling the firmness of his body pressing him into the mattress. Feeling the roughness of his jeans pressing on his bare thighs.

His legs part automatically, making room for Jake's body, and a gentle guidance of Jake's hand has Kyle wrapping his legs around his hips. Then Jake is shifting forward, thrusting his hips, and...

Kyle breaks their kiss as his back arches, head tossed back as pleasure ripples through him. It's unlike anything he's ever felt. Someone else pressing against him, grinding friction, hot and heavy, against his straining erection. It's almost embarrassing just how quickly he's this worked up, but in the moment, he can't bring himself to care. Especially not when Jake's hips pull back before grinding forward again, and this time Kyle can feel the hardness in Jake's jeans, rubbing against his own, and...*oh fuck*, that's new. That's new and it feels so, *so* good.

His hands scramble at Jake's body, clutching his shirt, fingers curling tight, nails clawing at his back with every slow thrust, slowly driving him mad. He gasps, soft groans falling from his lips, breath hitching in time with their movements.

Then Jake is gone, and Kyle is left reeling. Dazed and confused, he watches as Jake leans back, reaches behind him, and pulls his shirt over his head before tossing it to the floor. Kyle stares, mouth open, tongue wetting his lips as he's faced with Jake's well-defined chest, skin flushed and ribs heaving with each labored breath. He doesn't get to stare for too long because Jake's hands are scrambling at his waist, unbuttoning his pants and kicking them off to the floor.

Then he's back, settling between Kyle's waiting thighs, and Kyle gasps. He feels skin on skin, his thighs brushing against Jake's waist. Their stomachs press together where Kyle's shirt has ridden up, and his hands eagerly and desperately explore the wide expanse of Jake's back.

And when Jake grinds against him again, Kyle sees stars. He can feel everything. He can feel the shape and firmness of Jake's erection against his own, the cloth of their boxers doing very little to hide it. Jake is hard. Jake is hard *for* him. Jake is hard and pressing against him in ways he never expected to feel *so* good.

He tosses his head back, Jake's hips moving mercilessly against his own and his lips finding Kyle's jaw, moving down his neck, kissing and sucking and trailing his teeth.

Kyle feels the heat building way too quickly and all at once. He comes without warning, his entire body tensing and spasming, leaking out into his boxers as Jake continues to thrust against him. He thinks he makes a sound, but he's far too gone to notice.

Jake's movements slow, his kisses along Kyle's collarbones becoming gentler.

When Kyle comes down from his high, he's immediately hit with a surge of embarrassment and shame. He groans, holding onto Jake with one arm while the other moves to cover his face with his hand. "I'm so sorry. Oh my god, I..." He struggles to get his words out between breaths, chest heaving as he comes down. "I didn't mean to...so fast...it's my first time doing anything like this."

Jake chuckles, low and enticing, making shivers run down his spine and his toes curl. Jake noses along his neck, nuzzling him under his jaw. "Dude, it's okay, really. I take it as a compliment. So, I'm your first?"

Kyle nods weakly.

Jake kisses him beneath his ear, a rumbling purr in his voice. "Cool."

"I...I wanna get you off," he says, voice trembling as the words feel strange on his tongue. He moves his hand, tilting his head to look at Jake.

Jake props himself up, gazing down at him, a small, amused smile playing across his lips. "It's not a scoreboard. You don't have to do anything you're not comfortable with."

Kyle frowns, determination pinching his brow. "I know, but I...I want to."

Something shines in Jake's eyes, but he leans down before Kyle can read it. The smile is still on his lips as they hover over Kyle's. "Okay. Touch me."

"I..." Kyle stammers, suddenly uncertain. "I don't know..."

"It's easy," Jake leans to the side, still propped up on one elbow while he takes Kyle's hand with the other. "You've touched yourself, right?"

Kyle feels his face burn. "Yeah."

"It's just like that, but on me," he presses Kyle's hand to his chest, sliding it down over his stomach and past the waistband of his boxers. Kyle's fingers curl as they meet hair, but Jake keeps gently guiding him onward. He wraps Kyle's hand around himself, holding it there and helping him through his first stroke. "There you go, just like that. Stroke me like you'd stroke yourself."

Jake's hand leaves his own, and for a moment, Kyle hesitates. Jake feels so foreign in his palm. Larger and thicker than his own, but smooth and firm. It's exhilarating. He's holding another man in his hand, feeling his arousal, and something tickles low in his gut, heat building despite the fact that he just came.

Jake shifts again, putting his elbows on either side of Kyle and ducking his head until their foreheads are pressed together. "It's okay. I'll like anything you do. Just touch me. Touch me, Kyle."

At the sound of his name, a broken and shuddering plea on Jake's lips, Kyle moves. It's jerky at first, hesitant and uncertain. But the more he sees Jake enjoying it, the more confident he becomes. Jake's breathing picks up speed, eyes squeezing shut and brows furrowing as his lips part. His hips jerk in time with Kyle's strokes, and he tests different speeds and firmness of his grip, testing to see what gets a better reaction from Jake.

"Yeah, just like that. Oh god, *fuck*, Kyle. Faster. Yeah, just like that. Keep going. Don't stop. Don't stop," Jake pants, licking his lips, eyes squeezed shut. Kyle watches him, fascinated, as his hand works. His wrist hurts, but he doesn't care. All that matters is tipping Jake over the edge.

And watching as closely as he is, he sees the moment it happens. The moment Jake's mouth drops open, face scrunching up, body tensing, and then the warmth of cum spurting out over his hand and wrist.

Kyle strokes him through it, and when he's done, Jake collapses on top of him with a sigh. With his clean hand, Kyle idly trails his fingers up and down Jake's back, not caring that he can barely breathe. He enjoys the weight on him. He waits for Jake to come down from his high, but he can't wait long before the doubts and anxieties start to catch up to him, intruding on their little bubble of peace.

"Was that...okay? Was it good for you?" He asks, fingers idly picking at the bumps of Jake's spine.

Jake chuckles, the sound low near his ear and rumbling through his chest. "I think the fact that I came is proof of that," he sits up then, gazing down at Kyle with unexpected fondness. It takes his breath away and makes him squirm under the attention. Then Jake is leaning down, pressing a quick and chaste kiss to his lips. "Come on, let's take a shower."

Jake instructs Kyle to wrap his arms around his shoulders and legs around his hips, and when he stands, he easily picks Kyle up. He gasps, giggling and lightheaded as Jake's hands move to grab his ass.

Right here, right in this moment, he's happy. This he could get used to.

CHAPTER 13

*I*t's been a long time since Jake last enjoyed a joint shower. Cindi was never really a fan of them. She said Jake got in her way, and she had her routines to work through. He's showered with a few other ex's, but it was rarely for sex purposes.

He showered with Kyle simply because he wanted to. Because he wanted an excuse to touch him. To see him bare and wet and warm beneath his hands. And it was fun. Actually fun, which is something he never thought he'd say about showering with someone else. They slipped a few times, attempted to wash each other's bodies, laughed at each other and then had to hush their giggles before Kyle's neighbors heard them. Never once was it awkward, and at one point, Jake even managed to pick up Kyle, pinning him against the wet tile wall while he stole kisses from his lips and down his neck.

They could only stay in the shower for so long, however, and as time moves forward, they have to return to reality and to their lives.

They get dressed back in Kyle's room. Kyle stands near

his dresser, keeping his back to Jake, body hunched shyly as he pulls on boxers and jeans. Jake watches him, pulling on his own pants, taking his time, movements slow as he watches the movement of muscle beneath Kyle's skin. He's small and slight, but he's not dainty. Not in the way his ex-girlfriends had been. He's not as built as Jake or the rest of his friends, but Kyle is still very clearly a man.

And Jake is finding that's not a turn off in the slightest.

"I have practice I need to get to," Jake says, reaching down to grab his shirt and shaking it out. He sniffs it, and while it does smell of a bar and faintly of sweat, it'll do until he gets back to his apartment. Kyle doesn't turn around, but he makes a vague noise of acknowledgement. It's neutral, without any real indication that he's disappointed or relieved. Jake feels his brows pinch, but he forces himself to smile. "We should totally meet up after, though."

Kyle freezes, a t-shirt pulled onto his arms but not quite over his head. He turns slowly, peeking over one bare shoulder. His brows are creased, lips pursed into a small frown as he looks over Jake's face. "Why?" it sounds cautious and wary, and Jake can practically see those walls being rebuilt.

He refuses to let that happen. Not after he's finally managed to tear them down. So, he smiles, head tilting to the side. His shirt is held in his hands, but he makes no move to put it on. "Because I wanna see you again," he says, letting some of his amusement show, but also hoping it comes across as genuine as he feels. "I wanna take you out on a date."

Kyle turns around further, clutching his shirt to his chest. His frown deepens. "I...I don't think that's a good idea."

Jake feels his face fall, confusion dampening the budding giddiness. "What?"

Kyle shakes his head, "No," he pulls his shirt over his head, tugging down the hem of it and averting his eyes, focusing too much on straightening out his shirt. "No, that's not a good idea."

Jake feels it like a stab to his chest. Panic flickers through his veins, making his limbs tingly and light while at the same time feeling like lead weights. It's a strange feeling. One that he's not familiar with. Now that he thinks about it, he doesn't think he's ever been rejected before.

But after the wave of distress settles, he takes a good look at Kyle. He sees how stiff his posture is and how strained his expression is. He sees the worry in his eyes and the way he bites his bottom lip. He sees the way he won't make eye contact and the way his fingers fiddle with his shirt.

It's a rejection, but Kyle is clearly torn about it. He looks worried and nervous. And that's when it clicks for Jake. Kyle's uncertainty about admitting to his sexuality, desire for privacy, fear of being seen by people they know.

He's not rejecting Jake because he doesn't like him, but because he's afraid of getting hurt.

It makes Jake's heart ache for a whole new set of reasons. The cold, sharp pain in his chest melts into something warmer.

"Hey," he steps forward, reaching for Kyle. The boy flinches when Jake's hand comes down on his shoulder, but he doesn't pull away. Jake takes him by both shoulders, turning him to face him. "Look at me," he says gently, and slowly Kyle tilts his head to look up at him through his lashes, lip still caught between his teeth. "You know I didn't mess around with you just *because*, right?" Kyle looks away, and one of Jake's hands slips from his shoulder, knuckles going beneath his chin and gently tilting his head back up. He meets those uncertain eyes and smiles. "I actually *like* you, Kyle," he says, voice soft and breathless with the truth of it. It feels good to say aloud. It feels good to admit to himself. He feels his insides bubble with the giddiness of it. "I feel like I can be myself around you, and you don't judge me for it. I *like* being with you, and I'd...I'd like to explore that."

Kyle's eyes drift closed as he takes in a shaking breath. One hand comes up to Jake's arm, fingers closing around his wrist. Not pulling it away, but clinging to it, grounding himself. "I... I do, too," he admits it with a voice that shakes, but it feels like the same kind of relief that Jake had experienced. "I feel the same way, but..." his eyes open, uncertainty in their depths as he gazes up at Jake. "It's just...complicated."

Jake smiles, a fluttering in his chest that feels like hope. "Not that complicated," his hand slips from Kyle's chin, cupping his jaw in his palm as his fingers slip into his hair. Kyle tilts his head into it, and Jake feels his heart clench before it beats into overtime. "I like you. You like me. Go on a date with me."

Kyle sighs, breath squeezing from his lungs and rushing past his lips, body sagging in defeat. "Okay."

"Okay?"

"Okay," Kyle looks up at him, the ghost of a smile tugging at the corners of his lips, even as exhaustion hangs beneath his eyes. "On two conditions," strength comes back into his voice and his posture, expression hardening with that familiar confidence Jake has seen during tutoring. It makes something inside him flutter as he distantly wonders what it would be like if this commanding side of Kyle slipped into the bedroom, tearing off his clothes, pushing him down and riding him. "One, we go somewhere away from town and away from campus. And two, we take it slow. I don't wanna go fast. Can we just see how we feel tomorrow?"

Jake's smile is wide and uninhibited, a bubbling exuberant excitement coursing through his veins, giving him a high that's hard to duplicate. "I know the perfect place," he leans down, pressing his forehead to Kyle's, loving the way he can hear the guy's breath hitch. His thumb gently caresses his cheek. "And we'll take it day by day."

He kisses Kyle. It's chaste and sweet, but firm enough and lingering long enough to really feel Kyle's lips. To memorize the way their lips fit together and to feel the way Kyle stiffens before immediately relaxing, leaning into him just enough that Jake knows he wants it, too.

He pulls away far too soon, knowing that if he doesn't, he'll never be able to leave. A smirk curves his lips as he's left looking at Kyle's dazed expression, eyes lidded, and lips parted, leaning forward as if he were chasing Jake's retreat. Jake's thumb brushes his cheek one more time before his hand falls. "I'll text you after practice."

He goes before Kyle can fully gather himself, pride and glee bursting in his chest at leaving the man in such a state. The smile never leaves his face all the way back to his apartment.

* * *

"Hey, Jakey boy!" Marcus is there the moment Jake steps into the locker room. At the announcement of his name, a few of his other teammates lift their heads, calling out their greetings before going back to changing and checking their phones.

"Hey, dude," Jake offers his fist, which Marcus readily bumps with his own as Jake steps up next to him, opening his locker and tossing his bag inside. He's already changed and ready for practice, but he pulls out his cleats, sitting down on the bench as he kicks off his sneakers.

"Where were you last night?" Marcus asks, sitting down next to him with his own cleats.

"Yeah, man, you were just MIA all night," Steve closes his

locker, leaning against it with his arms crossed. "We tried calling and texting you, but you didn't pick up."

"The girls from apartment three were throwing a party and invited us down," Marcus says as he laces up his own cleats. "Total babes. *Totally* your type. They kept asking about you. Heard about you and Cindi breaking up."

"I was out," he says simply, slipping his feet into his cleats, starting to lace them up.

Marcus snorts, nudging his arm with his shoulder. "Yeah, no shit. *Where* were you? You didn't come home at all."

"Did you get some?" Steve asks, and hands drop onto Jake's shoulders as Steve squeezes them. "Oh my god, you *did*, didn't you? You *dog*. Who is she? Anyone we know?"

"I wasn't out with a chick," Jake snaps, shrugging Steve off his shoulders. He steels himself, sitting up a little straighter and preparing to tell them straight up. If this is going to be part of him, they're just going to have to accept it. And he'll take whatever teasing comes.

But as he opens his mouth, Kyle's face comes floating into his mind's eye, worried and nervous, and the words die on his tongue. His mouth snaps shut, as he looks back down to hastily tie his shoes. Kyle doesn't want to be outed, and Jake has to respect that.

"I was just out with a friend."

There's a beat of silence before he hears Steve echo. "A friend?"

"You have friends besides us?" Marcus says it like a jab, teasing and light, but there's a layer of confusion there. One of suspicion.

Something inside him twists, and the giddiness he'd felt the entire way here starts to sour. It tangles up inside him, making his breath short and his heartbeat too loud. Would they even understand if he told them? Would they treat him differently? Would they judge him? They're his friends, and he loves them, but would it change things?

He likes Kyle. He *really* likes Kyle. Even now, he's looking forward to seeing him later. He still feels haunted by their shared kisses and the *need* to have more. Like what they had wasn't enough. A pleasant heat rolls through him at the thought of kissing Kyle and the memory of his face twisted in pleasure.

He can't deny that he likes Kyle and that he's extremely attracted to him, but now that the giddiness has calmed down a little, he realizes he's not entirely certain if *he* wants to be out either. He's still ridiculously attracted to Kyle, but he's not exactly sure how he feels about this.

"Don't worry about it," he says, pushing himself to his feet and starting for the door. He doesn't turn around, but he knows his roommates are looking at him like he's crazy. He can feel the weight of their stares. "We'll get laps again if we're late to practice."

Even now, he would rather skip practice to get back to Kyle, which is a realization that hits him hard. Baseball is his life and his passion and realizing that he'd rather skip it to be with another man is surprising. And he wonders if he should take it as a warning sign.

CHAPTER 14

It feels like a waking dream. A daze surrounds him, he feels unsteady on his feet, and his limbs feel light and tingling. His heart flutters in his chest, unable to find a steady tempo. As he sits down at his desk, afraid his legs will give out beneath him. One hand lightly traces along his lips. He swears he can still feel a ghost of the warmth from Jake's kiss.

His kiss.

Holy *shit*, Jake kissed him. Several times? Oh man, it was several times. And this morning…Oh god. They…they got each other off. They *showered* together. He not only saw Jake naked, but he touched him, *washed* him, and pressed his body against him.

Kyle's hand slides down from his lips, gripping the front of his shirt as his breath falters. It still feels like a dream, but it's starting to settle into his gut that it was real. It just seems so impossible and surreal. *Jake* likes *him?* Jake actually wanted to…*wants* to…touch *him?* Wants to take him out on a date?

He must've stepped into some sort of alternate universe where things are topsy-turvy because this is just too strange.

Still, he can't say he didn't enjoy it, or that he won't continue to enjoy it. So, he might as well let himself enjoy it, right?

He sighs, long and shaky, body deflating as he turns to face his desk. He just needs a distraction, that's all. Something to keep himself from dwelling on this and all the things that could go wrong before he works himself up into an anxiety attack. If that happens, he'll no doubt get too overwhelmed with doubts and end up cancelling the date. And he *really* doesn't want to cancel the date.

He opens his laptop, going through the familiar and habitual motions of pulling up all his game editing programs. It's comforting to see the familiar displays fill his screen, the familiar lists, numbers and designs. Right. This is his world. Where everything happens by design and there are no surprises. He controls everything here.

He throws himself into it, letting his mind hone in and focus on the same problems he's been trying to solve lately. The damage calculations are coming along better, but there are a few bugs in a few instances that still need to be worked out. He just has to run a long list of simulations and possibilities, so he can pin point all the anomalies. Once he has a list of those, he can start to sift through them and look for the common denominator which will solve a majority of the problems, before going along the outliers and figuring out just what numbers seem to be throwing off his algorithms.

His stomach rumbles loudly, twisting enough that he sits back, torn from his thoughts. One hand automatically goes to his stomach, resting on it as the wave of hunger rolls over him. Oh. Right. He hasn't eaten yet today. He can feel the pin pricks and pressure of a headache building, no doubt dehydration from last night, so he should probably eat something, so he can take some painkillers. He doesn't have a lot of food in his dorm, but he doesn't really want to have to go out.

He's pulled from his thoughts when the door opens, and Jasper stumbles back into the room. His eyes are bloodshot and drooping, bags under them and he looks exhausted. His body hunches, feet dragging, his clothes a mess. Really, he looks no different than he usually does when he comes home, hungover.

"Hey," Kyle says, more out of reflex than anything else. He and Jasper have always had an easy camaraderie.

Jasper, however, doesn't look at him, just grumbles an irritable, "Hey," as he drops his bag to the floor. He stretches his arms over his head, groaning as his back pops before his body collapses again. He shuffles over to his dresser to rummage through it, and Kyle turns back to his laptop.

He's not too worried about it. Jasper is rarely talkative when he comes back after a weekend. After learning what it means to be truly drunk, Kyle can't blame him. If Jake hadn't been there to wake him up, he might've been in the same state.

His cheeks warm at the thought of this morning, and he shakes his head, forcing himself to focus on the string of numbers on his screen.

"So, uh..." Kyle looks up, blinking in surprise as Jasper hovers near his desk. He holds a pile of clothes in his hand and a towel is draped over his shoulder. He rubs his neck, eyes averted. "Sorry, about last night, or whatever."

He's clearly waiting for something, despite the fact that Kyle has no idea what he's talking about. What happened last night? Rather than ask, he just shifts in his seat, mutters an awkward, "Uh, it's okay."

Jasper nods sharply before spinning on his heel and

hurrying into the bathroom, shutting the door behind him. Kyle watches him go, uncertainty churning in his gut, mixing with the preexisting hollowness from hunger.

On second thought, maybe leaving his dorm would be a good thing. Get some food. Put some distance between him and whatever awkwardness Jasper is experiencing. Hope that later it'll just be resolved. He packs up his laptop, grabs his wallet, and slips out the door as the sound of the shower starts up.

The fresh air does wonders for his exhausted body. It feels cool and refreshing against his skin, which still feels heavy and gross from the night before, despite taking a shower. His eyes are heavy and tired, and the fresh air helps him feel more awake. It fills his lungs, breathing life back into his system, restarting him and rejuvenating him in a way he hadn't realized he'd been needing. Who knew fresh air was great for hangovers?

He goes to the sandwich place in the cafeteria and gets a sub, a bottle of water, and heads back out to the quad. He finds a place against a tree, off to the side and free from the minimal crowd on the small field in the middle of campus. Campus feels dead at this time of day on a Saturday. Slow and lethargic, people moving about in a dreary daze as they attempt to wake up from a long, busy Friday night. It's peaceful.

He pulls out his laptop, settling it on his lap and typing with one hand while he eats with the other. It's slow progress, but it's progress. A least a lot of his current work involves just analyzing data anyway, trying to pin point where the bugs slip through the algorithms.

He's pulled from his thoughts when someone unceremoniously plops down next to him, and he whips around, staring at a girl with a side cut, long wavy hair, and a plethora of piercings. She's smiling at him, edges of her eyes crinkling with a knowing amusement. "Hey."

Kyle gapes for a moment before his mouth snaps shut. He scowls, but it's done more in confusion than actual anger. "Uh, hi?"

"You must be Kyle," she holds out her hand, and Kyle stares at it for a moment. Despite the strange amusement in her smile, it seems genuine enough, and her expression is open and earnest. He takes her hand hesitantly.

"Uh, yeah. How do you know who I am?" Her handshake is firm and friendly.

Her smile widens just a fraction, lifting her cheeks. "I'm Liddy, Jake's ex from like, high school," she leans forward, over their gripping hands, tilting her head to give him a little wink. "And I know you've got your own little arrangement with him right now."

Kyle freezes, feeling his blood run cold even as heat rushes up his neck and onto his face. His body feels stiff, eyes widening as his jaw clenches. He thinks he might be squeezing her hand in his panic, but he can't be sure. Not when his blood is pounding through his veins and his heartbeat is loud in his ears. His vision tunnels in on her without really seeing her. His mind is just a broken record of, *oh god*, she knows, she knows, she knows, people know, how do people know, run, run, run.

Before his flight instinct can fully manifest, she chuckles. The sound is soft and gentle, understanding and warm. Not at all mocking or malicious. It catches his attention, and he focuses on it, blinking as his brows furrow. Her other hand lays over the top of his, forcing his grip to relax.

"It's okay," she says, and it's low and gentle and makes his body automatically react to her words. "It's okay. He didn't say anything about it. I've just been teasing him about it, and you know...your reaction kind of confirmed my suspicions."

He jerks his hand away, holding it to his chest as if he'd been burned. "I'm not...we're not...it's not like *that!*"

She blinks, knees pulling up and arms moving to wrap around them. She hums, tilting her head to the side. He doesn't like how she's looking at him as if she can see right through him. "But...you want it to be, right?"

Kyle bites his lip, looking away.

"Hey, hey, no judgement here," she chuckles, but somehow the sound is soothing rather than grating. "I have a girlfriend myself. She's beautiful, and I love her," Kyle looks at her sharply, and she smiles. "Yeah, I used to date Jake a long time ago, but we have no hard feelings. Now he's my best friend, and even though he denies it, I can read him like an open book."

Kyle looks down, eyes on his keyboard but his focus is distant. "What..." he licks his lips, trying to take deep breaths. "What has he said about me?"

She shrugs, waving a hand around vaguely. "Just that you're tutoring him, that you're super cute, and honestly, a bunch of other random little details that he wouldn't notice if he wasn't interested in you."

Kyle feels the heat burn his cheeks. A hand comes down on his shoulder, and he flinches, but he doesn't pull away. When he looks up at her shyly through his lashes, her smile is small and kind, almost pleading.

"He's a good guy," she says softly.

"I know," he whispers.

"Just give him a chance. He's a big oaf, and an idiot at times, but he means well. He's struggling with a lot right now, but I've never seen him *actually* interested in anyone before. Not like this. I don't know you, but from what I've heard, I think you'd be good for him."

There's a twist in his chest. A fluttering in his heart. His lungs squeeze, but it doesn't feel like he's suffocating. A buzz runs through his veins. He looks away, nodding just a fraction as he whispers. "I'll give him a chance."

The hand on his shoulder squeezes. "Thanks, Kyle. I don't think you'll regret it. Who knows? Maybe he'll be good for you, too," he looks up in time to catch her wink, and with a smile, she stands. "Well, I was on my way to the library for a study group, so I better get going. But it was nice meeting you!"

"Yeah," he says, smiling shyly. "You, too."

She waves and walks away, and he lifts his hand in a small semblance of the same gesture before it falls back down to his keyboard. She isn't what he expected from one of Jake's ex's, nor what he expected from Jake's best friend, but he finds that he likes her. There's just something about her that puts him at ease.

But enough about Jake. Enough about Liddy. He has work to do.

Unfortunately, that's easier said than done.

He has an increasing problem focusing. He keeps checking the time in the corner of his screen, frowning when he realizes barely any time has passed since the last time he checked. It takes him an embarrassingly long time to realize *why* he's so frustrated at the time.

Jake.

He wants it to be later, so he can be with Jake again. Date or not, he just wants to hang out with him, and that's stealing focus away from his work. Cry Thunder has been his sole focus for so long that it's strange and new to find something else nagging at his mind.

His thoughts drift back to that morning. To Jake's lips on his. On his neck, teeth grazing against his collarbone. To the feeling of Jake's weight settling over him, between his legs, pushing down on him and pinning him to the bed. Of the tantalizing feeling of skin on skin, and the sparks that raced down his spine. The heat building low in his gut as Jake moved above him, grinding against him. The feeling of his hardness pressed against Kyle's, a feeling he's always wondered about but been too embarrassed to dwell on for too long.

The sound of Jake's breath, fast, heavy and labored. The sight of him furrowing his brows, lips pinching as Kyle's name shuddered on his lips.

Them in the shower, bodies bare and skin slick as Jake picked him up. His legs locking around Jake's narrow hips as Jake pushed his back to the cold tile. Body hard, broad and firm, half chub pushing against his ass with interest as Jake's lips devoured his neck.

Kyle swallows hard, slamming his laptop closed. He has a problem. A *very* big problem. He looks around the quad, but no one is paying him any mind. Then he glances down, blanching at the obvious erection pushing against the seam of his jeans.

Fuck. *Fuck fuck fuck.*

He closes his eyes tight, trying to will it away, but his thoughts keep drifting back to Jake. To his large, calloused hands and how they felt on his…

Fuck.

He packs his bag quickly, standing and holding it awkwardly in front of him as he hurries to the student union. It's closer than his dorm, and this is an emergency. No one gives him more than a curious glance, and he hurries past them with his eyes firmly on the ground to hide his flush. The bathroom, thankfully, is blissfully empty.

He locks himself in one of the stalls, drops his bag to the ground, and leans back against the stall wall. His hand is at the front of his pants in seconds, shaking fingers fumbling with the button and zipper. His other hand covers his mouth, muffling his heavy breaths as he pulls himself out.

He strokes himself quickly and roughly, desperate to get it over with before anyone comes in. Panicking but unable to stop, he remembers the feeling of Jake's hand, of his lips, of his body.

And he comes embarrassingly quickly, a high-pitched whine slipping from between his fingers. He stands there, dazed and shaking as he comes down from his high, his breathing slowly starting to regulate.

Then he cleans himself up as best he can, grateful that his hand caught most of it and there's no obvious mess on his jeans to show his shame.

Oh god, his shame. It rushes through him, sour and sickening, settling like lead in his stomach. He just jerked himself off to images of Jake in a public bathroom. After Jake had gotten him off just that morning. How fucking pathetic can he be?

His downward spiral is interrupted by the sound of his phone going off. He jumps, scrambling for it and nearly dropping it in the toilet. His heart hammers in his chest as he rushes out of the bathroom, automatically swiping to answer the call without really thinking about it.

"Hello?"

"Kyle!" his mom's voice comes from the receiver. His steps slow as he walks through the student union, aimless and restless. He doesn't want to go back out to the quad, not after what just happened, but he has no other destination in mind.

His mind wanders as his mom's voice drones on. He's stopped paying attention, but distantly recognizes that she's telling him about something that happened recently at home. His thoughts linger on Jake, confusion, guilt, shame, and hope swirling into a nauseating mix that makes him wish he'd eaten a little slower.

Liddy said he would be good for Jake, but is it even

possible that whatever is happening between them can ever be anything more than just an experiment?

He thinks there's a small hope something might come of it, but he dreads that there's a bigger chance it'll blow up in their faces.

CHAPTER 15

*G*etting dressed for dates is second nature by this point. He knows what clothes he has, and he knows what makes him look good. For this date though, he finds himself standing in front of his mirror longer than usual, a contemplative frown across his face as he mentally dissects his outfit. After an internal debate, he rolls up the sleeves of his button up to expose his forearms because he knows it makes them look good. He has nice, strong arms, so he might as well show them off.

He straps a watch to his wrist. He barely ever wears it, but it looks nice and it complements the outfit. Plus, it has a way of making him look more sophisticated, which is never something he's really worried about with any of the girls he's dated, but with Kyle he doesn't want to look like a regular jock.

He sits on his bed while pulling on his shoes, a good step between formal and casual. Something to make him look good but without putting his outfit over the top. As he ties the laces, he mentally goes through a list. Deodorant? Check. Cologne? Check. Hair? Looking good. Clothes?

Pristine and spot on. Phone, wallet, keys, check, check, check.

When he's done, he stands, taking a deep breath and shaking out his hands. Despite his nerves, he adopts a casual posture, smooth and confident, and hopes he can manage to sneak out of his apartment without his roommates noticing.

He isn't that lucky.

As soon as he steps out into the living room, Marcus looks up from the couch. He does a double take, looking Jake over before letting out a long, low whistle. "Okay, so you are *definitely* going to see some girl."

Jake frowns. "How'd you know?"

Steve walks out of the bathroom at that moment, pauses when he sees Jake, then grins. "Dude, you're wearing your date clothes."

Jake sighs, moving quickly toward the door.

"Who's the lucky girl?" Steve calls after him.

Jake lifts a hand up, waving vaguely at him over his shoulder. "I'm too much of a gentleman to kiss and tell," he says vaguely, hoping it sounds confident and mysterious enough for them to stop pushing. It seems to do the trick, but then Marcus asks a completely different question.

"Dude, does Cindi know? She's gonna flip her shit when she finds out you're dating already."

Jake snorts a short laugh, rolling his eyes as he reaches the door and wrenches it open. "It's none of her business what I do. *She* dumped *me*."

"Ha! Amen to that. Good luck on your *date!*"

"Get some, Jake! *Get some!*" Steve calls after him as he closes the door.

Breathing out a sigh of relief, he hurries down the stairs and starts off toward campus to pick up Kyle. Hands shoved deep in his pockets, he wonders, not for the first time and no doubt not for the last, if anything would change if he admitted he was seeing a guy. He knows it's not a decision he can make on his own, but that doesn't stop him from wondering, for better or for worse.

* * *

Kyle's door swings open mere seconds after he knocks, and Jake grins down at him, hands in his pockets and rocking back on his heels. Kyle's smile fades as he looks Jake up and down, smile morphing into a frown.

Jake feels his heart twist, nervousness trickling through his veins. "Is, uh...everything okay?"

Kyle looks him up and down once more, frown deepening. "I didn't realize we were...like this was a *dressing up* kind of date," Jake blinks, but before he can really process that statement, Kyle is stepping back, and the door is starting to swing closed. "I need to change."

"Whoa!" Jake reaches out, stepping forward to catch the door before it closes. Kyle doesn't push it, already stepping away, deeper into his room. He doesn't try to stop Jake from entering after him, gently pushing the door shut behind him. "You don't *have* to change. It's fine. You're cute no matter what you wear."

Kyle barely seems to hear him. Even the compliment goes unnoticed as Jake watches Kyle's expression go into lock down, shutting off behind a torrent of thoughts and contemplation as he tugs open his drawers and rummages through them. "No," he mumbles, but Jake can't tell if it's to him or himself. "No, you put effort into dressing up, so I should, too. If this is a dress up date, then I should dress up. Plain and simple."

Jake finds himself smiling, amusement fluttering warm and fond in his chest. He's never heard anyone call it a *dress up* date before, and he thinks it's cute. It shows just how inexperienced and adorable Kyle is. Jake really doesn't mind if Kyle doesn't change, but if he insists, Jake isn't about to stop him. Not when Kyle is suddenly undressing, ripping off his shirt and tossing it to the floor and proceeding to stand shirtless with one hand on his hip and the other rubbing at his chin.

"I have to have *something* that's appropriate. Fuck, I never dress up. What's the dress code for a first date? What about this? No, not that shirt," he groans, and Jake knows Kyle's awareness of him has faded as he gets wrapped up in his thoughts.

He leans against the wall, arms crossed over his chest, and watches with increasing amusement as Kyle frets over his clothes. He pulls some out, holds them against himself, and then shakes his head before shoving them back. Jake has had the misfortune to watch some of his ex's get ready before, but they were never this adorable. He also has to admit he enjoys the show and the exposure of Kyle's bare skin.

It reminds him of this morning. Of what it felt like to touch him. To press him to the mattress, writhing beneath him. To have him pinned to the wall of the shower.

He has the increasing urge to touch, but he holds himself back. Now isn't the time. Date first. Woo him first. Show him he's actually interested in more than just his body. Jake's fingers curl into fists, and he simply resigns himself to waiting.

But he can only wait for so long before Kyle's frustration seems to be getting the better of him.

"Here," Jake steps forward, hand falling on Kyle's bare shoulder. He jumps, head whipping around to gape up at him, but he relaxes as Jake's hand slides soothingly down his back. "Let me help."

Kyle hunches, looking away. "Okay."

Jake takes a moment to rummage through Kyle's clothes,

moving through his dresser and his wardrobe. He has to admit, Kyle doesn't have a lot. It's mostly t-shirts and comfort clothes. He does, however, manage to find a button up and a bowtie. He's never been one for bowties himself, but as soon as he imagines one on Kyle, he can't let it go.

He helps Kyle get dressed. Nice jeans, nice shoes, a button up, and his bowtie. Kyle keeps his eyes averted the whole time, a pretty flush settled pink and rosy on his cheeks and on his chest. Jake lets his knuckles trail along Kyle's jaw as he steps back to admire his work. Kyle shifts awkwardly under Jake's gaze, but it only serves to make him even more adorable.

"Perfect," he says, smiling wide as he puts his hands on his hips.

Kyle tugs uncertainly at his collar. "Thanks," he mumbles. "I, um...I'm a little nervous."

"I know," Jake says stepping in close to wrap Kyle up in a hug, pulling him to his chest. His heart stutters when Kyle automatically wraps his arms around Jake's waist, nuzzling into his chest. "But you don't need to be."

They leave, and Jake has to shove his hands deep in his pockets to resist the urge to reach out and take Kyle's hand.

* * *

THIS IS AWKWARD.

Far more awkward than Jake was expecting, and far more awkward than things had been the night before. At least then they had alcohol to loosen their tongues and push them in the right direction. Now, seated at a nice Italian restaurant a little way out of town, they sit in silence. Jake rests his chin in his palm, free hand idly tapping at the table and picking at grooves in the wood. Kyle sits across from him, fidgeting with his sleeves and picking at his napkin. Jake idly muses that it's a good thing the napkin is cloth because paper would be shredded by now.

Jake's eyes wander the room. The lighting is dim, a candle on each table. There are a few people here, but none he recognizes, and mostly older couples. Soothing music plays, and it creates an atmosphere that feels private and intimate.

"Sorry."

His eyes snap back to Kyle, brows furrowing as Kyle scowls down at the napkin in his lap. "For what?" Jake asks, bewildered.

One of his shoulders rises and falls in a weak shrug. A bitter, dry laugh escapes his lips. "For being so awkward. I'm not very social. I don't know how to do…" he looks up, but carefully avoids eye contact as he waves a hand around in an annoyed gesture. "*This.*"

Jake feels a prickle of doubt shiver down his spine, cold and sobering. Dates are common enough for him. First date jitters are also common. But he never considered dragging someone out who doesn't *like* the idea of dates. Especially since last night they were fine.

"So, you want to make games," Jake says, abruptly changing the subject as the memory filters by. It seems like a safe enough topic, and one that Kyle actually enjoys, and he hopes it'll help clear some of the discomfort from the air.

Kyle stiffens, eyes widening as he finally looks at Jake. "I...did I tell you that?" There's a blush on his cheeks that Jake can see even in the dim lighting.

He chuckles. "You touched on it, last night."

"Oh," he clears his throat, shifting in his seat as he sits up a little straighter, lifting his chin. There's a defensiveness in his eyes and a pride in his posture. "Yeah, I wanna design and code games."

Jake perks up, leaning more on the table. "That's really cool. Are you working on anything now?"

Kyle's eyes light up, and the ghost of a smile tugs at his lips. "I am. It's called Cry Thunder, and I've been working on it for a couple years now."

He goes on, and on, and on, and on. A fantasy MMORPG unique in design and coding, custom made by Kyle himself. He launches into a description of it, getting side tracked onto tangents where he rants and complains about other RPGs and the downsides to them, going on to explain how he plans on fixing those problems and annoyances in his own game.

He talks, and Jake listens. They pause long enough to order their food, and Kyle continues with minimal prompting from him. And after the description of the game is over, Kyle delves into the details of his plans, and...

It's then that it really starts to dawn on Jake just *how* smart Kyle really is. He's really, really fucking smart. Like, Jake knew he was smart. He knew he got straight A's and barely had to work for them. He knew Kyle was a little nerd, and that was part of his reasoning when asking for tutoring in the first place.

He just hadn't realized Kyle was far more than just book smart. He was creative, too. He took math and numbers and coding and made art with it. He designed things. He looked at problems and came up with creative solutions. He was *creating* something *amazing* all on his own, based on his own vision and his own drive.

It's more than a little impressive, as well as extremely intimidating.

It even becomes a little humiliating when Kyle *really* starts to get into it and Jake has to ask him to kind of dumb it down for him. Explain things in layman's terms because he *wants* to understand, he really does, he just can't. He doesn't know what an algorithm is, and he doesn't understand any of what Kyle's unique damage calculations mean for actual gameplay.

For the first time in his life, Jake starts to feel like the person he's interested in might be out of his league. Which is a strange and alienating feeling. He's always been with hot girls on the same level as him, but Kyle...Kyle is adorable, cute, funny, kind, and way, way too smart for him.

Kyle doesn't just like him because he's hot, right? Oh god, is *Jake* the hot accessory? No, there's no way Kyle is that shallow, right?

"Jake?"

He blinks, lifting his head from where he'd been staring at the table. He doesn't realize he's been frowning until he feels it relax. "Yeah?" It's only then that he realizes he's been so wrapped up in his thoughts that he was tuning Kyle out.

Kyle shifts in his seat, fingers twisting in the cloth napkin on the table. "Sorry for rambling," he mutters, eyes downcast.

Guilt rolls hot and fresh in his gut, and Jake instinctively reaches out, putting a hand on Kyle's. "No, man, it's fine. Really. You're cute when you get excited about things," it's not a lie, and Jake feels like a jerk for not just appreciating it and instead going off on his own pity party.

Kyle's smile is small and shy. "Thanks," he pulls back his hand quickly when their food arrives, a blush on his cheeks as he refuses to make eye contact with their waiter. When they're alone again, Kyle asks, "So what about you? What kinda stuff do you do?"

Jake's smile is wry. "I play baseball."

Kyle rolls his eyes, smile still in place as he picks at his food. "I know *that*."

Jake chuckles, but there's no humor in it. An attempt to lighten the mood falls flat as it fills with self-deprecation. "No really, that's about all I do. Ever since I was a kid, my life revolved around sports. My grades in high school were okay, but I've always just kinda been, you know, the dumb jock," he tries to make it sound like a joke, but Kyle's smile falls. "No one really took me seriously, and I coasted by on average grades. Then I got into college on a baseball scholarship, and just kinda coasted again," he laughs again, this time dry and far more bitter. He looks down, poking at his pasta with his fork. "Until now, anyway," he shrugs. "No one's ever really thought much of me, so they never challenged me. I've never been good for much other than throwing a ball."

"I've always had the opposite problem," Kyle's voice is soft, and Jake glances up. He leans his cheek onto one hand, smile a mirror of Jake's, not quite reaching his eyes. "All people ever do is push me and challenge me."

Jake exhales a sharp laugh. "Well, yeah. I can see why."

Kyle frowns. "What do you mean?"

Jake rolls his eyes, lifting his fork to point at Kyle with it. "You're a fucking genius, dude. You're smart as hell, and you can do so much. Compared to you, I'm just an idiot with muscles."

He expects Kyle to smile, but instead his frown deepens. "I don't think so."

"What?"

Kyle sets his fork down, eyes intense as he glares across the table. "Jake, you're not dumb."

Jake smiles reassuringly as he chuckles. "Dude, it's okay. It's fine. I know what I'm meant for in life."

"No!" Kyle leans across the table, practically putting his shirt in his food as he snatches up Jake's hand. He stares at it, wide and blinking, following the length of Kyle's arms to meet his eyes. They're narrowed and fierce, lips tight as he scowls. "You're *not* dumb," he says with enough adamant force that Jake thinks he might just believe him. His voice softens then, scowl easing into a shy smile. "You're not an idiot. You're smart and kind and observant and courteous and a really good guy. You may not know a lot for your classes, but you learn really quickly."

"You're just a good teacher," Jake insists, but Kyle is already shaking his head.

"No, I've tutored before. Some people just really aren't that smart. No matter how often you tell them stuff, they never get it. *You* get it. You *learn*. You're determined and hard-working, and once things are actually explained to you, you *get* it. You're not dumb, Jake. It's just no one has ever given you a reason to try before."

Jake's smile is small, barely touching his cheeks, but it's genuine. He moves his hand, easily sliding his fingers between Kyle's. He stares down at them, at how they fit, and runs his thumb over Kyle's knuckles. "Thanks, Kyle."

"No problem," he says, breathless.

* * *

As THEY LEAVE the restaurant later that night, Jake tries to make a move. He bumps into Kyle's side, and his fingers stretch to lightly snatch at Kyle's.

As soon as his pinky hooks around Kyle's, he pulls his hand away fast. He shoves them into his pockets, subtly taking a step away to put distance between them. "Sorry," he says, head down and shoulders hunched. "I'm just not...ready for that." He pauses, glancing up through his lashes to search Jake's face. "Is that okay?"

Jake smiles, hoping it's calming and doesn't show any of the doubt he feels squeezing at his gut. "Yeah, that's fine. Don't worry about it."

He understands, but he wonders if it's going to hurt this much every time.

CHAPTER 16

*J*ake's car is nothing fancy, but it's clean and comfortable. It's a lot nicer than Kyle was expecting, given Jake's messy apartment, his disorganized backpack, and the fact that he's a jock. He expected some old take-out bags, some clothes or gym bags, and some other miscellaneous stuff. But his car is organized, clean, and smells nice.

He doesn't say anything about it, but his expression must be clear enough, because Jake calls attention to it. He tells Kyle not to judge him or stereotype him, and while he's teasing, Kyle's laugh is strained, and his cheeks feel warm. He really needs to stop doing that because Jake is just so much *more* than anything he expected.

But at the same time, he kind of hopes Jake never stops surprising him and exceeding his expectations.

"I don't drive my car often," Jake says as they pull out of the parking lot, turning onto the main road. "Campus and most things are within walking distance of my apartment. I mostly use it whenever we have to get groceries or something, but half the time Marcus or Steve drive."

Kyle hums, one elbow resting on the door of the car, cheek propped up by his palm. His other arm rests on the center console as he stares out the window. "I don't even have a car."

"You don't?"

Kyle shrugs. "I never really needed one. I never really went places, and if I needed to...my brother would drive me. And after his...his accident, I don't really feel comfortable driving."

Jake's hand comes down over his, startling him for a moment. He watches as Jake's fingers, warm and solid, slide between his own, putting their hands palm to palm, squeezing gently. It's far more comforting than words could ever be, and Kyle squeezes back.

It's dark now, and Kyle feels braver in the safety of shadows and in the blanket of night that covers the town. Here, hidden from the world, it feels like no one can touch them. No one can see them or judge them. It's just him and Jake. He feels like he's stepped outside of himself and hesitantly towards someone he isn't, but who he might like to be.

The cars moving alongside them down the main road blend into the background, their passengers disappearing into the darkness and becoming inconsequential. They're on the outskirts of town, a good twenty minutes from campus, but it might as well be hours.

The small, sly smile that curves his lips surprises him, as do the words that leave his mouth. "You know, if I've learned anything about dates from watching old movies, it's that you're about to take me to a make-out point or something."

Jake seems taken aback, but he chuckles nonetheless. "Holding my hand in the parking lot is moving too fast, but you want me to take you to a make-out point?" he's teasing, but there's a genuine curiosity in there and an eagerness that he can't quite hide.

Kyle keeps his eyes trained on the window, glad for the darkness to hide his blush. "Well, people could see us then. They wouldn't be able to see us in the car," he lets his thumb move across Jake's knuckles. It feels natural, and he hopes it's as intimate for Jake as it feels for Kyle. He also hopes his palms aren't sweating too badly. He takes a slow breath to steady his voice as he speaks. "Besides, I think it would be fun."

Jake laughs, hand squeezing Kyle's. "You're full of surprises."

Kyle smiles, but the silence seeps back in. It doesn't feel as calm as before. There's an undercurrent of anticipation and nervousness that runs between them. After another mile or two, Jake pulls off on an exit, and Kyle's heart hammers in his chest, spreading adrenaline through his veins. He knows this isn't the exit for town, and it's nowhere near campus.

He tries to regulate his breathing as they pull off on a scenic route that circles the town, showing off the more mountainous region that surrounds the area. Their speed slows to match the new speed limit, and with it, Kyle can feel his nerves rising.

For a moment, just a moment, he feels doubt. But then he glances over and takes in Jake's profile in the light of the moon and the glow of the car's dashboard. His eyes trail along the strong line of his jaw and the cutting edge of his cheekbones, his strong nose and the curve of his lips.

Desire hits him all at once, memories bleeding into fantasies. He wants to kiss those lips again. He wants to feel Jake's tongue on him. He wants to feel his weight, his hands, and writhe under them. He wants Jake's attention on him, solely him. He wants to see Jake's face again as he comes and know it was all because of him. For a moment, just a moment, Kyle wants to occupy all of Jake's thoughts. As selfish as it feels, it's what Kyle wants.

His heart beats faster and his skin tingles with anticipation because he knows what he has to do. No, what he *wants* to do. He wants this just as much as he hopes Jake does.

The car slows, and Jake pulls off onto the side where the road curves into a scenic overlook. It's tucked away from the main road, but even that road is off the beaten track and nearly empty at this time of night. They haven't seen another car since pulling off the highway. Jake puts the car in park and leans back, staring out the windshield with a small smile on his lips.

"It's not really a make-out point, but it's close enough," he chuckles, and if Kyle didn't know any better, he'd say it sounds nervous. Then it hits him, Jake probably *is* nervous. Jake is nervous over *him*.

Before the high can fade and before doubts creep in, Kyle rides his wave of courage. He unbuckles his seatbelt, the sound loud in the quiet car. "I think it'll do just fine," he says, licking his lips as he turns in his seat, letting go of Jake's hand to reach out with both of his. He takes Jake's face, firmly pulling him over the center console as he leans forward, pressing their lips together with sudden fervor.

Jake is surprised and caught off guard, and in his moment of hesitancy, Kyle feels his courage bleeding away. His hold goes lax, and he starts to pull away, but then Jake is surging forward after him. A firm hand finds its way behind Kyle's neck, cradling the back of his head, holding him firmly in place while Jake tilts his head and devours Kyle's lips.

Kyle returns the kiss, but he feels like he's fighting a stronger current, barely able to stay afloat. Jake has so much more experience than he does. He knows exactly how to turn his head, how and when to move his lips, how to sweep his tongue into Kyle's mouth and make his toes curl. His hands roam Kyle's body, leaving trails of fire in their wake. Even with his patient guidance, it's all Kyle can do to just cling to him and kiss him back, trying to follow his lead and explore on his own.

He enjoys it. He really does. He loses himself in Jake's lips, and the feeling of his hands, and the smell of his cologne. But it doesn't take long before he realizes that Jake is being cautious. Jake's hands roam over him but stay courteously outside his clothes. His kisses are urgent and desperate, but he doesn't push for more.

It's strangely sweet. He's respecting Kyle's boundaries and not pushing him for more. It makes Kyle's chest tighten and a fluttering fills his lungs.

It's sweet, but he wants more. He wants to see Jake come undone, and he wants to be the one to do it.

He puts a hand on Jake's chest, pushing back until he can see his face. It takes a moment for Jake to come out of his haze, blinking as he pulls back. His eyes are lidded, lips wet and parted as he looks at Kyle, confused. "Do...do you want to stop?"

Kyle shakes his head, licking his lips. "No, I want...I want..." oh god, it's embarrassing to say. A lot more so than he was anticipating. He leans forward, burying his face in the crook of Jake's neck to hide his expression, but presses his lips to his throat as an excuse. His hands slide down Jake's broad chest, coming to rest decisively at the front of his jeans, tugging lightly at the button.

"You want to touch me?" He sounds breathless, one of his hands already moving to help Kyle unbutton and unzip his pants.

Kyle nods, face rubbing against his neck. He licks a spot there, running his teeth along tender flesh before latching on and sucking lightly. It's instinctual, something he's not entirely sure about, but he hears Jake's breath hitch and knows it's alright. He kisses the spot and forces himself to speak. "Yeah, but...not with my hands," he runs his nose and lips lightly up Jake's neck, trying to tell him without saying the words.

It seems to do the trick. He *feels* Jake's full body shudder and the hand on him tighten. "Oh," he sounds winded, and it sends a thrill through Kyle. "Oh, okay. Yeah, yeah, totally. We can. We should move to the backseat. Yeah, okay, let's go."

It takes a lot of awkward maneuvering for them to get into the backseat. First Jake forgets his seatbelt is still on and gets tangled up in that. Then they take turns sliding through the two front seats to fall into the back, limbs spread as they lose their balance and laughing as they elbow and knee each other. Kyle follows Jake's lead as he settles in.

Jake ends up sitting with his back to the car door, one foot on the floor and the other on the seat, knee bent and resting against the back of the seat. Kyle sits between his spread legs, eyeing the front of his jeans. Jake doesn't hesitate to reach down, eager as he pushes down the waist band of his jeans and boxers far enough to pull himself out. He's as big as Kyle remembers, flushed, red and thick.

Kyle swallows hard, embarrassed when he feels his mouth watering.

He manages to get down between Jake's legs, one hand wrapped loosely around the base of his cock, mouth hovering several inches above it, before he loses his nerve and his courage gives way to nerves. He looks up sheepishly, gazing through his lashes at Jake, leaned against the car door and watching him intently through lidded eyes.

"I, uh...I'm not really sure..." he swallows thickly, eyes flickering back down to the swollen cock head. He's never been this close to one, and while his body *burns* with the need to touch, it's still incredibly intimidating. Especially when he wants this to be good for Jake, whose no doubt done this plenty of times. "I've never done this before."

"Hey," fingers slip beneath his chin, lifting his head until he's looking up at Jake again. He's smiling, encouraging and kind. "It's okay. I guarantee I'll like anything you do," his fingers run through Kyle's hair, gently applying pressure to push him down. "Just go slow and explore. It'll feel good for me, I promise."

Kyle takes a deep breath, closing his eyes as he lowers his head and opens his mouth. It feels strange, and tastes stranger. But it's not bad. It tastes of salt and skin, smells musky and so much like *Jake*. There's something about it that fuels the fire in his belly. He licks along Jake's shaft, first with the tip of his tongue and then with the flat of it.

"Yeah," Jake breathes from above. "Keep going. Take it into your mouth, yeah, slow. Just like that."

Kyle suckles on the head, curiously moving his tongue over it, pressing into the slit to taste him. He feels Jake jerk, but then he's exhaling a shuddering moan, and shivers run down Kyle's spine.

It gives him the confidence to continue, to take a little more into his mouth, to slide his lips over the shaft. "Yeah," Jake says, panting now as his chest heaves with each word. "Make your lips tighter, just like that. Use your hand as a stopping point so you don't go too far. Use your tongue...*holy shit!* Yeah, holy fuck, okay, okay."

Curious, Kyle moves down as far as he can before he feels his gag reflex start to trigger, and then he hollows out his cheeks and *sucks*.

The sound Jake makes is low, guttural, and sends sparks of pleasure sizzling down Kyle's spine, especially when the moan trails off into his name. Kyle wants to make him sound like *that* again. He'll do anything to hear that sound. To hear Jake say his name like *that*.

So, he keeps going, following Jake's instructions that are getting less informative and more like babbled encouragements. Jake, as it turns out, is surprisingly talkative. With his mouth unoccupied, he pants, and each exhale has words and moans escaping his lips. He babbles, begs, and pleads with Kyle for *more*, go faster, just like that, do that again, harder, oh god.

Kyle can feel his own hardness straining against his jeans, and his hips jerk shallowly, seeking any sort of friction he might get against the seat of the car.

Jake's fingers tighten in his hair, back arching and his head hitting the window. "Kyle, I'm gonna…I'm gonna…"

He comes then, spurting hot and sticky into Kyle's mouth. Despite the warning, it takes him by surprise. The texture and taste are strange, as is the way it fills him suddenly and quickly. He pulls off Jake as his last spurt settles and surprises them both when he puts a hand to his lips and swallows, wiping off the last bit at the corner of his mouth with the back of his hand.

"Holy shit," Jake says, staring at him, wide eyed and mouth gaping. "That was so hot."

Kyle giggles, surprised and pleased and still riding the high of making Jake look like *that* and sound like *that*.

Jake takes a moment to come down from his high, breathless and chest heaving as he stares at Kyle. Kyle stares back, unable to look away, feeling caught in the headlights. But his hips can't stop moving, even if it's just a shallow cant. His hard on strains against its confines, and his blood still boils. The taste of Jake lingers on his tongue. He licks his lips, and watches as Jake's eyes flicker down to the movement.

Then Jake is moving, surging forward to capture his lips again. They fall backwards onto the seat, and Jake settles over him, between his legs. Kyle wraps them around his hips automatically, and one of Jake's hands moves to cup and squeeze his ass. He gasps, and Jake's tongue pushes inside his mouth.

His hand moves, fingers creeping beneath the waistband

of his pants, grabbing a handful of his bare ass with his palm, squeezing before his fingers move again, slipping between his cheeks, prodding at…

Kyle jerks back, hands pushing Jake's chest. He doesn't move far, but it breaks their kiss, and Jake moves back far enough to look down at him. Kyle stares up at him, eyes wide and chest heaving with every breath. His heart hammers painfully in his chest, entire body tight.

"I'm not…" His voice cracks, and he has to swallow past the lump in his throat. "I don't think I'm ready for that."

The confusion on Jake's face melts into understanding, followed quickly by relief. "Okay," he says, bending forward to press a gentle kiss to Kyle's lips. "That's fine. We can wait. I can do something else."

He moves down Kyle's body, trailing kisses as he goes, pushing up Kyle's shirt to spread his attention around his chest and stomach, moving lower and lower. He pulls Kyle's pants and underwear down to his thighs, exposing him to the cool night air. Kyle feels vulnerable, but the thrill of it isn't bad. Anticipation runs hot through his veins as Jake stares down at him.

He holds eye contact as he lowers himself over Kyle's erect cock, swallowing him whole until Kyle feels himself touch the back of his throat and Jake's nose is pressed to Kyle's curls. Kyle gasps, jerking automatically, but strong hands hold him down.

He doesn't last long, and Jake makes quick work of him. Swallowing him down again and again, sucking hard as he pulls up. He pauses long enough to suck on a finger before going back to work, and while he sucks, that finger slides between Kyle's cheeks. He stiffens at first, but Jake doesn't push. He simply rubs his finger around Kyle's entrance. It's strange, but after he gets used to it, it feels wonderful. It adds a new thrill and a new friction to the already overwhelming sensation of Jake's mouth.

His fingers tensing and curling into Jake's shirt are the only warning he gets before Kyle comes, and Jake swallows it down casually, causing Kyle's heart to thump painfully in his chest.

Good god, that *is* hot.

Jake collapses on top of him, and his arms wrap around his shoulders. Together, they come down from their high, breaths evening out slowly and sweat cooling on their skin. Kyle idly plays with Jake's hair, carding his fingers through it as Jake nuzzles into his chest.

"Maybe...maybe next time we could try...*that*," Kyle says, hesitantly and haltingly into the silence of the car. "If you go slow."

Jake chuckles, voice rough and ragged as he buries his face in the crook of Kyle's neck, sending shivers dancing across his skin. "I'll never hurt you, Kyle."

It's a sweet sentiment, but one that causes a trickle of doubt and sour reality to enter his heart, cracking the fragile contentment they have. Surprisingly though, it doesn't hurt as much as Kyle thought it would. He finds he's already braced for it. Walls hidden around his heart and barbs in place to keep Jake's sweet words from reaching his core.

Because as nice as it sounds, Kyle knows there's no way a guy like Jake would want to be with Kyle for very long.

CHAPTER 17

*A*s they pull into the parking lot of Kyle's dorm, Jake is stilling running on the high of the night. It was a successful date in far more ways than one. Not only did he get Kyle to open up and diffuse the awkwardness between them, but Kyle had actually been incredibly kind and encouraging. He'd told Jake that he's smart and that he *can* do the things he puts his mind to, which is far more than anyone else has ever told him.

Then, of course, there was the blowjobs. Not his first one by any stretch of the imagination, but no doubt one of the most memorable ones. The memory of Kyle's lips stretched around him, brows furrowed in concentration, lightly humping the seat while he looks absolutely *wrecked* is gonna stay with him for a long, long time.

The drive back is quiet, but Jake doesn't mind. He's wrapped up in his own thoughts anyway, the afterglow still a warm buzz in his veins. He's been holding Kyle's hand the entire way back, but he lets go now to put the car in park and turn it off.

He's reaching for the door handle when Kyle's hand grabs

his arm, fingers curling rough and insistent. He stops, turning to look at him with an eyebrow raised.

Kyle's eyes are downcast, his bottom lip caught between his teeth. "I, uh...you don't have to walk me up."

Jake's eyes soften, a smile on his lips as he puts a hand over Kyle's. "I know, but I *want* to."

Kyle glances up at him, lips pursing more before he looks away. "No, I mean...what if...what if *I* don't want you to?"

Jake feels his heart sink in an instant as his smile fades. "What do you mean?"

Kyle looks up sharply, hand squeezing Jake's arm. He looks momentarily panicked, words leaving his lips quickly, stumbling over each other. "No! That's not...I didn't mean it like that! It's really sweet that you want to walk me up to my room, really. It's sweet. I appreciate it. I really do. I just...Jasper is probably here right now. He doesn't usually go places on weekdays. And if you walked me back, he'd probably think something was off or suspicious, and I'd rather avoid that."

Kyle isn't looking at him, and he looks incredibly nervous. Nervous and vulnerable and small. It makes Jake's chest twist unpleasantly. He hates seeing Kyle like this, doubting himself and *them*. He hates seeing Kyle worry about what other people think of him when he's so...so *incredible*.

Most of all, he hates that Kyle's fear is coming between them, keeping them from actually being happy. He's keeping *himself* from being happy.

He peels Kyle's fingers off his arm, sliding them between his own. Squeezing his hand, he brings it to his lips, pressing a soft kiss to the back of Kyle's hand. He stares and waits. Slowly, Kyle's gaze flickers back to him, hesitant and side-long, but it's good enough.

"Just so you know," Jake says, voice low and even, making

sure Kyle knows *exactly* how serious he is. "I wouldn't mind being a little more open about us. What do you think?"

He doesn't get the smile he was hoping for, nor does he get any sort of fond look. Instead, Kyle looks away, gaze trailing out the windows and into the parking lot. A group of students walk by on the sidewalk a good distance away, but it's close enough to hear their laughter.

Kyle pulls his hand away, and Jake tries to ignore the sting he feels in his chest. "I...Jake, we basically *just* started seeing each other. If this...if we don't work out..." he cuts himself off with a groan, running his finger through his hair and tugging at the strands. He scowls as he tries to gather his thoughts. Jake's hands curl into fists on his lap, nails biting into his palm as he tries to be patient, but his heart hammers painfully in his chest. "It's just...if I come out, I'm out. Permanently. If I come out of the closet, there's no going back in, and I...I like it here. It's *safe* in here. I don't have to worry about people judging me or picking on me. I can just continue to go unnoticed and not be *bothered*."

Jake tries for a smile, hoping the shadows in the car hide how shaky it feels. "We could come out together? It's not like I'm gonna make you do this alone," on some level, the idea terrifies him. He doesn't know how people will react if it becomes public knowledge, but he knows that he likes Kyle. Kyle makes him happy, and he wants to treat Kyle right. Even if that means being public about their relationship and dealing with the consequences.

But Kyle is already shaking his head. "No, you don't get it."

Jake grabs his hand again, weaving their fingers together but holding their hands over the center console, below the view of anyone outside. This time Kyle doesn't pull away, and he reluctantly meets Jake's gaze. "Then *make* me understand."

Kyle stares at him for a long time, face still scrunched into a scowl. Then he sighs, defeat making his expression fall and his shoulders sag. He looks down at their hands, and when he speaks, his voice is quiet. "It's...It's *easy* for someone like you to come out. You're popular, you're a sports star, and you're hot. If *you* came out as gay, they'd probably write inspirational articles about you. They'd call you brave and exceptional. They'd make you out to be this amazing gay role model or whatever."

He sighs, leaning back in the passenger seat. His head tilts back, eyes open and gazing out the front windshield, but they're unfocused and distant. Jake wants to reach out to him but holds himself back. Instead, he just squeezes his hand. Surprisingly, Kyle squeezes back, clinging to him like an anchor.

"If...If *I* came out as gay..." His voice shakes, nearly cracking before he pauses, licking his lips to find the words. "I would be even *more* of an outcast. I'm already a nerd. A freak. A quiet, ugly wallflower. The only reason people don't pick on me more is because I'm quiet and I keep to myself. If I came out, I'd be even *more* of a target. I'd be even *more* of a loser. And once I come out, I can't go back."

Something boils in him, hot and angry. He turns in his seat, dropping Kyle's hand abruptly as he reaches out to cup his face. He tries to keep his grip gentle, but he fears it might be too rough as Kyle squeaks in surprise.

"Okay, first of all, listen up," Jake turns Kyle to face him, holding his face firmly so he can't look away. He tugs him forward just a bit, leaning so they're both hovering over the center console, faces a mere six inches apart. He wants to make sure he's all Kyle sees and all he'll focus on. "I want you to listen and listen carefully. You. Are. Hot. As. Fuck."

He says it firmly, pointedly, leaving no room for argument. He needs Kyle to realize he's one hundred percent serious. This is not just what he believes, but what he knows to be true.

"You just got me off like, half an hour ago, which, by the way, was one of the hottest blowjobs I've ever received, and the sight of you beneath me is gonna stay with me forever, but the point is, we got off like thirty minutes ago, and I already want to tear all your clothes off and do it again because, let's face it, last time you were wearing too many clothes, and I want to see what you look like naked and squirming and flushed red and moaning my name. That bowtie is adorable, your face is adorable, and I want to do unspeakable things to you. I never want to hear you disparage yourself like that again."

In the yellow light from the parking lot street lamps, Jake has the immense pleasure of watching Kyle's face slowly redden to a dark and beautiful color. It stretches all the way up to his ears and down his neck. His eyes are wide, and lips parted as he gapes. He looks startled and embarrassed, but he doesn't look turned off by the confession. Quite the opposite, really.

Jake sighs, closing his eyes briefly as he leans forward, still holding Kyle's face still as he presses their foreheads together. "Second of all, I understand. I really do," he leans back, meeting Kyle's gaze with a small, wry smile. "Look, I can't promise we'll be together forever or anything. I can't promise a year or a month. This is new territory for me, too, but I want to be here, and I like being here. With you. We can just take it one day at a time. But, just so we're clear, I'm not and will never be ashamed to be seen with you."

Kyle's smile is slow to form, but as shaky as it is, it's real. His hands come up, and he lightly grabs Jake's wrists before pulling his hands away. "Thank you," he whispers, voice rough and eyes suspiciously glassy. "Really, just...thank you. For this. For everything. I'll..." He swallows hard, licking his lips as his eyes flicker away. "I'll think about it," he releases Jake's hands then, unbuckling his seatbelt and turning away to open the door. He pauses before sliding out, glancing over his shoulder with a shy smile. "Thanks for tonight."

And then he's gone. The car door slams shut, and Jake is left in the shadows and silence as he watches Kyle retreat to his dorm. He walks quickly, shoulders hunched, and hands shoved in his pockets.

Jake's chest feels tight with a deep seated, pulsing *ache*. Kyle didn't kiss him goodbye, nor did he say they could do it again. He knows that might be rushing it, this could be nothing. Kyle might just need time, but that doesn't stop it from hurting.

He sighs, gripping the steering wheel, but he doesn't go anywhere. Instead he groans, leaning forward until his forehead rests against the wheel, eyes squeezed tightly shut against the burn he feels.

The realization that what he has with Kyle probably won't last feels like a punch to the gut, knocking the wind out of him and leaving his entire body aching. He doesn't know when or how, but Kyle has already wheedled his way into his heart, giving Jake *hope*. That hope crumbling to dust feels like a kick to his heart. He could break it off first, but he's enjoying his time with Kyle. He wants to ride this wave for as long as he can.

He just has to steel himself for the inevitable fall.

CHAPTER 18

*T*he next two weeks feel like a waking dream.

It's the happiest Kyle has ever been, and he feels like he's living on a constant high. Every time his phone buzzes with a text from Jake, his heart leaps into his throat. Every time it rings with a call, he feels a buzz of excitement in his veins. Every time he sees him, his heart flips and there are butterflies in his stomach. He's not sure how long this part of it is supposed to last, but he hopes it never ends.

It feels freeing.

He's never allowed himself to openly admire and like someone like this, and he never thought he'd ever be able to be with and touch and kiss someone like *Jake*. He's so incredibly out of his league, yet he looks at Kyle like he's the answer to the universe.

It's just as terrifying as it is exhilarating.

It's harder to see each other in the week, but they make it work. Tutoring becomes an excuse to see one another, even when they have no real need to do so that often. Jake is learning quickly and well, and certainly isn't dumb enough to require tutoring every day. But he likes seeing Kyle, and Kyle likes seeing him.

And the rewarding make-out session following each tutoring session is worth it.

They've been going out most weekends, keeping to the outskirts of town and to less crowded areas. Kyle doesn't care where they go as long as they can be more or less alone.

They've also been experimenting more. Pushing their physical boundaries. Well, Kyle's boundaries anyway. Jake is down for pretty much anything and usually takes the lead to guide Kyle through it. He can't say that he minds. He hasn't been able to work up the courage to, you know, *go all the way* yet, but he thinks he's getting there. Everything else feels good. *More* than good. He loses himself in Jake's touch. In a pleasure he's barely dared to dream about. It's easy to let everything slip away when he's in Jake's arms and simply *feel*.

There's a problem with dreams, though. You always have to wake up from them, and they always come to an end.

Kyle wakes abruptly from his living daydream on a Wednesday.

It's like any other Wednesday. The middle of the week. The weekend in sight to keep him going. His homework is done, like always. He doesn't have a tutoring session with Jake planned, but he fully expects one to come up last minute. His classes for the day are done, his roommate is gone, and he's just relaxing in his room. He has his Cry Thunder files pulled up, but he's not working. He's lost in a memory of two nights ago, when a post tutoring make-out session had turned into Jake slowly fingering him until he was squirming and moaning at the mercy of those fingers.

He checks his phone, eagerly waiting for Jake's inevitable text or call, but while there are no notifications, his eyes settle on the date.

And it's with a jarring start that Kyle realizes that he missed the anniversary of his brother's death.

His chest feels tight, breaths coming shallow and quick. Eyes wide and mouth parted as he tries to breathe, he tries to find his mom's contact, but his fingers are shaking, and it takes a few tries. His entire body feels like it's quivering. His fingertips and toes start to feel numb. His eyes burn and his head spins in a spiral.

Everything is too loud, but his ears are ringing. His skin feels too tight, too hot. He can't breathe. He can't breathe.

"Hello?" his mom's voice is a grounding point, and he clings to it. He latches on, focusing on it to keep him from spiraling out to space.

"Mom?" he can feel how his voice cracks, but he can barely hear it.

"Kyle, honey, what's wrong?" her voice is instantly concerned, low and hushed and soothing. Just the sound of it starts to ease off his panic attack. It's familiar and comforting.

He pulls his feet up onto his chair, an arm wrapping around his knees to keep them close to his chest, and he squeezes his eyes shut. He shuts out everything but the sound of his mom's voice, trying to calm his breathing enough to speak. "I...I forgot to call you yesterday. I'm so sorry, Mom. I'm so sorry. I forgot. I forgot, and..."

"Honey, shhhh, it's okay, breathe, okay? Breathe with me," she breathes loudly and exaggeratedly, slow and steady, and he listens. He matches his breaths to hers, and slowly, so slowly, he starts to calm down. The feeling comes back to his limbs, and his chest feels a little less tight. "That's better. You feel better?"

He makes a sound of confirmation but doesn't quite trust his voice yet.

"To be completely honest, Kyle, we were almost glad we didn't hear from you yesterday."

"What?" Kyle's voice cracks, confusion making his brows furrow.

"It's just...we were hoping it meant you might finally be moving on, you know?"

"Mom, what? *No!* I'm not *moving on!* I'm not going to just *forget* him!"

"You don't need to forget him, Kyle. We'll never forget him," her voice is calm and soothing, even as her words are a knife in his chest. "But we can't be held back anymore. We need to move forward. All of us. We didn't...We didn't go to his grave this year."

"What?" Kyle breathes, tears burning in his eyes.

"Honey, listen. It's not that we don't care. We *do*. He was our son. We loved him, we still do, and we'll never forget him. But we can't carry grief around forever. He wouldn't want us to. It's not just you, I...I need to move on, too."

"Mom, I...it's not that easy," his voice is thick, words edged with tears he feels slipping down his cheeks.

"I know, hon. I do. I really do. But just think about it, okay? Just try. If not for your sake, then for his. He wouldn't want you holding yourself back."

"I'm not!" he says far too quickly and far too defensively. He firmly ignores the nagging voice in the back of his head that agrees with his mom.

"We love you, Kyle. Just think about it, okay?"

"Okay," he sounds small and defeated. "I gotta go, mom."

"Okay, thanks for calling."

"Yeah. Love you."

"Love you, too."

He hangs up and slams his phone down with far too much force before burying his face in his arms. His chest heaves with shaking breaths, tears burning his eyes and searing down his cheeks. He curls into as tight a ball as he can, and he feels small.

Guilt claws at his chest, raking across his ribcage and gnawing at his heart.

He can't believe he forgot. He hasn't thought of his brother in...in far too long. He hasn't been working on their game. The game they were creating together before he passed. It's one of the last connections he has to his brother, and he's been letting it fall to the wayside. He's been selfishly wrapped up in himself and letting himself drift away from what's actually important.

His shoulders shake, breath hitching and heaving. He lets it out because he has no choice, and he's just glad his room-mate isn't around. He's glad he's alone. He needs to be alone.

When his phone vibrates loudly and Jake's name flashes across the screen, Kyle ignores it. He turns it on silent and throws it across the room to land on his bed.

With temptation removed, he can focus on his guilt.

* * *

THE CALLS from Jake don't stop. They start out few and far between but get more insistent the longer Kyle ignores them. He texts between them, in moments where he can't call. Kyle just gets an onslaught of messages.

If he's being honest, they're cute. Jake is cute. He openly flirts with Kyle through text and doesn't bother to censor himself and what he wants. Kyle's never had anyone flirt with him or compliment him like this, and in some ways, he likes it.

But where messages from Jake had once made his heart skip a beat and butterflies go wild in his chest, where they had once drawn a smile to his face, now they just make him sick. Guilt twists in his gut and makes him nauseous. Guilt over forgetting his brother bleeds into guilt over ignoring Jake's messages, but that doesn't stop him. He still ignores them.

For the first time in his life, Kyle skips classes. Not all his classes. Just the one he has with Jake. He avoids the places on campus he knows Jake lingers and steers his path around the spots where they would usually meet up.

The texts get less flirty and more anxious and worried, and that just makes Kyle's guilt and shame worse.

He keeps his phone on silent and stops looking at it. He feels slightly less guilty if he doesn't see how many things he's ignoring. He starts letting his phone die and waits hours if not days to charge it.

He focuses on Cry Thunder because it's what he should be doing, and he's not sure what else to do to stop the near constant churning in his gut.

* * *

IT'S a week later when Jake finally gets fed up with him and takes a more direct route. That direct route means skipping the class they have together, which Kyle has also skipped to avoid him, and showing up at Kyle's door in the middle of the day.

Kyle ignores the initial knock, heart slamming painfully against his chest as he looks through the peephole to see Jake standing in the hallway, arms crossed over his chest. He stays quiet, hoping if he does, Jake will eventually go away.

Instead, he knocks again. "Come on, Kyle. I know you're in there just open up. Please?"

It's the please that gets him. It's on the verge of breaking, sounding desolate, confused and worried. It's a knife to Kyle's gut, and in that moment, the guilt becomes too much to bear. It has him reaching out and opening the door, lips pressed together to hold his composure as he stares at Jake's feet. He steps back, holding the door open, and refuses to look up as Jake steps into the room.

With the door closed, Kyle turns to face him, but he can't lift his gaze above his knees. He hunches his shoulders, arms crossed tightly over his chest as he glares stubbornly at Jake's shoes. Jake stands in the middle of his room, facing him, and Kyle fears whatever expression he's wearing.

"What do you want?" he asks, stiff and demanding. He can feel himself shaking, but he fights against it and tries to hold firm.

The pause is almost a moment too long. Kyle can feel his strength crumbling in the wake of the thick silence. When Jake finally does speak, it's surprisingly neutral. It's not angry or indignant, worried or sad. It's just blank. Even. Flat. "You've been ignoring me."

"I've been ignoring everyone."

"Why?" it's not so much demanding as it is pleading. It hurts. It twists that knife in Kyle's chest. He doesn't like hearing Jake sound so forlorn.

But he made this bed, and now he has to lie in it. "I've just been needing some space."

"Yeah, I got that much, but *why?*"

Kyle bites his lip, feeling a hiccup bubble up his throat. His eyes have that phantom burn, and he *really* doesn't want to cry right now. He watches Jake's feet as he takes a step forward. Kyle stiffens, but doesn't retreat as Jake comes closer. As warm, comforting and familiar hands rest gently on his shoulders. "I can give you space if you need it, but I just want to know *why*," his voice is far too soft. Far too gentle. Kyle can feel himself falling apart, held together barely by the seams.

"I just need space," he repeats, but his voice cracks. His tongue feels thick.

"Was it something I did? Whatever it is, I want to know. I don't want to upset you or push you away. Please, Kyle, just talk to me."

He hates this. He hates that Jake thinks he's done something wrong when it's just Kyle who's fucked up. He hates that he's doing this to Jake. He hates that Jake won't just realize how terrible he is and leave him.

He squeezes his eyes shut, feeling the tears building up around his lashes. He squeezes his hands into fists, feeling the bite of his nails against his palm. "Can't you just *go?*" he snaps, voice full of bite and venom, because if he doesn't, he knows he'll break.

The hands on his shoulders squeeze. "No. Come on, Kyle, just talk to me? I'm here for you, whatever it is."

A hiccup breaks through his defenses, followed by a sob. And that's all it takes before everything starts to break down. Tears escape down his cheeks, and he breaks, feeling the way his lungs shudder. When he breathes out, the words come out in a rush. "I forgot the anniversary of my brother's death," his voice breaks off as a sob tears from him, bubbling in his throat and rattling in his chest.

Jake pulls him in instantly. Arms wrap around his shoulders, and hands rub up and down his back. Kyle's arms wrap around his waist, fingers clutching the back of his shirt as he holds on desperately. He presses himself into Jake's warmth, using the solidness of it as an anchor. He buries his face in Jake's chest, and he cries.

It all comes bubbling up, no longer able to be contained. He shakes, and he sobs, and each one wracks through his body. Tears stain Jake's shirt, but he can't stop. And when his knees start to give out, Jake picks him up, carries him to his bed, and sits down, cradling Kyle in his lap. Kyle curls into him, letting his arms ground him.

He takes the comfort. The hands running soothingly

along his body. The soft, wordless sounds Jake makes under his breath. The way Jake nuzzles into his hair. The smell of Jake, spicy and earthy and overwhelming. He breathes it in, and he lets himself escape.

Escape from the pain, from the guilt, from the sorrow, from himself.

When Jake pulls away from him, frames his face with large gentle hands, and wipes his tears away, Kyle doesn't resist. And when Jake bends down to kiss him, long and languid, he pushes up into him. He pushes his tongue against Jake's lips, seeking solace, seeking a distraction, seeking anything to make him feel good when he feels like otherwise he'll come crashing down.

Jake's hands on him turn more insistent, hungrier, and Kyle whines into his mouth. A shiver runs down his spine as Jake growls, as Jake holds him firmly in place, as Jake's lips and tongue devour his mouth.

Kyle wants more. He *needs* more.

His hands grab at Jake's clothes, desperate and uncoordinated, but so very, very needy. He whines, high pitched and pleading. Jake's shirt is barely off before Kyle is squirming in his lap, peeling off his own and throwing it aside before readjusting. He straddles Jake's lap and presses eagerly into his mouth, presses them flush together and shivers at the feeling of Jake's strong, broad chest against his own. His hands run down it, nails biting into his abs before sinking into the waistband of his jeans. He rubs himself desperately against Jake, already growing hard, heart hammering at the sound of Jake's breath hitching. He bites Jake's lip and is rewarded when he moans, long, low and *deep*.

Then Jake's hands are on him. All over his body. Running down his back and gripping his arm, firmly squeezing and pulling Kyle against him. Their hips rub together, grinding until Kyle can't take it anymore. His fingers scramble at the button of Jake's jeans, and he gets the message.

He scrambles off Jake's lap, and the two of them fumble and struggle to take off their pants as quick as possible. Instead of sharing embarrassed smiles, awkward laughs, and fond kisses, they work in silence, each movement frantic and hasty, the sound of their panting filling the space. There's a tension in the air that drives them forward. A need for something to happen *now*, lest they fall apart completely. It's a desperation, and Kyle feels it deep in his core, radiating throughout his body.

He steps to his desk, digging in a drawer for the bottle of lube and box of condoms Jake had bought for them a couple weeks ago. He had insisted they keep it in Kyle's dorm. Not for then, but for whenever they were ready. Kyle is ready now.

He steps back to the bed, handing them to Jake who stares at them with wide eyes before looking up at Kyle. "Are you sure?"

He tightens his lips, not quite trusting his voice, and nods.

Jake takes him by the hand, pulling him gently onto the bed. He kisses him sweetly, deeply, and passionately. There's so much in his kiss. So many things he doesn't say. Like he's trying to communicate through touch alone. Kyle takes it all, desperately trying to forget, even if it's just for this moment.

Despite Kyle's eagerness, Jake takes his time with him. He stretches him out slowly and carefully. Kyle squirms under the ministrations of his fingers, whines and begs and pleads for more in a cracked and broken voice, barely able to form coherent words. Jake presses kisses to his neck, to his chest, hands touching down his waist and his hips, stroking his cock in time with his fingers.

Then Jake pulls out, and Kyle whines at the sudden emptiness. But Jake is prepping himself and settling himself between Kyle's legs. He lines up, and Kyle's back arches at the thick pressure at his entrance. His hands grasp at the bedsheets, body tense as he waits.

Jake leans forward, pressing a kiss to his chest, his collar bones, his lips. "Relax, babe. You have to relax," Jake kisses him softly, gently, hands on his waist and hips and petting along his quivering thighs until Kyle relaxes. "Hold onto me and breath through it, okay?"

Kyle wraps his arms around Jake's shoulder, nodding against him.

Jake pushes in, slow and steady, stretching him and filling him. Kyle cries out, body arching and eyes squeezing shut.

"Kyle, Kyle you feel so good, holy shit, fuck, fuck, fuck," Jake mumbles against his skin, mouthing wet kisses along his shoulder, his neck, his cheek. "I'm gonna fuck you so good. I'm gonna make you come. Are you ready?"

He feels so *full*. Stretched nearly to his limits. He feels the slight burn and the dull ache, but it also feels so *good*. Jake is inside him. Deep, deep inside him. Jake. Hot, beautiful, baseball star Jake is inside *him*. Is fucking *him*. Stretching him and filling him and babbling praises as his hands move relentlessly over Kyle's skin like he can't get enough.

It's all Kyle can do to nod, arms tightening around him and legs wrapping around his hips.

Then Jake moves, pulls back and thrusts into him, over and over again. He babbles filthy things in Kyle's ear, praises that he never thought he'd hear, and Kyle hangs on. Holds on for dear life.

And then he lets himself unravel. Lets himself go. He gives himself into the pleasure of it, and he sees stars.

* * *

"HEY, bathroom's all yours if you need it," Jake says, stepping back into the dorm.

Kyle doesn't respond. He lies on his bed with his back to the room, staring at the cinderblock wall. His body aches and it burns, but it's not a bad feeling. He feels spent, exhausted, and just wants to sleep for hours. The satisfaction, however, faded quickly. The post sex high crashed down quickly, giving way to all the things he had been bottling up and hiding from.

The guilt is consuming. It tears into him, ripping his heart to tatters. It makes it impossible to enjoy the fact that he just had sex with a man way out of his league. He should be happy. Instead, that happiness has soured in his gut, becoming heavy and leaden.

Because he knows he can't keep him.

The bed shifts as Jake sits on the edge of it. "You sure you don't want me to carry you to the shower?" he touches Kyle's arm, and Kyle flinches away. He immediately feels bad about it, feels just another twist of that knife in his chest as guilt chokes him. But every touch makes his skin crawl. He's too sensitive in the worst way. In the way that always proceeds an anxiety attack.

"I'm fine," he manages to choke out, but he knows he doesn't sound fine.

"Kyle…"

"Just go," Kyle snaps, then squeezes his eyes shut, already feeling the tears forming. He takes a deep breath and tries again, aiming for something calmer but just as firm. "Please. I…I just want to be alone. I need some time. I promise I'm fine."

He doesn't believe it, and he knows Jake doesn't either. He doesn't say anything, but he also doesn't move. His hand touches Kyle's arm again, and while Kyle doesn't pull away, he does tense.

"Jake, please," he hates how broken he sounds and the raspiness of his breath. "I just need some space right now."

"Fine," he says, and the bitterness in his voice makes Kyle's stomach roll. His breath comes in short gasps as Jake stands, moving around the room to get dressed. Kyle refuses to turn around. Refuses to see the hurt on his face. Hearing it in his voice is bad enough. "Just call me if you need me okay? I'll be here for you, anytime. You can talk to me. You know that, right?"

The lump in his throat is too thick to speak around, so he nods instead.

A moment later he hears the door open and close, and he's alone.

He asked for this, but it still hurts. His chest feels tight and hollow. He curls in on himself, knuckles going white as he grips the blankets. "I'm sorry," he mutters through broken sobs. They wrack through him, and he can't stop the tears or the shaking. He can barely breathe. "I'm sorry," he says to no one. To Jake. To himself. To his brother.

He's sorry for having sought escape. He didn't mean to escape from his brother. He didn't mean to forget. He's losing himself in Jake. In his smile. In his touch.

It's because of Jake that Kyle forgot, and that causes a deep-seated ache to pulse in his heart.

He doesn't want to choose between Jake and his brother, but he feels like he's going to have to.

CHAPTER 19

"Come on, dude," Liddy says, running up alongside him on the path. "Do you know how many details I gave you on my first real relationship with a girl?"

Jake's lip curls. "Too many."

"*Exactly*. So, give me too many details!"

He frowns. "It's not really any of your business, Liddy," he pulls ahead, pushing his legs to run faster and to lengthen his stride putting distance between them. He's more of a sprinter anyway, and Liddy has always been more endurance. She bides her time and eventually his pace slows, allowing her to catch up.

"Okay, so I know it's not technically my business, but you've *made* it my business for the past couple months. You *always* make it my business. You talk to me about these things because you *like* to, and you don't feel like you can with your dude-bro friends," she barely sounds out of breath, and Jake's chest aches as he heaves with each inhale. It's not fair.

She also has a point, and he hates it. He *can't* talk about this with his other friends, and he desperately *wants* to talk about it, but he's afraid to. Talking about it makes it real, and Jake is scared of what that might mean.

His words sound stilted and heavy as he pants. "It's just..." he groans, tossing his head back as he runs. "It's *complicated*."

"Okay, pull over for a stretch break," Liddy nudges him off the path toward a patch of grass, both of them slowing to a jog until they walk off the path. Jake immediately starts rotating his arms across his chest and rolling his shoulders while Liddy grabs her ankle and pulls it back. "Okay," she says, balance wavering as she hops around on one foot. It's amusing enough to lighten the atmosphere. "Now that you can *breathe* and think, tell me what's up."

Jake groans again, stretching his arms high above his head. "It's just...weird, okay? Kyle isn't really in the closet, but he's not really out of it either? Like...he *knows* he's gay, and he's pretty open with *me* about being gay, but he doesn't really want other people to know. Which...yeah, fine, I get it. He explained it to me, and I *get* it, but that doesn't make it any easier. Especially when we haven't really talked about *us?* Like, we meet up, and hangout, and go on dates, and make out, and we fuck, but I have no idea where we stand."

Liddy lets out a long, low whistle, switching to her other leg. She reaches out, putting a hand on Jake's shoulder to help balance herself. "That's rough, buddy. But you're enjoying fucking him, yeah?"

He snorts, rolling his eyes, but he smiles when he looks at her. "That's all you're interested in?"

She grins. "No, but I'm trying to sound like a bro to put you more in your element. How's the sex?"

He sighs. "Fucking amazing. He's so goddamn cute, and ridiculously sexy without even trying, and I have a hard time holding myself back, but we go at his pace and it's still so good."

"He enjoy it?"

Jake laughs. "Oh yeah, from what I can tell? Definitely."

"Well, that's a good step."

Jake drops to the ground, stretching his legs out in front of him and leaning for his toes, eyes on the ground as he mumbles. "Too bad I can't tell if he enjoys being with *me*."

Liddy spreads her legs shoulder width apart and leans over to stretch down one leg. "To be honest, Kyle seems like a really sweet guy, but, you know your first is always complicated and never really lasts. In relationships in general, but *especially* in your first gay one," she switches to her other leg, a wry laugh on her tongue. "I mean, I dated several girls who were just *experimenting* or whatever. Like, sure Kathrine. You're three fingers and a tongue deep in my pussy, but you're completely straight. I believe that," she glances over, eyes sparkling and a smile on her lips as she hopes to share a laugh with Jake. But his face is anything but amused, and her smile fades. "Oh, but like...you guys are probably the exception to that rule, you know? Kyle *knows* he's gay, so that's a step above my experiences. He just needs some help stepping out of the closet. You guys might have something that lasts."

He knows what she's doing. He's not stupid. She's trying to make him feel better by saying the things he wants to hear and by encouraging him. Sometimes he needs a dose of blunt reality, and sometimes he needs hope. Turns out, right now, neither is making him feel better.

He leans back, pulling his knees up and resting back on his hands behind him. He stares at a spot in front of him, lost in thought and unable to meet her eyes. He doesn't want to see her pity or her sympathy. "Honestly, I'm not really sure that's the track we're on."

"Oh?" she sounds surprised by that, and she sits down next to him with a light groan. Facing the same direction, staring down the path at other runners and joggers, she nudges his shoulder with hers. "Tell me about it."

"It's just..." he sighs, running a hand through his hair, feeling sweat make it stand on end. "I like him, Liddy. Like...a lot. I have feelings for him, like...real, strong, deep feelings," he groans, fingers twisting into his hair and pulling at the roots. He falls back, lying on the ground and letting his arms fall out as he glares up at the sky. "I hate this. I haven't felt like this with any of my ex's before. No offense."

"None taken."

"But I've never felt *this* much for someone. I've found them hot and fun, yeah, but not like this? I know I'm not making any sense, but it doesn't *feel* like it makes sense. I think...I think I might love him? I dunno. Maybe. I don't think I've ever really loved someone, so who the fuck knows. I'm trying to be patient, because I know he's not ready to come out, but... maybe it doesn't matter, you know? It just feels like he's holding me at arm's length. Not physically, but emotionally. On the inside? Fuck, this makes no sense," he runs his hands over his face, digging the heels of his palms into his eyes.

Liddy chuckles, and he feels her hand come down on his shoulder, rubbing and squeezing comfortingly. "Man, I didn't know you were such a girl."

He spreads his fingers, glaring up at her through them.

She grins, reaching out to playfully press a finger to his nose. "It's not a bad thing. It just means that you're in touch with your emotions, and it's what a lot of guys are afraid to do. I've always known you were sensitive. You feel a lot, and you let yourself feel. Some of your dude-bro friends could learn a lot from you."

Jake swats her hand away, throwing his arms up over his head as he sprawls out on the grass. "Feeling my feelings sucks."

She chuckles, pulling her knees up and wrapping her arms around them. "Yeah, it does. But it makes you a better person. It makes you *human*. And hey, if this thing with Kyle doesn't work out, at least it was a good step for you. Maybe you'll learn to broaden your horizons and try again."

"Yeah, maybe," he eyes her through narrowed eyes, lips tight. "When did you get so wise?"

She grins, preening as she lifts her chin. "I've always been wise, thanks for noticing."

He snorts, rolling his eyes. "Is that why you once challenged me to a habanero pepper eating contest?"

She kicks him lightly. "Which I *won*, by the way."

"We burnt off half our taste buds!"

"But I *won*."

They laugh, and she stands, holding out a hand to help him back to his feet. They start off down the path again, jogging back towards campus. Liddy rambles between panting breaths about her girlfriend and her classes, just to fill the space. Jake makes the appropriate and expected noises of acknowledgement, but he's not really paying attention.

He's realized, through that conversation, that he's already started to think of him and Kyle as broken up, which leaves a sour taste on the back of his tongue and his gut twisted in knots. The worst part is, he's not sure if he can consider them broken up if he's not even sure if they were together to begin with.

It's not a conversation he wants to have, but it's one he knows he *needs* to. He needs to know if they're officially together. He needs to know if Kyle is worth fighting for, or if they really are just drifting apart before they ever had a chance.

* * *

173

THEY MEET up later that night to study. Jake had been on his way to Kyle's dorm when Kyle texted him, asking if they could meet up in the student union instead. His roommate was there, and Kyle doesn't like the ideas his roommate has about them. Jake tries to ignore how much that stings.

They find a secluded small lounge area on the third floor. It's an area that's rarely crowded during the day, but here and now, well after class hours, it's even more empty. It's quiet and private, yet Jake feels like there's an ocean between them.

Kyle sits across the table, his laptop out and open, and a notebook sitting next to him. Jake's book and notebook are out, but he's not looking at them. His pen idly taps the page as he leans on the table, cheek resting against his open palm and elbow resting on the table. His eyes are on Kyle.

Kyle has barely looked at him since they arrived, and he's as fidgety and flighty as he has been for the past week or so. He looks nervous and shy, which is something Jake had thought they were long past. It reminds him of their first couple of study sessions, but even then, the tension was different. Then it was a new kind of uncertain tension, but now it feels harsher, more nervous, and it makes Jake's stomach twist itself in knots.

They should be past this by now.

"So..." he starts, aiming for slow and casual. Kyle's eyes flicker up automatically, but then snap back down to his computer screen. Jake frowns. "This Saturday we have a practice match against a nearby school," Kyle raises a brow, humming lightly, and Jake takes that as reason enough to continue. "It's not a big deal. Just a game for fun before the real season starts next semester. It'll be here, but they're not like selling tickets or anything. Anyone is welcome to come, though it's mostly friends, family, and...partners."

He sees Kyle freeze and hears the rhythmic typing stop.

Slowly, his gaze lifts, carefully blank as he stares at Jake. Jake smiles, trying to go for casual and encouraging. He doesn't want to push. He knows from experience that when he does, Kyle tends to back away. But he needs to get this out in the open.

"I was thinking maybe you could come?"

Kyle's eyes narrow slightly, brows pinching as his lips press into a thin line. "As your...friend?" He asks cautiously.

Jake's smile is sheepish as he tilts his head. "Well, yeah, kinda. Though I was thinking more like...boyfriend?"

Kyle stares at him for a long time, silent and tense. Jake can feel it thick and choking, suffocating him and forcing him to take shallow breaths. His stomach rolls, and his heart feels like it's lodged itself in his throat. All he can do is stare and wait.

The anticipation feels like there's an axe hanging over his head.

Kyle sighs, reaching forward to close his laptop with a finality that feels like the axe falling.

"Actually...I've been thinking about that," he trails off, busying himself as he closes his notebook and sets it neatly on his laptop. He then leans forward, resting his elbows on the table and rubbing his temples with his fingers, closing his eyes. "I don't think I'm *ready* for that. To be...gay," he whispers it, glancing around nervously as he lowers his voice. "I mean, I am gay. But I don't think I'm ready to be *open* with it."

Jake tries for a smile, but it feels shaky. His pulse hammers in his veins, making him feel dizzy. "That's fine. We don't have to come out about it yet. We don't have to tell anyone."

But Kyle is already shaking his head, leaning back and putting his hands on his notebook and laptop, fingers splayed wide. There's a stubborn determination there that makes Jake's heart sink into his stomach. He knows that look, and he doesn't like it in this context.

"No, Jake, I mean...maybe it would be better if we just called this off?" he waves a hand in the air, lips pursed as he looks everywhere but at Jake. "You know. *Us?* I like you. I really, really do. I can't deny that. You're really great, and you deserve so much, but I don't think I can be the one to give it to you."

Jake feels himself tense. Heart like lead in his chest. His breaths shallow, and his blood static in his veins. He's heard this all before.

It's not you, it's me.

You're a great guy, but I don't think we fit.

I like you, I really do, but we should break up.

He's heard it so many times, but it's never hurt like this. He feels like he can't breathe. There's a ringing in his ears, and his limbs feel tingly. This can't be real. This has to be a bad dream. Not real, not real, not real...

"I'm sorry," Kyle continues, oblivious to Jake's panic. He's already packing up his things, movements quick but stiff. "I'm really sorry, but with school and my game and your sports...I just think it's a bad time. We should focus on other things. I asked around, and I found another tutor who can help you. I already emailed them your information, so they can start teaching you from now on."

"Wait," Jake croaks, voice cracking. He can't bring himself to care. He sits up straight, eyes wide as he gapes at Kyle. "You're not going to *tutor* me either?" he can't tell if he feels offended or hurt. Probably both. Hurt is underlying everything at this point. "You don't want *anything* to do with me?"

Kyle zips up his bag with far more haste and force than necessary, stiffly getting to his feet and throwing the strap over his shoulder. He holds onto it, staring at the ground. "I just think this is for the best. I'm sorry, but...you'll find someone better. To tutor you, and to be with."

He turns to leave, already scurrying away. Jake leaps to his feet, nearly tripping in his haste and scrambling after him. He grabs Kyle's wrist, jerking him to a stop. Kyle doesn't try to pull away, but he doesn't turn around either. He keeps his head bowed, body stiff.

"Kyle," Jake says, keeping his voice low. There's an urgency there, but he tries his best to sound reasonable and soothing. He can't let Kyle walk away. "Come on, just think about this."

"I have," it sounds cold and indifferent, and a shiver runs down Jake's spine.

"I don't *want* someone else."

Kyle's body heaves with a sigh, shaky and wavering. "Just because you're pretty doesn't mean you can always have what you want," he turns then, pinning Jake with a watery gaze. His eyes are red rimmed and glassy, but there's an unwavering determination there. His lips form into a tight frown. "Just..." he speaks softly, almost pleadingly. "Don't make this difficult. Don't follow me. Just...let me go."

He turns then, and when he tugs on Jake's grip, Jake lets him go.

He's left standing there long after Kyle is gone, eyes distant. Breathing hard. Each breath threatens the well of emotions further up his throat until he's choking on a sob.

His stomach is twisted, and his skin buzzes with static. He's pretty sure his knees are shaking, but he still stands there, afraid that if he moves, it'll make this moment real. It's stupid, really, the idea that if he stays still, it won't be real.

He doesn't know what to do. He feels frantic and manic. Energy buzzes beneath his skin, but it has no focus and no direction.

He'd been expecting this. He hadn't wanted to accept it or

face it, but deep down, he had been expecting this. He'd already been considering them broken up. He's broken up with people so many times before, but like with everything else, Kyle is different. Kyle has always been different.

It's through blurred vision and with shaking hands that he calls Liddy. She's the only one who will understand.

CHAPTER 20

*H*abituation.

The process of becoming so used to a continuous stimulus or condition that your psychological and emotional response to it becomes diminished or altogether disappears.

Conditioning.

Desensitized.

The pain no longer aches. Or rather, the pain is so damn near constant he's forgotten what it's like to feel any different. It's just part of him now. At first it felt like a knife buried deep in his chest, stuck between his ribs and tearing at his heart. It hurt to move and think. Every breath brought a fresh wave of pain.

But over time, he's gotten used to it. The sharpness of the knife has dulled. He's gotten used to its presence between his ribs. He's used to the ache in his heart. The way his stomach rolls no longer feels dizzying, and the nausea is constant enough to ignore.

The first few days had been a fresh new hell. He hadn't been able to sleep, but he also hadn't been able to get himself out of bed. Going to class was simply going through the motions, but he barely heard anything his professors said. Jasper tried to make conversation with him several times, but eventually gave up when his only responses were one-word mutterings or grunts.

He threw himself into his game.

It was the only thing to truly distract him, and the only thing he could throw himself wholeheartedly into. It was the only thing that mattered, and the only thing that has mattered in the past few years. It's the only thing that should matter now. This is his life's work. This is what his brother wanted him to do. This is what he *promised* his brother he would do. He has to finish it for him.

Time becomes a strange concept. It seems to drag by, sluggish and thick, sliding past him like molasses. And at the same time, it rushes. It flies past him without his awareness or consent. It drags and speeds in intervals, switching without warning, leaving him in a constant state of vertigo. He zones out and the clock says three hours have past, but his memories remain blurry and uncertain.

He disregards time as much as he can. He sets alarms for his classes, so he won't miss them, but other than that, he lets himself forget.

He loses himself to numbers and calculations and algorithms. He loses himself to pixels and fractals that make up his designs. He loses himself in walls of text. In dialogue options. In damage calculations. In weapon selections. In game market prices. In item selections. In ability brainstorming.

His fingers are a slave to his mind, flying across the keyboard and feeling as numb as the rest of him. His eyes burn, and he only trudges to bed when the burn becomes too much to bear and his eyes refuse to stay open. Then he curls up in bed, sometimes still fully clothed, often without brushing his teeth, and lets his body shut down.

It feels less like sleeping and more like a slip into unconsciousness. It's dreamless and dark. He wakes with a start most mornings, unable to go back to sleep and his mind immediately latching onto the things he doesn't want to think about. He drags himself out of bed to his desk, boots up his computer, and loses himself all over again.

Jasper, thankfully, is a heavy sleeper and doesn't seem to mind Kyle's odd hours or his new, sleepless schedule. If the light from his laptop screen bothers Jasper, he doesn't say anything about it. Kyle can usually hear him snoring just minutes after he's crawled into bed. He envies him for that.

Jasper does, at one point, bring up his behavior. It's offhanded and casual. Just a comment about Kyle being in their dorm a lot more often now and asking if he's still seeing that jock guy. Kyle answers with a stiff and guarded *no*, but Jasper doesn't get the message. He pushes. Asks if they broke up and that's why Kyle is condemning himself like a hermit.

He says it as a joke, teasing and light hearted, and Kyle *knows* he doesn't mean anything hurtful by it. But it's too close to home. It finds that knife that's dulled in his chest and *twists*.

Kyle snaps at him. He doesn't remember all of what he says. He doesn't remember the words or his phrasing, but he remembers the venom. He remembers the anger. He remembers how, in that moment, he wanted to hurt Jasper as much as he was aching himself. He remembers saying some pointed things. Hurtful things.

He remembers Jasper's face.

He remembers it like a snapshot. A picture that remains in his memory even as the words around it fade. Jasper's eyes wide and mouth hanging open. His face contorted in surprise and shock. Another picture of it fading into hurt, confusion and betrayal. Another picture of it twisting into anger, closed off, cold and indifferent.

Jasper hasn't talked to him much since, and Kyle feels terrible. Whenever he sees his roommate, he feels a fresh wave of guilt roll through him. But soon enough, even that starts to dull. He gets used to the constant emotion of it. He stops looking at Jasper when he moves around the room, and keeps his eyes focused on his laptop screen.

If he just works on his game, everything will be okay. Everything else will fade. The pain will go away. He just has to work until it goes away.

He just has to work.

He just has to focus.

He just has to forget.

* * *

WHILE HE'S WRAPPED up in his game, in his coding, in his planning, and his work, he's fine. It's easy to push everything else aside and simply run calculations and plans in his head. It's when he stops that things get bad.

Cry Thunder is an unsteady dam. It's barely holding back the flood waters that threaten to crash in and sweep him away, drowning him violently and without care.

The moment he stops working and stops focusing, he barely gets to take a breath before the waters start to trickle in. Thoughts of his brother and thoughts of Jake. They rush into his mind in tandem, creating havoc and swirling him down into dark, watery depths. He feels like he can't breathe. He feels like he can't *think*. His body starts to go numb as his mind drifts away from it, breath coming ragged and fast as a panic attack edges closer.

The numbness keeps him from feeling the anger, brittle and white hot. Whenever he stops working, whenever he lets himself breathe and the thoughts come crashing in, his anger burns *hot,* and it burns *fast.* It rips through his veins, aching in his heart and simmering in his lungs.

He's angry at Jake. Jake, with his stupidly pretty face and stupidly attractive body and his stupidly adorable laugh and smile that make Kyle *melt* every time. Jake made him forget his brother. *Jake's presence* in his life made him forget the one person he promised never to forget. Jake made him forget his priorities, swept up in the excitement of the moment and the heat of passion. He never thought he'd be one to be blinded by a pretty face, but here he is.

He's angry at his parents. They should have called him when he forgot to call them. They should have gone to his brother's grave. They claim to be moving on, but to Kyle, it feels like giving up. He refuses to give up or let go. He doesn't want to let his brother go.

He's angry at *himself.* He's disappointed and guilty and *mad* at himself for letting himself forget. He let himself get distracted. He let himself live in some stupid fantasy where someone like Jake might actually like him and let himself believe that maybe if he came out, it wouldn't be so bad. He let himself forget what's really important, and he knows better than that.

And honestly? He's mad at his brother. His brother *left* him. He said he would always be there for him, and he left. Kyle knows he didn't mean to *die,* but he still left, and now Kyle has no one. He feels alone, and no one understands.

He works until his eyes burn and his body begins shutting down. He works until he's exhausted enough to fall into bed and go to sleep without having to think. He works until he's ensured a dreamless, thoughtless sleep.

And then he wakes up, and he does it all over again.

* * *

HE WORKS WELL into the night, as has become his habit. He doesn't think he's looked away from his screen in hours. He knows Jasper has already gone to bed. He heard him get ready an hour ago, and somewhere around that time he turned the lights off.

Kyle feels himself getting frustrated. It's a tick beneath his skin, crawling and restless. His eyes narrow, blurring at the edges and burning as he looks over a paragraph of coding. It's wrong. It looks *wrong*. But he can't figure out why. He's been stuck on this bug for *hours*. He hasn't gotten past it. His vision has been going in and out, and his focus hasn't been much better. He thinks there might have been a while there where he passed out. He can't remember much.

With a grunt of frustration, he saves everything and closes his laptop. Tomorrow. He'll come back to it tomorrow. He should sleep now before he passes out on his keyboard.

He rubs his eyes, feeling water well up at the corners in an attempt to relieve the persistent dryness. When he opens them, gray dots dance at the edges of his vision. He can see them, even in the dark of the room. And they don't fade. That can't be a good sign.

He pushes himself to his feet, intent on going to the bathroom, but his balance wavers. His knees lock up, and his vision swims. He stumbles a couple steps, hitting the wall next to the door to the bathroom. His breaths are slow and ragged as he clings to the wall, trying to stop the vertigo. Everything is spinning, slow and disorienting.

It takes far too long for everything to come back into focus.

He steps into the bathroom, closes the door, and turns on the light.

He's caught by his own reflection. He looks far too pale. His skin feels greasy, and his hair looks matted and gross. He honestly can't remember the last time he took a shower. He realizes with a start that he's pretty certain he's only taken one since he broke it off with Jake. He tried once, and the thoughts came swirling in and pushed him toward a panic attack, so he's been avoiding the shower ever since.

Dark and heavy bags hang under his eyes. His eyes themselves look hollow and distant. His clothes are rumpled and dirty, and he's not sure when he last changed them.

He looks terrible.

It's then that his stomach rumbles, loud and twisting, clenching his gut painfully. He grits his teeth, wrapping one arm around his middle and using his other hand to prop himself up on the counter.

He can't remember the last time he ate. Yesterday? He thinks it was yesterday morning. He hasn't drunk much either. He knows he hasn't been eating very well lately, but this is the longest he's gone.

He knows he needs to eat. Logically, he knows that. He needs to put *something* in his stomach to keep him going, but the thought of food makes his stomach roll. No matter how hungry he is, he feels nauseated by the thought of eating anything. His throat feels thick, tongue sluggish and swollen. He's not sure he'd even be able to get himself to swallow if he tried.

It's a bad sign. A very bad sign.

He stares at himself in the mirror, eyes wide with the mounting horror of realization.

The last time he was like this was right after his brother's death. He isolated himself. He lived in the dark of his room. He didn't talk to anyone, not even his parents. He didn't eat anything and barely drank anything. His sleep was sporadic and far between.

He ended up passing out and having to go to the hospital.

He hadn't meant to starve himself, but he was too upset to eat. He'd been put on fluids until his body could work back up to food. It had been a terrible experience. He'd worried his parents, who'd just lost a son. He'd been stuck, surrounded by nurses with pitying eyes. He hadn't been able to work on anything.

He knew his brother would've hated to see him that way.

He'd hate to see him *this* way.

He can't let it happen again. He doesn't want to fall that low again. He *can't* fall that low again. If he does, he's not sure he'll be able to come back, and he doesn't want that. He has to be strong. For his brother, and for himself.

He needs help.

He can see the tears welling up in his eyes in the mirror, vision blurring with them. They're warm as they run down his cheeks.

He needs help.

He collapses into bed that night, teeth brushed, body showered, and wearing clean pajamas. He feels better, but only a fraction. His stomach still hurts, his body aches, and he still feels emotionally numb.

Tomorrow. Tomorrow he'll go to the counseling office and make an appointment. Tomorrow, he'll find a way to get better.

For his brother.

For himself.

CHAPTER 21

*J*ake has been on autopilot for weeks. He wakes up when his alarms tell him to. He goes to class when he needs to. He eats when his body tells him it's time to eat. He sits with his roommates in the evenings because it's better than being alone. He laughs when he gets the cue to laugh, but even that sounds strangely hollow and fake. He knows they notice. He can see it in the way they exchange worried glances. But they don't comment on it, and for that, he's grateful. He doesn't want to talk about it.

He does his homework with almost a religious reverence, throwing himself wholeheartedly into it. He keeps his head busy with numbers and problems and critical thinking, and that helps distract from the void in his chest. He studies, and he fills up his thoughts with information, focusing on storing that away rather than thinking about how much he hurts and why.

Studying and homework have become easier. He knows how to focus through the homework and how to phrase his answers. He knows how to read through the text and decipher it into something he actually understands. He tries to focus on that and not on the person who taught him how to do it.

Not thinking about *him* is hard, though. *He* lurks in Jake's thoughts all day, hiding in the shadows, waiting for him to be distracted for just a moment before he starts to rise to the surface. His cute smile. His shy laugh. His pouting scowl. The way he glared at Jake with tears in his eyes when he told him sternly and firmly that there was no future for them and they should just never see each other again.

Bad thoughts.

He ignores those thoughts. He pushes them far, far away.

He's made it over the last big round of tests and papers, and he can see that his grades are steadily improving. It's not enough to kick up his GPA yet, but there's obvious improvement that'll allow him to keep his scholarship, as long as he keeps it up. He has proof that he's trying and it's working. He can see his professors are impressed, and when he has his counselor meeting to discuss it, he seems impressed as well.

It's just a shame that while Jake smiled, he felt too numb to really feel proud. Especially when they started talking about how smart he was to go out and find a tutor, and then he just got stuck thinking about Kyle.

Kyle had, true to his word, lined up another tutor for Jake. He's not sure how he managed to find this guy, but he seems nice enough. He contacted Jake through their school email and sounded all professional and stuff. But Jake doesn't *want* another tutor. He'd rather suffer through it on his own. Maybe it's his stubborn pride talking, but it's working out just fine. Between make-out sessions and Jake staring helplessly at Kyle's profile, Kyle actually did manage to teach him good study techniques, and they've managed to stick. Jake is doing just fine on his own.

His grades aren't the only thing that's been improving.

Jake's laser focus and hyper fixation have come in handy during practice as well.

He charges into each practice with the single-minded focus of a bull in an arena. He runs hard. Hits hard. Throws hard. He works and works and works until his body is exhausted and close to collapse. He takes every piece of advice his coach has to offer and does his best to improve. He focuses entirely and hyper fixates on improving. He sees all the things he's doing wrong and all the things he *could* be doing, and he works. And he works. And he works.

He gets to practice early, and he's the last to leave.

He works until his muscles are screaming and his body aches, but he doesn't care. It keeps his mind clear, it feels good, and it helps him fall asleep at night before the thoughts he's been keeping at bay can catch up to him.

Distantly, he notices the affect it has on his teammates. He can see how startled they are at first. He can see how confused and rattled they are, and he can hear their whispers behind his back. He pays them no mind, focused wholly on himself and his own performance. Let them gossip. He doubts they'll ever come close to being right, anyway.

After the initial shock wears off, he actually notices his teammates rallying around him. Fall semester practice has always been slower and lazier than spring. Spring is when the actual season starts, when they have to crack down and actually work hard. Fall is when they tend to goof off despite trying to stay in shape. But the semester is coming to an end, spring is coming up, and Jake is determined to do better and to *be* better.

And seeing his intensity, his teammates start to step up to the plate as well. They start to follow his example, cracking down on their own performances. He doesn't know if it's because they're inspired by him, because they don't want to fall behind, or because they don't want him to show them up.

Whatever it is, it rallies a team wide improvement in focus and drive that isn't entirely a bad thing.

His coach, however, isn't fooled.

"Hey, Jake," the man says, leaning against the fence and watching as Jake goes at a round in the batting cages. And by a round, he means several rounds. The rest of the team has already left, and there Jake is, taking swing after swing.

"Hey, coach," he grunts as he swings, hits the ball, and resets his stance. He can feel sweat trickling down his chest, beading on his forehead, cold in the autumn air. "Need me to get out of here?"

"Yeah, but that's not what I came to talk to you about. You've been pretty intense at practice lately, and don't get me wrong, you're doing great. But I can't help but feel like there's something else going on. How've you been lately?"

Jake grits his teeth and swings, relishing in the jarring slam of the bat against the high-speed ball. He resets his stance. "Fine."

"Sure as hell don't look fine."

"I'm *fine*," swing. Hit. Reset.

"Heard some gossip from the boys that your lady dumped you a month or two back."

Swing. Hit. Reset. "It was a mutual dumping."

"Jake, I say this because I care about my players, and while you've been doing great on the field, you need some stability off the field. It doesn't take a genius to see that you've been tense as all get out the past few weeks. The whole grades thing been stressing you out?"

Jake just hums vaguely, letting his coach believe that's all it is. Just him stressing out about grades. Not his tutor slash almost-boyfriend leaving him.

"Thought so. Exercise is great to get your mind off things, but there are other ways to relax. I know you don't have a girl right now, but you've never had trouble finding one.

Maybe you should go out with the boys. Have some fun. Get laid. Would be good for you. Get that tension out before you work yourself into the ground."

The light goes off, indicating that his round is over. He lets the bat drop, straightening as he laughs. It sounds hollow and bitter, but he doubts his coach will notice. No one else seems to. How long has he been good at faking being happy? "Maybe you're right. Thanks, coach."

"Anytime, son. Now get out of here so I can close up."

The idea of getting laid makes his stomach roll. The idea of going out and finding a random girl to fuck, having it mean nothing, it makes him nauseous. Once upon a time, he might've been all over that. Not now. Something has changed, and he knows it has everything to do with Kyle.

Still, his coach might have a point. He *is* tense and stressed, and maybe he *should* get laid. He's been so hung up on Kyle for the past few weeks, barely daring to think about him but being caught up on him all the same. It's pathetic. Especially when Kyle made it extremely clear that he wants nothing to do with Jake anymore.

~~Jesus Christ~~, he's never been this hung up on a break up before, and he and Kyle weren't even officially dating.

What's *wrong* with him?

He's far too lost in his spiraling thoughts and doesn't see Cindi until it's too late. She's waiting for him outside the practice field, leaning against the fence with an air of impatience that smoothly fades into something more coy at his approach. He hasn't seen or heard from her much since their break up, but she looks exactly the same. Waiting for him exactly like she has before. Hot, confident, sexy, but strangely enough, it doesn't do anything for him anymore.

"Hey," she says, pushing off the fence and sauntering over to him, hips swinging.

"Hey," he says, and doesn't stop until she puts herself in

his path, blocking his way and putting a hand on his chest. He looks down at it, brows pinching with confusion as he looks up to meet her eyes.

He knows that look. That's the look she used to give him when she wanted something from him. That gaze that's filled with lust that used to drive him crazy, but now he can see how disingenuous it is. How fake it is. How it's crafted to toy with him. How that lust may be real, but it's not for *him*. It's just a general horniness.

He frowns, sighing loudly. "What do you want, Cindi?"

She leans in close, fingers toying with his shirt, her voice pitched low. "I just came by to see how you've been doing."

"Fine," it's a clear dismissal, but she doesn't get the hint.

"I forgot how hot you smell after practice, and how good you look playing," she leans in close, tilting her face toward his neck. He leans back, pulling away as he feels her breath against his damp skin.

"Cindi."

"I've missed you, Jake," she reaches up, running her fingers lightly over his lips. And that's when the smell hits him. It's familiar and pungent, and it sends him reeling, but not for the reasons she no doubt wants. Her fingers smell like her vagina, her arousal, but instead of making him weak in the knees, it makes his stomach twist.

He catches her hand by the wrist, pulling it away as he steps back. She looks shocked as he glares at her. "If you just want a fuck toy, you can go find someone else. Or better yet, go buy one at the store."

Her surprise shifts quickly into indignant rage. She scowls, eyes narrowing as she snatches her hand back. He's not fooled, though. He can see the pink on her cheeks from her embarrassment at being called out. "Jake, what the *fuck?*"

"You don't care about me," he says, plain and simple, standing tall and meeting her glare with one of his own.

She scoffs, rolling her eyes as she crosses her arms over her chest, hip cocking out to the side. "Like you ever cared about *me*."

That makes the knot inside of him loosen, shoulders slumping slightly as his glare falls. "Actually, I did."

"If you *really* cared about me, you'd fuck me now. What's the matter? You're not with anyone. I'm not with anyone. You're still hot, even if we're not dating. If you really liked me, then you'd fuck me."

Something hits him then. It's the cold wash of clarity. It freezes in his chest before melting out through his veins, cool and calming. It eases the tension from his body, slithering as a welcome reprieve through his veins.

He realizes what he's learned from being with Kyle.

He realizes just how much of an asshole he's been.

He realizes who he wants to be.

He reaches out, putting his hands on Cindi's shoulders. She looks startled, staring at him with wide, confused eyes. He smiles, hoping it looks as genuine as it is. "I'm sorry," she gapes at him, and he forges on. "I'm sorry I never took the time to get to know you. I'm sorry no one has. You're more than a quick fuck, and you should be treated as such. And I'm sorry I never did that. I hope you can find someone who will."

He leaves then, walking away without waiting for a response. He leaves her looking shocked and confused, gaping and frozen.

He leaves her and everything she represents behind.

He feels like he's leaving a part of himself behind. A person he once was and no longer wants to be.

He walks away feeling like a new man.

* * *

"ANYWAY," he says, swirling around the dregs of his coffee. "I think you were right. I'm thinking about going out to a gay bar or something tonight. Try to pick up a dude. I...I think I'm ready to explore that part of me."

Liddy sits across from him, lounging in her seat with one hand wrapped around her own coffee cup, finger tapping it idly. There's a lazy smile on her lips. It's the one she wears when she finds something privately amusing. "You know," she says slowly, gently tapping her cup on the table before lifting it to her lips. "For someone so pretty, you're not very bright."

Jake bristles, frowning as his eyes snap to hers. "What's that supposed to mean?"

She takes her time downing the rest of her coffee. When she's done, she sets it down, leaning forward to put both elbows on the table. Her grin is positively shark-like. "It *means*, Jakey boy, that you're being an idiot. Do you even realize that for the past *hour* you've talked about *nothing* besides Kyle?"

Jake blinks, frown fading. "What? No, fuck off, you're exaggerating."

"I'm not. I've even been timing you," she glances at her phone. "One hour and seven minutes to be exact," she glances back up, tilting her head to the side. Her piercings shimmer in the light. "I even tried steering the conversation away a couple times, but you just kept dragging it back to Kyle. You're really hung up on this dude, aren't you?"

Jake groans, slouching in his seat and running his hands down his face. "Fuuuck, I'm so sorry. I didn't even realize. ▬▬▬, this is so pathetic. *Yes*, okay, I'm hung up on him, but like...that's getting me nowhere. What I need is to, you know, rebound," he lets his hands fall, glaring at the wood grain on the table, brows furrowed. "Or something."

Liddy's laugh is light and airy, thick with amusement.

And while he bristles, scowling at her, he can tell that she may be laughing *at* him, but there's no judgement there. "Has that ever worked for anyone? Fuck no. Rebounds are a *terrible* idea. Especially when you're this hung up on someone. What do you want, Jake?"

He frowns. "I want to get over…"

"I *said*," she cuts him off, sharply but not unkindly, eyes intense as she stares. He feels her pick him apart, ripping open his chest and leaving him vulnerable, exposed and raw. She smiles, reaching out to take his hands, voice softening in that way that always draws the truth out of him, whether he wants it to or not. "What do you want?"

It rushes through him, echoing out of that numb void in his heart and aching through his chest. It comes out in a whispered rush, a truth he can't deny but doesn't want to let loose. "Kyle."

Liddy's grin is wide, eyes dancing. "Then fucking *fight* for what you want."

Jake scoffs, rolling his eyes as hurt and hope fight within his chest. "It's not just up to *me*, Liddy. He has a say in this, too."

"You gotta fight for what you want, Jake. You're afraid of rejection, and you're afraid of not being good enough. That's been your problem for-fucking-ever. That's why you go after girls you're not interested in and who you know just want you for your looks. Because you're confident in your looks. Kyle makes you feel like a *person*. He sees *more* than just your looks. And you're scared it's not enough. But, think of it this way, maybe he feels the same. Maybe he's scared *he's* not enough for *you*."

Jake frowns. "That's not fucking possible. He's amazing, and so much better than I am, and…"

"Have you told *him* that?"

"I…of course, I have," he has, hasn't he? Kyle *knows* how he feels, doesn't he?

Liddy squeezes his hands, bringing his attention back to her. "Look, if you don't do anything, you're gonna end up regretting it. And I don't know about you, but I don't want to spend the next few months trying to pick up the pieces of your broken heart. From what you've told me, he wasn't a hundred percent behind the break up either. Sounds to me like he was just protecting himself. Go to him, ~~dude~~. Bare your heart and open up to him. Let him see all of you," her smile softens, head tilting to the side. "If you do that, no one can turn you away."

His smile is timid. "Thanks, Liddy."

"No problem, ~~dude~~."

"Why did I let you go, again?"

She laughs, light and lilting. "Because you were an asshole and I wanted to fuck girls."

"If you were single, I'd snatch you up in a heartbeat."

Her eyes lower, sweet tinged with sadness. Her thumbs brush over his knuckles. "It's no surprise I'm still a little in love with you, but, it's changed. It's a friend love now. And Becca has my whole heart."

Jake chuckles. "Becca would castrate me if I tried anything."

Her smile is gentle and fond. "Yeah. Yeah, she would," she shakes her head, patting his hands. "Anyway, get out of here, you big idiot. Go plan some grand gesture and get your boy back. Fight for your happy ending, dumbass."

He stands, leaning forward and kissing her quickly on the forehead. "Thanks, Liddy."

CHAPTER 22

*T*he counselor's office is just like Kyle expects it to be. The waiting room looks like any other waiting room around the school, same carpet, same chairs, same generic paintings on the walls. He sits, and he fidgets, doing his best not to make eye contact with anyone else in the room. He does, however, catch a few glances. Not all of them look bad. Tired. Distant, maybe. But not bad.

He wonders how bad he looks. He *knows* he looks nervous. He can feel it. His stomach rumbles because while he managed to eat a banana and a small thing of yogurt this morning, it doesn't really make up for all the meals he's skipped lately. He can practically *feel* the bags under his eyes. He didn't exactly look great in the mirror this morning, but at least he forced himself to shower and put on clean clothes. His hair, however, is a fucking disaster that he hadn't bothered to tame.

When his name is called, he stands and greets a woman. She looks somewhere in her thirties, smooth copper hair curling around her shoulders, dressed nice but casual. She smiles at him warmly, and he tries to return it as she leads him back through the hallway to her office.

It's a nice office, he supposes. It's small. She has a chair that looks comfortable. A desk nearby. Some bookshelves made of dark wood that give it a homey feel. There are paintings on the wall as well as her certificates and diplomas. The curtains framing the window are deep and rich in color. She's obviously taken time to turn her cinderblock cubicle of a room into something more comfortable.

As soon as the door is closed, he feels his panic rising. It's a tight knot forming in his gut, nauseating tendrils coiling and curling upward through his chest, squeezing his lungs.

She takes her seat, and he slowly lowers himself to the couch opposite her. It's comfortable, the smooth, worn leather creaking beneath him as he shifts and adjusts. His eyes dart everywhere, avoiding eye contact with her as she shuffles through some papers.

He shouldn't be here. He doesn't *belong* here. He doesn't have any deep-seated issues to work out. He doesn't have any traumas, right? He's not like the other kids who come in for counseling. He's *fine*.

She introduces herself during his haze of trying to get a grip on his self-control. He knows he must respond to it and introduces himself, because his lips are moving, and his voice is on autopilot, but his mind is elsewhere, giving himself a stern pep talk to just *get* this over with.

Then she's settling back in her chair, lounging comfortably. Her clipboard rests on her lap, and her elbows rest on the arms of her chair, fingers meeting and steeping together as she smiles at Kyle. It's a warm smile, disarming, welcoming and gentle, but he *knows* it's carefully crafted to be that way, and *that* puts him on edge.

"Right, well, Kyle, is there any particular reason you're here?"

He shrugs, shifting his weight, eyes on the coffee table between them. "Just to talk...I guess." Yet despite that, he can't figure out what to say. The thoughts and words jumble on their way to his mouth, building up and clogging his lungs. He doesn't know where to start. Oh god, what is he doing here?

She must sense his rising panic because she says, "Hey, there's no pressure. You don't need to open up right away. A lot of people come in here just to talk. How about we start with the basic starter questions, so I can get a general idea of everything. Does that sound good?"

He nods, biting his bottom lip. Answer questions. He can do that. That doesn't require a lot of thought.

He eases back into the couch, letting it envelop him in an illusion of safety as she begins.

They're easy questions at first. Simple questions about himself. How's college life so far? Does he get his school work done? Does he go to classes? How does he feel about them? Is he too stressed about grades? What's his relationship with his family like? Does he talk to them often? Does he socialize much on campus? What does he do in his free time? Is he eating properly?

She pokes and prods at him, trying to get a good picture of who he is and what his problems might be without asking directly. She beats around the bush, poking from the side until she can get a full outline of him. He answers on autopilot, truthful if not a little ashamed whenever he gets this look that tells him that whatever his answer was, it's not *good*. He knows that. He *knows* it's not good. That's why he's *here*.

Then, when it becomes clear that he's not in a good place, she digs deeper. He tells her about the past few weeks. He tells her how he's been isolating himself, snapping at his roommate. He tells her how he barely showers and forgets to eat. He tells her how it's *hard* to eat, like his body refuses to accept food. He tells her how he's thrown himself into his work, and he's getting things done, but it doesn't feel *good*. He tells her how he has to practically work himself into a coma every night to avoid the nightmares.

That's when she starts asking more pointed questions.

"Have you been abusing a substance?"

"No," he thinks he's too much of a coward to do that.

"Have you thought about hurting yourself?"

"No."

"What's your support network like?"

He squirms in his seat, fingers picking at the skin around his nail beds. He stares at them to keep from making eye contact. "You know..." he mumbles. "Classmates and stuff."

"Classmates?" he doesn't look up, but he can *hear* the surprise. He bites at his bottom lip, feeling the hot rush of shame to his cheeks. "Not friends?"

He shrugs, slouching further into the couch, wishing for all the world that it would swallow him up. "I don't have a lot of friends. I...I had *one*, but..." another shrug and the sharp twist of his heart as his stomach knots and drops. "It didn't work out."

She moves then, and he glances up through his lashes. She leans forward, setting her clipboard on the table and off to the side without looking at it. She rests her elbows on her knees, interwoven fingers held up in front of her face as she leans forward. She pins Kyle with a curious stare, eyes narrowed slightly as she looks him over.

It's a forced sense of intimacy and of privacy. He feels like she's picking him apart with her eyes. He squirms under the scrutiny.

But when she speaks, it's not demanding nor is it confrontational. It's soft and inviting. She doesn't so much pull him out of his shell as peel it back and step aside, waiting and offering for him to step out on his own. He knows this is just part of her job, a presence that she's crafted specifically to feel like this. But it's so natural that maybe she was like this all along and just found a job that fit her.

Either way, it eases the tense knot in his gut and makes him *want* to step out of his shell. From behind his walls. That's why he's here, right? And she makes him want to talk. Or maybe he's been dying to talk anyway. To get it off his chest.

He's such a mess.

"Why are you here, Kyle?"

He shifts his weight, eyes darting around the room. He opens his mouth, but no words come out, and he snaps it shut again.

"I know that you know why you're here," she says gently, a soft smile on her lips. It doesn't look like pity, but instead like sympathy and understanding. "It's clear to me that you don't think you need help, and you're scared to want it, but you came here for a reason. You came here to talk about something that you can't talk to anyone else about, and I'm here to listen. All you have to do is talk."

His eyes flicker to her, sidelong and wary. He glances at the door, licking his lips as he finds his voice, shaky and nervous. "You, uh...you can't say anything to anyone, right? What I say is private?"

She nods. "Unless you're a danger to yourself or others, nothing you say leaves this room."

He nods. "Okay," he licks his lips again, mouth feeling incredibly dry. Closing his eyes, he tries to swallow down the lump in his throat and tries to breath deep into his tight lungs. As he exhales, he lets it out in a rush. "I've been seeing this guy. Well, no, I *was* seeing this guy. Sort of? We weren't really dating, but, we kind of were? It doesn't matter. We're not seeing each other anymore."

He opens his eyes, expression tight and pinched as he

winces at his own words. He glances at his counselor, expecting the worst. He expects surprise, maybe confusion, and definitely thinly concealed disgust. What he doesn't expect is for her to be completely nonplussed. Nothing about her expression changes, and there's no tension to assume that she's merely hiding it. She just looks unsurprised and unaffected by the admission.

"So, you're gay? Or at least bisexual?" it's not said in any of the ways Kyle expected it to be. It's casual and offhand, like she's trying to figure out where to put this new piece of his puzzle.

Still, he tenses. His blood runs cold and his heart hammers painfully in his chest. He stares down at his lap, where his hands are clenched tight, knuckles white. He grits his teeth and lets out a long, hissing sigh, forcing himself to nod once, sharply. "Yeah. I guess."

"And you and this guy broke up?"

Another twist of pain. Another sharp nod. "Yeah."

"And you're having a hard time getting over it?" he shrugs, and she continues. "That's understandable. We all break up, but we heal with time, and we learn how to move on. If he can't see you for who you are, then that's fine. You'll find someone who can."

Kyle shakes his head, dread and shame twisting hot in his chest. "I, uh...I was the one who broke up with him."

"Ahh," she hums. It's noncommittal and blank, without any expression to tell him what that *means*.

He finds himself scrambling to explain himself, eyes narrowed on his lap as he picks at a loose thread on his sleeve. "I wasn't ready, you know? I've...I've never been in a relationship, let alone...I'm not out? People don't know that I'm...yeah, and I wasn't ready for that, I don't think."

"Well, what *would* make you ready?"

Kyle purses his lips tight, brows furrowing. He pulls his feet up onto the edge of the couch, knees bent as he slouches, as if he might hide behind them. He picks at the sleeves of his hoodie. He remains silent because he doesn't know. He digs around in his head and turns the question over, but he just *doesn't* know. And with every passing second, his scowl grows deeper from his frustration.

She lets him have time to process and to think, but when he doesn't respond, she eventually speaks again. It's kind and gentle, soft in a way that comes from experience and understanding rather than a textbook. "Listen, Kyle. No one is ever truly ready for life. No one is ready to experience loss, or to be vulnerable with someone, or to fall in love, or to have children, or to go to college, or to be out in the adult world and survive. Being ready? It's an illusion. Few of us are ever ready for what life throws at us. Not completely. No one is ever a hundred percent confident. We just get better at taking chances and learning along the way."

She sits back a little, slouching in her chair and hanging her hands over the arms. He watches as she looks around her office, almost wistful as she gestures to it vaguely. "I wasn't ready to take this job. I kind of just fell into it. I wasn't sure it was the right move, but I took it anyway. And I'm so glad I did." She looks at him again, head tilted and a smile in her eyes. "If you wait until you're completely ready to do anything, you'll never truly live."

They're silent for a moment. She lets him absorb her words, and she doesn't push him to speak. Nor does she bombard him with more. She just sits and waits and lets him have a moment to himself. It's an easy silence, and her words slowly sink into Kyle's head. They drift down, settling into his bones. He feels the knot in his chest loosening, even as his stomach continues to twist.

"My..." his voice cracks, and he has to stop to clear his throat, licking his lips. He closes his eyes, taking solace in the darkness. "My brother died a couple years ago," he whispers, the breath of truth feeling numb on his lips. "He was my best friend, my *only* friend, and now he's gone. How am I supposed to move on from that?"

He doesn't see her face, but her voice takes on another gentle level of understanding. "The pain of that will always be there. I don't think loss is something we can ever forget. Not completely. But it does get easier. Everything is loud right now. The wound is fresh. But in time, it will scab and heal. It may scar, but it will heal. And you'll be surrounded by so many good things, so many new things and new people."

He opens his eyes, feeling them burn as he stares at her.

"If you let the good things happen, your loss will fade into the background emotional noise of your life. And that's okay. Our loved ones wouldn't want us to grieve forever. They'd want us to be happy and live our lives to the fullest. If your brother loved you as much as I think he did, he wouldn't want you to swear off happiness," there's a pause, and Kyle takes in a deep, shuddering breath. The next question is a gentle prod. It's a question, but it doesn't feel like one. "Is that why you broke up with this guy?"

He nods, a hiccup squeezing his chest. Kyle squeezes his eyes shut, feeling the stinging bite of tears forming as he desperately wills them away. He feels his lip quiver, and he bites it in an attempt to stop it. When he speaks, however, he can't stop the waver in his voice. "I forgot the anniversary of my brother's death. I got distracted. *He* distracted me. I let our, whatever we were, I let it distract me."

"Kyle," she says, gentle and patient. She waits for him to open his eyes. She waits until he looks at her, vision blurry with tears he doesn't want to shed. She smiles, calm and patient and so understanding. It reminds him of his brother. "You weren't *distracted*. You were *healing*."

His breath hitches, another hiccup seizes his chest, and gives in to his tears.

CHAPTER 23

$\mathcal{F}$ueled by a stubborn determination, a blaze of hope, and a twisting, urgent worry that he might be too late, Jake finds himself standing in front of Kyle's door.

He's been thinking about this all day. Sitting through class had been a pain, and he'd barely been able to focus, but he knew he had to be there. Kyle would *kill* him if his grades dropped because he skipped class to see him. The whole point is to make Kyle *happy*, not upset.

But as he's standing here, facing Kyle's dorm door, he starts to feel the first cold edges of doubt rising. How the *hell* is he supposed to make Kyle happy? What does Kyle *want*? He's not exactly a typical guy, or a typical person even. He's complicated and sweet but rough around the edges and likes clichés but hates that he likes them and...

Get on with it, a voice in his head says, sounding suspiciously like Liddy. *Just* do it. Dive right in. You have nothing to lose and everything to gain.

Before his nerves can get the better of him, reflex and adrenaline have his hand lifting to the door, knocking sharply. Then he stands back and waits, heart pounding painfully in his chest and making him dizzy. This is it. This is it. This is it.

His breath catches when the doorknob turns, body freezing stiff as it swings open.

But it's not Kyle. Jasper stands in the doorway. His hair is a mess, but no messier than usual. Half of it is tucked away beneath his gray beanie. He looks bored, tired and exhausted, but no more so than the average college student. When he sees Jake, he blinks, surprise coloring his boredom for a second before his eyes narrow suspiciously. "What do you want?"

Heart in his throat, standing up a little straighter and trying not to fidget under Jasper's weighted gaze, Jake manages to answer. "I'm looking for Kyle."

All at once, Jasper's demeanor changes. His shoulders sag, and he leans against the door, pressing his head to it as his eyes flutter briefly closed. "Oh, thank god," he sighs, pushing off the door and disappearing back into the room.

The door is left open, but Jake isn't sure if that's an invitation or not. After a moment of internal debate, he cautiously steps through the doorway, pushing the door a little wider and peering into the room.

"He's not here right now," Jasper says, hunched over his desk. His backpack sits in his chair, and he shoves books and his laptop into it haphazardly. "But this is the first time he's left the room except for class for like, fucking *weeks*. He's been on a fucking *downer*. Like, more so than usual. Before he was just kinda a homebody and broody, you know? But he's been in the pits of some shit, man, lemme tell ya. It *radiates* off him, and I feel worse just *being* here. Not eating. Not showering. Yeah, that's noticeable. And whenever I try to say *anything*, he just snaps at me or looks like he's about to break down, and I do *not* do well with tears."

Jake stands to the side of the doorway, shifting his weight from foot to foot as he makes a show of looking around the room. "Oh, uh..." he clears his throat. Does he sound as nervous as he feels? Come on, just play it off. He can do this. "I had no idea."

Jasper zips up his backpack, swinging the strap over his shoulder as he turns. He gives Jake a flat stare. Flat and blank and seeing *right* through him. Jake tries not to fidget, but he knows he is. "It was pretty obvious you and Kyle were a thing, man," he says, bluntly, yet sharp and striking right to the heart of the matter. Jake stiffens, eyes going wide. But before he can scramble for words, Jasper shrugs, bending over to pull on his shoes. "Just like it's pretty damn clear something happened between you two," he straightens, rolling his shoulders. "So, like, if you have a plan to get him back into a good mood, or at least drag him out of this Debbie downer pit, that's great. Or better yet, get him to move in with you so I can finally bring people back here. But I'll settle for the whole better mood thing," he moves toward the doorway, pausing with his hand on the door as he narrows his eyes over his shoulder, giving Jake a stern look. "So, look, don't hurt him anymore. Get your shit and his shit together. As long as you fix whatever this is, I don't care if you guys fuck around in here. Just not on my bed, got it?"

Jake holds up his hands, heat flaring to his cheeks. "Dude, I would *never...*"

"Good," he nods, slipping out the door and calling a loud, "Good luck!" Before the door slams shut.

And then Jake is alone. In Kyle's room. He looks around, hands on his hips and nervous excitement bubbling in his veins.

He has a lot of work to do.

* * *

WHEN HE HEARS the telltale sound of a key in the lock and the doorknob turning, it sounds like the bells of his demise tolling. Which sounds kind of dramatic, but he's freaking out.

He freezes with the candle lighter in his hand, entire body going rigid and eyes widening as his heart pounds into overtime in his chest. It bruises his ribs, makes his breath come quick and shallow, and makes him light headed. *Not good. Not good.*

Only half the candles he's scattered around the room on every available surface are lit.

Not good. Not good.

He had gotten a sweet rosé wine, but what if that's not what Kyle likes? What if he *hates* sweet wines?

Not good. Not good.

Maybe he should've…

But it's too late now. The door is opening and Jake spins on his heel, setting the lighter down on the table as he does so. *"Hey,"* he says, a nervous grin spreading across his face as he freezes, arms out to put the room on display. He's striking a pose. Oh god, he probably looks stupid. *Not good. Not good.* "Surprise?"

Kyle stands in the doorway, hand on the doorknob, backlit by the florescent hallway lights. He looks frozen, face captured and stuck in a moment of complete surprise and bewilderment. He stands frozen, and Jake stands frozen, staring at each other as the tension builds and builds, filling his chest, threatening to burst.

Kyle's eyes are wide, lips parted and moving as he struggles to find words and eventually fails.

Then his gaze shifts from Jake, moving around the room. Jake watches, heart pounding loudly in his ears, as Kyle takes it all in.

The room is dark, with just the pale orange glow of the

setting sun peeking through the closed blinds. The lights are off, and the only sources of light are about twelve candles scattered around the dorm in his attempt to set an atmosphere. The other eighteen remain unlit. On Kyle's desk is the bottle of wine, framed by two glasses that look simple and nice enough and that he managed to find for cheap at the store in his mad dash to collect everything.

Slowly, so very slowly that Jake can count it in heartbeats, Kyle closes the door behind him. The soft *click* resonates around the room, sealing his fate. For better or for worse.

Kyle licks his lips, and Jake tries to pretend he isn't as mesmerized by the movement as he is. "What…what are you *doing* here?"

And it's then that the tension in Jake's chest reaches a head, bubble bursting in a cacophony of nerves and embarrassment, kicking his fight or flight reflex into overdrive as his posture crumbles. He laughs, and it sounds hollow and forced, shaking at the edges. He gestures vaguely with one hand, the other scratching the back of his neck. His eyes dart around the room. "I, uh, I admit it's not my best display. It's not really what I hoped it would be, and I dunno if it was my planning or the execution or the timing, I just…"

His shoulders slump as he sighs, breath shuddering out of his lungs. He looks up at Kyle, feeling lost and forlorn.

"I just didn't know what to do," he says softly. "I've only ever dated superficial girls, and they love the shit out of romance movies or whatever. And I've never tried to get any of them back when they broke up with me, so I'm a little out of my element here."

He's floundering, and he knows he is, but the word vomit won't stop.

Thankfully, Kyle saves him from himself. He takes a cautious step into the room, slow and deliberate. He drops his backpack to the floor by his desk, eyes on the bottle of wine and empty glasses. Jake finds it hard to read his expression, unsure of what he sees and what he *wants* to see. "Is that what you're trying to do?" Kyle asks softly. "Trying to get me back?"

Jake laughs, but it's barely more than a nervous huff of breath. "Y-yeah, I... that's exactly what I'm trying to do. That's the idea anyway. Clearly, I don't know what I'm doing, and I suck at this, but..."

He stops when he hears it. It sounds so foreign for a moment. So out of place that he has a hard time processing it. But then it continues, and he's sure. *Giggling*. Kyle is giggling.

It starts out small. Bubbling, light and soft, slipping past his lips even as he presses them tightly together. Jake stares at him, eyes widening, as Kyle leans a hand on his desk, hunching over to hide his mirth. But his shoulders shake, his chest heaves, and eventually he can't hold it back anymore.

He *laughs*.

Loud. Bubbling. Bursting from his lips in a rush of sound, shaking his entire body. He laughs. And he laughs. And when the sound begins to dissipate into giggles, it starts all over again. Rising and falling. A melody of enjoyment and mirth that once would've made Jake's heart soar.

But now it only sinks.

He feels a rush of embarrassment, hot and shameful. It's followed by the sting of hurt in its wake, fueled by the brief panic of Kyle laughing at him. But the longer his laughing fit continues, the more his panic recedes, and Jake realizes Kyle has never laughed *at* him. Never once. His laughter, dare he hope, sounds more like the hysterics of relief than anything else.

His hurt fades to amusement, a smile breaking out across his lips. And then he's laughing, too. His own relief that Kyle isn't mad is its own source of adrenaline and endorphins, flooding his system and making him feel light and giddy. The tension and nervousness that had been building in his chest bubbles out in the form of laughter.

"In my panic, I almost got balloons," he confesses between rounds of laughter, a chuckle still edging his words. Kyle looks up at him, eyes crinkling at the edges and face red. His smile is so wide and genuine, and it takes Jake's breath away.

"Really?" he giggles, covering his mouth as if that might stop it.

"Yeah, nearly got a bunch of balloons, and I thought about scattering flower petals all over your dorm, but then I wasn't sure if you or Jasper were allergic to flowers, and I think he'd kill me if I did something like that. Plus, I couldn't find any pre-picked flower petals, and I didn't have time to do it myself," he shrugs and snorts another bout of laughter, running his fingers through his hair as he tries to catch his breath. "*Then* I wasn't sure if I should like, be naked on your bed or something? But I never got around to that anyway. Like I barely started to light the candles before you came back."

He isn't sure when or how Kyle ends up in front of him. He doesn't think he moved, but he doesn't remember Kyle moving. All he knows is that one moment they're laughing across the room from each other, and in the next, they're standing toe to toe.

Kyle looks up at him shyly, eyes lidded beneath thick lashes. His hair is a mess. His clothes are oversized and wrinkled. The bags under his eyes are dark and huge. He looks paler and, quite frankly, exhausted. But he still manages to be the cutest damn thing Jake has ever seen, and his chest is fluttering with that knowledge.

He bites his lip, but doesn't say anything, and Jake takes that as his cue.

"I just..." he says, hands aimlessly waving in vague, helpless gestures. His shoulders slump, and his voice drops low. Defeated. "I didn't know what to do. I kind of panicked. The truth is..." he takes a deep breath, trying to steady himself. He straightens a little, closing his eyes as the truth rushes out of him with painful honesty. "I think I love you, Kyle. I didn't mean to, and I didn't expect to. I didn't start all of this with that in mind, it just sorta...*happened*. I never wanted you to forget the other people in your life, and I understand that you need time. You're not ready to come out, and I get that. I really do. I know you're not done grieving, and I'm not trying to put pressure on you, I just..." his hands curl into fists at his side. He bites the inside of his cheek. He opens his eyes to meet Kyle's gaze, feeling far too exposed and far too vulnerable. But this is what he's supposed to do, right? Expose himself and let Kyle judge for himself. So, he rips his heart out and holds it out on a silver platter. He meets Kyle's gaze unflinchingly and hopes he can see his honesty. "I don't like the thought of you going through all of it alone. It's a lot to deal with alone, and I'm not selfish enough to abandon you just because you're not ready to be, you know, public with me," he tilts his head, a wry smile touching his lips. "Every day without you is painful."

He watches as Kyle's eyes drop, and he lifts a hand, fingers curled and hesitating before he reaches out. He lays it, palm flat, on Jake's chest. The touch is gentle and hesitant, but there all the same. Jake feels the breath freeze in his lungs.

"I may not ever really be ready," Kyle says, low and soft enough that Jake has to strain to hear.

When he does, he feels the hot knife of rejection stab deep into his heart, twisting and gutting him. But then Kyle's fingers curl into his shirt, clinging to him like an anchor as he lets out a shuddering breath.

"But, I suppose that's not really the point. No one's really ever a hundred percent ready for something, right? Games are tested and tested and tested, but when they're released, they still have bugs. Hiccups. They have to release patches to fix things," his head tilts a little to the side. "Maybe being ready is just a goal post that's always a football field away."

"Did you..." a breathless laugh escapes him. "Did you just try to use a sports analogy for my sake?"

Kyle glances up through his lashes, a shy but amused smirk on his lips. "Did it work?"

"Yeah," he breathes. "I think it did."

Kyle closes his eyes for a moment, taking another step closer. Hand still on Jake's chest, they stand barely inches apart. He tilts his chin up, meeting Jake's eyes with a fiery but vulnerable intensity that makes his heart stutter in his chest. "So...if you can forgive me for being selfish, and weird, and not good at *anything* like this, then, maybe...we can give it another shot?" his smile is hopeful. Nervous. Wavering at the edges as he tries to hold it steady. "Just take it one day at a time?"

Jake lifts a hand, ignoring the way it shakes as he puts a knuckle beneath Kyle's chin to lift it. Running his fingers along his jaw line to his neck, fingers diving into his hair to cradle the back of his head. His heart beats wildly in his chest. Hope making his skin feel light and tingly. A new fire burns and itches beneath his skin. One of eager anticipation and disbelieving wonderment. "Yeah," he says. "One day at a time sounds good."

The moment stretches between them, soft, tender and new. It's fragile, and it's precious. Something neither of them have felt before and both of them cherish.

Kyle is the first one to look away, glancing around the room with a teasing smirk finding a home on his lips. "So, you decided *not* to be naked on the bed?"

Jake laughs, loud and uninhibited as relief washes through his system. "Would that have even worked?"

Kyle reaches out, fingertips running lightly up the neck of the wine bottle. He glances at Jake sidelong, capturing him in a gaze that's dark and *smoldering*. And holy shit, Jake didn't even know Kyle was *capable* of looking at him like that, but he's into it. He's really fucking into it.

He licks his lips, smiling when he sees Jake's eyes flicker down to watch. He tilts his head, playful and coy as he says, "Wanna find out?"

CHAPTER 24

*J*ake's lips come crashing down on Kyle's in a strange mix of eagerness, rough desperation, and tender reverence. There's no hesitation. An arm wraps around Kyle's lower back, pulling him forward until he's pressed flush to Jake's larger frame. Another large hand cups his head gently, tilting it at the perfect angle as their mouths come together.

Kyle stiffens for only a moment before he's melting into Jake's embrace.

He missed this. He missed this so much. And he hadn't realized just how much he missed it until he has it again.

Jake is hot to the touch, firm and solid against him, and he awakens something in Kyle that he never knew existed. Embers that sparked and burned before, but Kyle had never allowed them to ignite into a full blaze. He's been scared of it. Scared of losing himself and scared of letting himself go. Now he lets the burdens, the doubts, and the guilt drop away. He lets those embers flare into a blazing inferno, burning and aching in his chest.

It's too much.

It's not enough.

He wants *more*.

His hands slide up Jake's chest, feeling the tight definition of his pecs and shivering at the knowledge that right here, right now, for today, Jake is *his*. His body is *his*. He can touch, and no one else can.

Jake is so far out of his league, yet here they are. The handsome jock, cocky and sexy, is quivering and moaning at Kyle's shy touch.

It feels like a dream. His head is buzzing, dizzy with adrenaline and the rush of endorphins. His chest is tight with emotions. He's felt too much in the past twenty-four hours. He's sunk to his lowest point and started to rise, only for Jake to show up and teach him how to soar. His heart has gone from feeling numb and empty to feeling so much all at once. So full and warm, and fit to burst. It *aches*, and it *hurts*, but it's not uncomfortable or unpleasant.

It feels like…

Holy shit, he thinks he loves Jake.

Holy shit, holy shit, holy shit.

His hands slide up, arms wrapping around Jake's neck and shoulders. His fingers dig into Jake's shirt, grounding him as his body threatens to float away. He goes up on his toes and pushes his lips firmly against Jake's. He knows his attempts are sloppy and uncoordinated. Despite the times they've made out before, he still feels like he doesn't know what he's doing. But he knows what he *feels*, and he feels like if he doesn't get more of Jake, he'll end up drowning.

Jake stumbles back a step with the force of it, and Kyle has the immense satisfaction of hearing his breath hitch in his throat.

Then Jake's hands become insistent. One arm wraps around his lower back, pulling him tight enough that the breath leaves his lungs. His other hand slides down Kyle's back, palm large and fingers spread as it settles over his ass. He squeezes, rough and possessive, and Kyle's hips jerk forward. The friction of grinding against Jake's thigh, if only for a moment, has him moaning into Jake's mouth.

"*Fuck*," Jake hisses, breath against his lips. "You're so fucking hot."

It's surreal. Kyle has never considered himself hot. Never thought anyone else would either. But the way Jake says it leaves no room for argument. He says exactly what he means, and that sends a thrill shivering down Kyle's spine.

The hand on his ass tightens, encouraging his hips to grind forward, and Jake's thigh slides more comfortably between Kyle's. He gasps, trailing off into a high whine as he moves against Jake's thigh. The friction is amazing. It's not long before he doesn't need Jake's insistent hands. He's grinding all on his own, clinging to Jake for dear life while his hips snap forward again and again, chasing that delicious friction.

Jake's tongue licks into his mouth, hot and heady, swallowing his moans and devouring him.

The angle, however, is uncomfortable, and Kyle can feel the pain building in his neck. He breaks the kiss, turning his head to the side to relieve the pressure and to give himself a chance to breathe. He barely manages to catch his breath before Jake's lips are on the curve of his neck, sucking dark marks just below his ear.

Kyle gasps. He moans. His hips snap forward and his toes curl, hands sliding up to bury themselves in Jake's hair. "*Jake*," the name slips past his lips. A plea and a sigh. Desperate and fleeting.

Then Jake's hands are pushing at him. Maneuvering him. Lips still at his throat, he guides Kyle around and back. The back of his knees hit the bed, and he abruptly falls down. He lands alone, sitting on the edge of the bed with his hands behind him to catch his balance. He's reeling, having been suddenly thrown out of Jake's embrace. The cold air rushes in to cool his heated skin. His body is buzzing, and while the space helps clear his head, he misses the touch.

Jake stands over him, eyes lidded and dark. His chest heaves, lips parted, red, and wet. He licks them, slow and deliberate, and Kyle shivers as he stares. Then Jake's hands reach behind him, grabbing the back of his shirt and pulling it over his head, only to toss it aside.

The breath shudders out of Kyle's lungs. It's not the first time he's seen Jake shirtless, but it fucking gets him every time. Leaves him reeling and dazed. He's so fucking hot, and he still finds it hard to believe Jake is looking at *him* with those heated bedroom eyes.

Jake drops to his knees on the floor in front of him, hands on Kyle's thighs to spread them while he settles between them. They then slip around to his ass, grabbing on tight while he pulls him forward. Kyle's hands automatically go to Jake's shoulders, wrapping around him while he ducks down to Jake's awaiting lips. The kiss starts where it left off, hot and heated and stealing his breath away.

His hips slide forward, seeking friction, but it's difficult at this angle. It doesn't work, and a whine of protest escapes him, causing Jake to chuckle lowly.

"Jake," he breathes, a desperate plea at the tail end of his voice.

"Hmm?" Jake hums, breaking the kiss to duck his head down, teeth nipping playfully at his collarbones, tongue dragging over them in a slow tease.

"I want you," Kyle says, hips jerking forward as Jake sucks a mark against his throat. He tilts his head back, eyes fluttering closed as shivers of heat run through his body. "I want you. I want you. Please," he wants it. Not like before, when it was a desperate attempt at escape. He wants Jake now, wholly and completely.

"Are you sure?" Jake mumbles against his skin, pressing tender kisses to the abused flesh. "I can wait. We can just…"

"*Please*," Kyle repeats, nails digging into Jake's bare shoulders. Then, again, quieter, "Please. I trust you. I want you."

Jake lifts his head, meeting Kyle's gaze and holding it. He can see uncertainty there, searching for any sign of doubt from Kyle. He doesn't blame him. Last time they had sex, Kyle kicked him out and broke up with him. Not again. Not this time.

His hands move to cup Jake's cheeks, leaning forward until their foreheads are pressed together. He closes his eyes, letting out a shaking sigh. "All I want is you," he says it softly, achingly, putting his whole heart into it and hoping Jake can understand, hoping he can hear it, too.

When he leans back, opening his eyes, Jake is smiling. Small and fond, eyes lidded and still dark with hunger. Without a word, he turns, reaching out and grabbing a plastic grocery bag. He pulls it toward him, reaching inside to pull out…condoms and lube?

Kyle feels heat surge to his already warm face, hot on his cheeks. "You're prepared," he says it as a statement but doesn't try to hide his shy bafflement.

Jake chuckles, setting the box and bottle on the bed next to Kyle. "Wishful thinking, I guess."

Kyle takes his face again and pulls him forward, kissing him lightly on the lips. He feels Jake smile under him before he deepens the kiss, tongue twisting with Kyle's.

The kiss doesn't last long. Jake pulls away, and before Kyle can protest, Jake's hands are on his shirt, tugging it up and over his head. It barely has time to hit the ground before Jake's hands are on the front of his jeans, popping the button with expert ease and sliding jeans and boxers down his legs quickly.

Then Kyle is naked. Bared and feeling vulnerable as Jake kneels on the floor in front of him, eyes raking down his body, dark and hungry. It's only that hunger, the clear desire, that keeps Kyle from curling away out of embarrassment. Instead he freezes, knees drawn up, lying back while being propped up on his elbows. His breath stills in his lungs, and he can see his chest red with a flush. He has no doubt that his face looks the same.

Then Jake's eyes meet his, something in them makes Kyle's entire body shiver. He reaches out, running his hands gently but firmly along Kyle's thighs, trailing fire in their wake. He grabs Kyle by the hips, roughly dragging him forward to the edge of the bed. Kyle gasps, falling to his back.

"You're so hot," Jake mumbles, ducking his head to press kisses along Kyle's inner thighs. He bites down, sucking a dark red mark into Kyle's pale flesh, and Kyle gasps and squirms. Jake smiles, licking the abused skin. "So cute."

He hooks Kyle's legs over his shoulders, tilting his head to gaze up the length of Kyle's body, meeting his eyes. His heart hammers in his chest, and he feels dizzy with anticipation. Jake smirks, giving a hungry and predatory edge to his handsome face. Then slowly, holding eye contact, he lowers his head and parts his lips.

A strangled sound escapes Kyle's throat as Jake sinks slowly down his length, lips hot, tight and wet. His back arches off the bed, fingers flying to Jake's head to card through and tangle in his hair.

It's not the first time Jake has sucked his cock, but holy *shit* does it feel wild and new.

He squirms under the attention, body overwhelmed and overstimulated. He's not used to it. He's barely touched himself in over a month. But it feels so, so good. Jake bobs up and down on his length, tongue pressed to the underside and lips tight. He sinks down, nose pressed to Kyle's dark curls before he sucks hard and moves up the shaft.

Kyle feels like he's falling apart at the seams.

He writhes, unable to stay still. He jerks, and Jake puts his hands to his thighs and hips, pinning him to the bed. One hand clenched in Jake's hair, the other grasps at the bed sheets, curled tight. His head tosses to the side, eyes squeezed shut, brows furrowed, and mouth open and panting. Whenever he opens his eyes and looks down, Jake is watching him, and it causes more heat to curl and coil in his gut, making his chest ache and forcing him to look away.

Too much, too much, too much, it's too much.

Then Jake pulls away, and Kyle is left reeling. Cool air hits his wet erection, and he shivers. All the buildup and sudden lack of stimulation leaves him relieved, dizzy, and disappointed. But at least now he can breathe. If only for a second.

He lays there, eyes closed, chest heaving with every panted breath, fingers finally relaxing and falling to the bed next to his head.

Then he hears the snap of the lube bottle opening, and his eyes snap open. He lifts his head, watching with anticipation, excitement, and nervousness as Jake coats his fingers, rubbing them together to heat it up just a little before his hand disappears between Kyle's legs.

He's tense. He knows he is. He's nervous and wired up from all the stimulation, but he wants this.

Jake presses a few fleeting kisses to his inner thigh, nuzzling it and resting his head against the soft flesh as he turns his eyes to Kyle. His smile is gentle, and his stubble feels good against Kyle's over-sensitized skin. "Just relax," he mumbles, and Kyle's body jerks as a wet finger presses to his entrance. "Relax for me, babe. I'll take care of you."

Kyle takes a deep breath, letting it out slowly as he forces his body to relax. Jake helps him through it. He presses his lips to Kyle's inner thigh and his free hand gently massages his hip. He teases Kyle's entrance, spreading the lube and rubbing circles until there are goosebumps on Kyle's flesh and his breath becomes more labored.

When he finally pushes in, Kyle immediately tenses, body relaxing once Jake starts to mumble encouragements against his skin. It stings at first. He's still new to this, and it feels foreign and strange. But he trusts Jake, and he wants this. He relaxes, lets Jake slowly and steadily get him used to a finger and after a while it starts to feel good.

Like, really good. Heat starts pooling in Kyle's gut again, and his fingers clench and unclench into the sheets. He squeezes his eyes shut, head turned to the side as he bites his lip. Jake whispers against him, breath hot and humid. Voice gentle and awed. "You're so beautiful. You're doing so good. Holy shit, Kyle."

Kyle is surprised by the second finger, but he adjusts quickly. It's not long before Jake is working him steadily. Fingers pump into him with an easy rhythm, pausing occasionally to stretch him. His lips have moved from Kyle's thigh back to his dick, licking lazy and messy stripes up the length of it, suckling on the tip.

Kyle writhes beneath him, breath coming short and shallow at the onslaught of sensations. He's so lost in it that he barely notices the third finger. So far gone that he doesn't even realize his hips are grinding down, seeking out Jake's fingers as they pump in and out of him.

Then Jake suddenly swallows him down just as he curls his fingers and Kyle's back arches off the bed, fingers clutching tight as a loud sharp gasp leaves his lips, trailing off into a long moan.

Jake pulls off him with a *pop*, grinning up at Kyle and looking far too proud of himself. Kyle wants to scowl at him, but he can't. His muscles aren't responding. All he can do is lay there and attempt to breathe as Jake pulls away. He shivers when his fingers pull out of him, leaving him empty and hollow. He whines, bordering on a whimper, but Jake's hands are already on him. He pulls on Kyle's hips, tugging him effortlessly off the bed until he's straddling his lap on the floor.

Jake leans in, and Kyle rushes to meet him. His arms wrap around Jake's shoulders as Jake holds him tight. His mouth is hot and wet, tongue exploring his and guiding him deeper into it. He tastes different, saltier and muskier, but Kyle doesn't care. The realization that it's *himself* he tastes on Jake's tongue is thrilling.

"Are you ready?" Jake asks, voice low and hoarse against Kyle's lip.

He nods, not trusting his own voice as he pushes forward, seeking out Jake's lips again and again, even as he pulls away to reach for the condoms. He chuckles at Kyle's attention as he struggles to open the box. His laughter turns to a gasp and a low groan as Kyle trails his lips down Jake's neck, experimentally nipping at the sensitive skin with his teeth. Every sound he manages to pull from Jake sends a shiver down his spine, sparking something hungry and primal within him.

Then Jake's hands are on him again, turning him around. He moves easily with the guidance, loving the feeling of Jake's hands on him. He ends up on his knees, bent over the edge of his bed. Jake shuffles behind him, and he can hear the sound of him struggling to kick off his jeans. Then his legs are being spread wider, and Jake bends down to bite playfully at his shoulder.

Kyle's body jerks and he gasps as Jake's erection presses between his cheeks. Thick, hard and hot. It presses into him, and Jake angles his hips, chasing friction against Kyle's bare ass. It's barely anything, but Kyle's head tilts back, hips automatically pressing back into him with each shallow thrust.

"*Fuck*," Jake whispers into his skin. His hands bite bruises into Kyle's hips.

He pulls back, and Kyle can hear the ripping of a condom wrapper. It's only a moment later that Jake's hand comes down on his shoulder, urging him to bend over a little more as the slick head of his cock presses against Kyle's entrance. He gasps, burying his face in the blankets on his bed as Jake slowly pushes in, in, in, spreading him wider and wider and…

He bottoms out, and the two of them simply stay like that for a moment. Jake leans forward, one hand on Kyle's hip and the other on his shoulder. His forehead presses to his other shoulder, and his breath is hard and labored. It's clear he's holding himself back to let Kyle get used to it, and something surprisingly fond flutters in his chest. Jake is big, but while the stretch burns, it doesn't hurt. He feels *full*. So full. And he likes it. Jake is inside him. Jake is filling him up, stretching him wide. His hips and thighs are pressed to the curve of Kyle's ass, his breath fanning out over his heated skin.

He can't believe he's here, that this is happening. It fuels something in him. A need for *more*.

His hips move gently, pushing back against Jake until he gets the hint. His hips begin to rock shallowly, pulling out just a little before pushing back in, getting Kyle used to it, building a rhythm. It's slow, steady, and surprisingly sweet. But after a while, Kyle's fingers are curled into the sheets, breath panting and sweat beading on his brow. His toes curl and he needs *more*.

"Jake," he breathes, voice cracking. "Jake, please."

Jake pauses, almost freezing behind him, and Kyle whines in protest. "What's wrong? Do you want me to stop?" he sounds so worried. So concerned. It warms Kyle's heart.

He shakes his head. "No! No, please. More. *Harder.*"

There's a pause, like Jake is trying to digest that information. And then all at once he pulls back, almost pulling out entirely before roughly snapping his hips forward.

Kyle's back arches, a strangled and broken moan escaping his lips as his entire body tenses. He grips the blankets as an anchor as he feels himself floating away.

Jake doesn't need any more encouragement after that. He picks up a faster rhythm, pounding into Kyle over and over again until the erotic, almost obscene sound of slapping flesh and harsh breath fills the room. Kyle covers his mouth, biting into the blankets to keep himself quiet. But then Jake is there, leaning over to harshly pant into his ear. "Don't. I want to hear you. Let me know how good you feel."

And so, he unclenches his jaw and lets the sounds spill out. Every heavy exhale that's punched from his lungs by Jake's snapping hips trails off in a moan. He keens when Jake adjusts the angle and hits the spot inside him that makes him see stars. He thinks he might have screamed, but he can barely hear his own voice over the ringing in his ears.

The whole time Jake keeps talking. He rambles, mumbling into Kyle's skin, breathing into his ear. Simple words. Curses. Encouragements. Endearments. It garbles into nonsense, half the words choked and broken with his own pants and half formed moans, but that doesn't make it any less hot.

The pressure inside him builds and builds, the heat pooling low and sensation pushing his senses into overload. His toes curl. His thighs tense. His moans get higher in pitch and he thinks he's saying Jake's name. He thinks he's begging, but he can't control himself.

Jake's thrusts become more ragged and less coordinated. Wild and crazed. The slap of flesh loses rhythm but is no less loud. Kyle can hear his ragged breath. His broken moans. A hand slides from his hip, fingers wrapping tight around his leaking cock before roughly jerking it in time with the frantic thrusts.

Kyle's body tenses when he comes, lips parted in a strangled cry as his eyes squeeze shut. His body spasms as Jake rides him through it, wave after wave. And then Jake pushes in deep, burying himself with a long, low groan as his teeth sink into Kyle's shoulder.

After the waves of their orgasms fade, they lie there, draped over the edge of the bed, Jake's body blanketing Kyle's. Their fingers twine together on the sheets, and they desperately attempt to catch their breath.

* * *

A LITTLE OVER AN HOUR LATER, the two of them are showered, clean, and lying naked on Kyle's bed. They'd been too content without clothes. Jake stretches out on his back, one hand behind his head and one arm around Kyle, who curls into his side, head resting on his chest. His eyelids feel heavy as he listens to the steady sound of Jake's heartbeat. He lets it lull him into a state of fuzzy bliss, body pleased and mind quiet for the first time in...well, in a very long time.

He knows they'll have to get dressed eventually. He has no idea when Jasper is going to come back, but for now, he's happy. He's not too cold pressed up against Jake's side, and his skin shivers pleasantly where Jake trails his fingers along his hip.

The silence is broken when Jake's stomach rumbles, loud and demanding. It's followed by a low, sheepish chuckle. "Guess I'm hungry."

Kyle lifts his head, resting his chin on Jake's chest to gaze up at him. His fingers idly trail through the light patch of chest hair across his pecs. "I could go for some food. I haven't been eating much."

Jake's arm tightens around him for just a moment. Something comforting and acknowledging without drawing too much attention to Kyle's recent misery. He appreciates it. "We can order in," Jake says, already reaching for his phone.

But Kyle reaches out, putting a hand on his arm to stop it. When Jake looks at him, one eyebrow raised, Kyle shakes his head. "I, uh...I kinda wanna go out? It's been a while since I've left the dorm for anything but classes, and I think it'd be nice."

Jake's grin is far too soft and far too fond, making Kyle's heart stop and flutter all at once as he leans in for a gentle peck on the lips. "It's a date."

They get dressed as quick as they can, laughing as Jake keeps reaching out for him, pulling him close to feather his skin with fleeting kisses. Kyle bats him away good naturedly but can't resist letting his own hands drift across Jake's exposed skin before he can slip his shirt on. They grab their keys, phones, and wallets, and head out the door.

Despite having just been outside a couple hours before, the crisp autumn air feels far more refreshing now. It no longer feels like sharp pin point knives digging into his flesh. Now it feels simply, refreshing. He's freshly showered, body aching but humming pleasantly in post orgasmic bliss. Jake is at his side, and the crisp air feels like it washes away the remaining negative energy from his lungs. It cleanses the shadows away.

It feels like a new beginning.

The guilt is still there, but he thinks he'll be able to manage it this time. Or at least, he'll be able to work on managing it. His counsellor was right. His brother wouldn't want him making himself miserable. He was always pushing Kyle to go out, to meet people, to *live* and be unashamed of it.

He thinks his brother might be proud of him.

They walk across campus, buzzing with people now that dinner is approaching, and most classes are done. There's a respectful distance between them, but every once in a while, Jake is forced to step closer to let other's pass. His hand brushes against Kyle's, and...

Kyle grabs his hand before he can overthink it. Before he can start to doubt it. He grabs Jake's hand and intertwines their fingers. He glances up to see Jake staring at him, eyes wide and lips parted in cute surprise. He tries to offer him a smile, but it feels shaky.

His heart is pounding in his chest, and he's certain his palms are sweaty. His skin crawls with anxiety as he feels the weight of stares around them. Every time he sees movement out of the corner of his eye, he assumes people are turning to look at him. Every time he hears words he can't make out, he assumes they're talking about them. Maybe it's his paranoia, but then again, maybe it's not.

He can't bring himself to look at any of them. He stares at the pavement beneath their feet as they walk, trying to regulate his breathing and calm his rapid heartbeat. Jake squeezes his hand, holding it tightly and confidently. It's an anchor point that grounds him, and Kyle squeezes back to let him know it's appreciated.

When they reach the quad, Kyle is pulled to a stop, and he turns to face Jake with eyebrows pinched, head tilting to the side. He wonders if maybe this was too much, if *Jake* isn't ready to let it be known publicly that he's dating a guy, but that doubt is wiped away the moment Kyle sees him.

Jake is smiling at him, soft and gentle. There's a fondness that melts Kyle's nerves and his heart beat quickens for new reasons. It makes everything else fade away. The quad. The people. The stares. The worry.

Jake lifts his free hand, cupping Kyle's face and lightly

running his thumb across Kyle's cheek. He recognizes it as a question. He lifts his hand, covering Jake's hand with his own. He leans into it, head tilted and a shy smile on his lips. He doesn't trust his voice, so he nods.

Jake leans down, capturing his lips. The kiss is firm and passionate, without being sloppy or rushed. It's gentle. Lips moving against lips. Deepening slowly until Kyle's breath hitches and his toes curl. He leans into Jake, and Jake's arm slides around his back to support him. The crisp autumn air feels good against his heated skin.

When Jake pulls away, Kyle feels breathless. Jake pulls back just far enough for Kyle to see his face. He smiles, and Kyle feels his own lips curve. He can still feel the stares and hear the whispers around him, but for once, he doesn't care.

Jake is in front of him, taking up his whole vision and his whole world.

Soft, kind, gentle Jake. Jake, who has never been anything short of encouraging and understanding. Jake, who has been so patient and kind with him.

"One day at a time, right?" Jake whispers into the space between them, sounding just as awed and breathless as Kyle feels. It makes his heart flutter.

"One day at a time," he agrees, squeezing his hand.

Kyle's still not sure if he's ready. He's not sure if he'll ever be ready. Maybe they won't last. Maybe it'll just be for college. Maybe it'll be less than a year. A few months. Maybe it's just for now. He doesn't know about the future, but living for the day, that he can do.

Today, he loves Jake.

Today, Jake loves him.

He doesn't know how they'll feel tomorrow, but he supposes they'll find out. One day at a time.

EPILOGUE

*J*ake doesn't think he'll ever get tired of the field. The hard-packed dirt. Dust kicked up behind feet and clean painted lines. The muffled sound of the ball hitting squarely against a waiting mitt. The clang of a ball colliding with a bat. The call of the umpire.

Nope, he'll never get tired of it.

Even when he's no longer playing.

"Come on, Jessica!" he shouts, waving a hand in the air to encourage her onward. "Keep running! Go on! Run it home!" the other team is still fumbling for the ball in the outfield, and the little girl grins as she rounds third base and pushes it home. She hits home without any problem and the crowd cheers. He grins, clapping his hands and reaching out for a high five as she passes, skipping back to her team. "That's our heavy hitter. Good job."

The kid grins wide, a gap in her teeth. "Thanks, coach!"

The game is called, and his team wins. Predictably, he'd like to say. They've been on a winning streak lately. It's going right to the girls' heads, but that's alright. They're allowed to be proud as long as they're having fun.

He leads the girls through their team cheer before he urges them to line up, shaking hands with the other team. After that, they scatter. They run back to the dugout to get their things, gathering where the snacks are about to be handed out, courtesy of this week's volunteer parent. Some of them dive out into the crowd, searching for their parents.

He watches them go, hands on his hips and a fond smile on his face. There's a warm pride bubbling in his chest. They've all improved so much in the past few months, and he likes to think it's because of his own efforts. It doesn't hurt that out of all the other volunteer coaches in the league, he actually has the most baseball experience. He's also the youngest amongst them, and he makes an effort to connect with the kids, which makes them more inclined to listen to him.

Once he's certain the volunteer parents are taking care of passing out the after-game snacks, he turns to the task of gathering the equipment. He moves around, picking up all the discarded bats and helmets.

As he bends down for one, sharp pain shoots through his leg. It's quick and gone in an instant, but the ache in his knee remains, throbbing dully. He sighs as he stands, keeping his weight off his right leg as much as he can. It's nothing new, and he knows the pain will fade soon enough.

It's an old injury at this point, and it doesn't sting as it used to. He had been upset at first, realizing that he'd never get to play professionally. But after the initial shock wore off, as he recovered, he realized that he didn't need it. There's a lot more he can do and a lot more he's capable of.

Still, as much as he misses it, he's happy with how things turned out. Life could've gone differently, but it didn't, and that's fine. Besides, coaching his daughter's softball team is nice. It brings back memories, he still gets to be involved, and he gets to help kids grow. It's far more rewarding than playing pro could've been.

"Dad!" He turns, barely managing to brace himself before a small body collides with his legs.

"Whoa, there, Katie. Try not to knock me over, 'kay?"

"Sorry," she says, though she doesn't sound it. She holds up the cupcake in her hand. "Look! Mandy's mom brought cupcakes this time. They all have this weird filling in the middle, but I like it. She said there's one for you, too."

He grins. "Maybe later. You had a good game out there. Didn't let anybody steal third."

"Not on my watch," she says, face mockingly grave as she salutes.

"That's my girl," he chuckles, turning and bending down as he offers his back. "Hop on up, princess. Let's go find your daddy."

She climbs onto his back, one hand hooked over his shoulder and around his neck while she eats her cupcake. He holds onto her legs, turning to walk off the field and around the fence where the rest of the crowd of parents and families gather.

It doesn't take him long to spot Kyle.

He stands with a couple other parents, talking to them politely, smiling like he's used to it. Jake's proud of him. He's come so far since they were in college. He's learned how to interact with people, and while he's still an introvert, he doesn't fear social interaction as much as he used to. He's gotten pretty good at it.

As if sensing Jake's eyes on him, he turns, catching his gaze from across the crowd. Jake grins, and Kyle smiles, small, fond and private. He excuses himself from the conversation and makes his way over, and Jake just stands there admiring him.

He's grown a lot since they first met. He's a few inches

taller. His hair is a little less messy. He smiles a lot easier, and he stands a little taller. His game is a huge hit, and he still has a tendency to overwork himself, but Jake is always there to take care of him. He never thought he'd end up as the trophy stay at-home-dad, but here they are. And he can't say he minds.

"How many people did I tag out this time, Daddy?" Katie asks as he gets near.

Kyle stops when he reaches them, tapping his chin as if thinking. He's wearing one of Jake's jackets again. It's a habit he picked up, and Jake has never cared to stop him. He looks adorable and small in Jake's larger jackets, sleeves hiding much of his hands. "I think it was nine."

"No, it was thirteen!" she argues.

He smiles, tilting his head. "Was it? I must've miscounted."

She makes a noise that sounds like dismissive acceptance, and Kyle steps closer. His hands find Jake's hips, leaning in close and tucking himself into Jake's chest. He tilts his head back, eyes lidded as he smiles. "Hey."

"Hey, yourself," Jake leans down, rubbing his nose against Kyle's, loving the way he chuckles under his breath, hands pulling Jake closer.

"You looked good out there," he says, tilting his chin to line up their lips, leaving sparse distance between them.

"You're supposed to watch the game, not me."

"I can do both."

Jake presses his forehead to Kyle's. Their lips brush when he speaks. "I love you today."

He can feel Kyle's smile. "I love you today, too," he moves up on his toes, pressing their lips together in a firm but chaste kiss. He tastes sweet and feels like home.

For ten years, Jake has loved him. For ten years, Kyle has loved Jake. One day at a time.

They'll see how they feel tomorrow.

Made in the USA
San Bernardino, CA
27 November 2018